From the award-winning
Where the Rainbow Ends and *...*
comes a witty tour de force of spirits, spooks, and sinners,
a supernatural roller coaster set in the Big Easy that is
giddy, soulful, and sentimental.

The Wolf at the Door

a novel by Jameson Currier

When a death occurs at Le Petite Paradis, a guesthouse in the French Quarter of New Orleans, the spirit world becomes unsettled, or so Avery Greene Dalyrymple III, the co-owner believes. The son and grandson of Southern evangelists, Avery is also an overworked and overwrought middle-aged gay man, a cynical "big-time drinker and sinner" fairly certain he can maintain a family of "other deviants and delinquents stumbling along Bourbon Street" to keep him company.

But Avery is also the only person in contact with the spirit world on his property—ghosts from the house's origins during the 1820s—and he must use the history left behind from another ghost—a gay man from the 1970s—to find a way to restore peace to his household and rejuvenate his faith.

"Currier is one of the few writers who can be equally literary, erotic, dramatic and damn funny, sometimes all in the same sentence."
Sean Meriwether, *The Silent Hustler*

The Wolf at the Door

Also by Jameson Currier

The Wolf at the Door

Jameson Currier

Chelsea Station Editions

New York

Cover paintings by Bryan Cunningham

Book design by Peach Boy Distillery & Designs

Published as a trade paperback original by Chelsea Station Editions,
New York, NY 10018
www.chelseastationeditions.com / info@chelseastationeditions.com

ISBN: 978-0-9844707-0-9

Library of Congress Control Number: 2010922641

First U.S. edition, 2010

Printed in the United States of America

To the hearts and souls of gay New Orleans

Follow your bliss and don't be afraid,
and doors will open where you never knew
there were going to be doors.
——Joseph Campbell

One

The problem with Creole cooking is that I can no longer appreciate its subtleties: my stomach has long ago rotted away from all the spices and sauces and what peptic tissue has remained behind in my digestive tract has been eaten away by nerves and ulcers. That doesn't mean that I don't partake of the finer, fierce morsels of the Big Easy; on the contrary, a good shot of cheap four-year-old bourbon will comfortably numb my prevailing gastric reflexes long enough for me to wolf down a gourmet four-course meal, though I must confess that my indulgences are not without their aftershocks, what with all the acid reflux, night sweats, and insomnia left in the wake of my appetite. I usually eat whatever hot-off-the-grill special Parker has on the menu for the night, and I still enjoy sampling the newly concocted megacholesterol entrées he has decided to feature on the menu, though I love to come back to my old favorites day after day, detecting the nuances of Parker's changing moods, heavy one day on the cayenne, lighter another with the roux.

My inflating weight and waistline reflect all this eating and drinking, of course; I've now reached the ungraceful age where sweating through the swampy heat of the city no longer helps me shed even the lightest of calories, and it doesn't help having Parker's kitchen in such close proximity to my office (twenty-three steps, to be exact, as I measured it one night when I was ravenous). Most of Parker's customers, and mine at the guesthouse above and behind his café in the French Quarter, are satisfied, over-indulgent travelers who found us unexpectedly on a honeymoon or while attending a convention, and this, along with a good word-of-mouth campaign, has been what has helped us float through the recent leaner and tougher times. We've both refused to advertise in any glossy lifestyle magazines or travel guides because every other day we vow to give up our crazy businesses, and though we don't cater exclusively to a gay and lesbian clientele, we proudly announce to anyone who'll listen to us that we're both gay-owned-and-operated businesses. In fact, we've tried to keep up with the times by launching a modest self-designed Web site as a subtle marketing tool in that regard, but you're not likely to find pictures of either of us tired old queens on it because we're both a bit too camera shy and worried about revealing our ever-expanding girths.

Parker's restaurant, Café Surtout, is accessible from Dumaine Street—tall arched windows and water-stained gold-painted walls inside the front dining room give it an elegant, blue-haired atmosphere, particularly after the sun has gone down, the tapered candles are lit, and the wobbly ceiling fans are spinning away. The crisp white tablecloths and goblet-sized water glasses give a formal first impression, but the assorted cutlery and serving china Parker has acquired from flea markets and odd-lot buyouts, along with the lavishly gilt-framed portraits of bright blue skies and buttery cloud patterns painted by a local artist in exchange for a couple of years of free meals bequeath a more tongue-in-cheek ambiance to the place. There is always enough foot traffic from Bourbon Street to keep his place full at *any* hour of the day were he ever to decide to go at it 24/7 (which I hope is *never*). Café Surtout seats no more than fifty malnourished customers at a time and during the heavy tourist season there is often a wait, sometimes up to a full hour or more. There's only a staff of two—Buddy, a clean-cut porn-star quality waiter who works the tables, the bar, and the door, and José, a macho Eve Harrington kitchen assistant who helps Parker cook and clean—and Parker, a strict, no-nonsense sort of guy, refuses to take reservations and locks the door promptly at half past ten each night, even if there is still a wait, not wanting to feel as if he has to accommodate the whims of famished and anxious tourists. This policy sends some of my customers into a panic, especially when they want to stop in for an after-dinner drink (or after-bar nightcap).

The Creole mansion where we both work—and share a second-floor apartment—was built in 1820 to house the family business and living quarters of Antoine Dubuisson, who ran a general dry goods store in the ground-floor room where Café Surtout is now located. The family lived in the second- and third-floor rooms of the main house until the death of Antoine's son, Pierre, when the store went out of business, and in the early 1900s the main house and the attached slave quarters in the rear of the property were redesigned into individual apartments. The first year Parker and I were both in business I put up wooden signs elaborately carved and painted by a local carpenter on our Dumaine Street facade (which mysteriously kept falling off until I finally gave up on rehanging them and merely propped mine up on the kitchen counter of my office), and other than our replacing some occasional rotted planks in the staircases and two of the large blue-painted wooden window shutters after a particularly awful hurricane season, all of the original architectural details remain intact, from the large wooden French patio doors and black wrought iron grillwork on the street-side balconies to the dented, interior brass doorknobs and chipped marble mantelpieces of the fireplaces inside the house. I can't even imagine the younger and thinner version of myself who ten years ago passionately named and decorated each of the guest rooms we unleashed on our unsuspecting paying visitors, all named and designed around a specific color scheme or period style of furnishings. (French Provincial in the Burgundy, Toulouse, Dauphine, and Orleans suites; high camp Southern floral in the Gardenia and Magnolia suites.)

The Royal Suite, the largest and most elaborately furnished of our guest rooms (and still my favorite, though there are days that it seems, when I am cleaning it, as insurmountable as de-boning a beached yellow whale), has an antique four-poster bed, beveled mirrors on the walls, and creamy gold floral linens and velvet bedspreads that deliberately match the curtains and upholstery.

There are only seven rooms available to rent in my guesthouse, Le Petite Paradis, but that is more than enough to keep me and Hank, my latest very attractive but high-maintenance boyfriend-slash-employee, worn out and irritable. My office is located as far as possible from the street, down the alleyway at the side of Parker's restaurant (which he will sometimes use for outdoor seating when he's interested in working even harder to make some extra money, usually around the end-of-the-year holidays when he realizes he needs to dispense some bonuses and paybacks and the weather is cooperatively cool and mild). The alleyway leads to a courtyard surrounded on two sides by the ivy and bougainvillea-covered brick walls of the adjacent buildings and on the others by the decaying, mossy back of the main house and front doors of the original slave quarters. The two stories above the ground floor are surrounded by the original wood balconies and below, in the courtyard, we've placed three small sparkling white enamel rust-free wrought iron café tables where our guests can sit outside and enjoy our ruin. We've also indulged in a host of lush potted ferns, rubber plants, and other exotic greenery, and there is a lichen-covered fountain of a flying fish spouting water into a tiny pond stocked with neurotic, darting Japanese goldfish, and as many hanging baskets of scarlet impatiens or white geraniums or varicolored pansies surrounding the space as have the will to live in this turgid heat and madness. My office door is at that far end of the courtyard and its remote location has never hampered a single obnoxious or well-intentioned customer from finding me at my tiny desk (which supports an equally small computer), unless I am purposely hiding out and napping in the back room where Hank and I also happen to spend our evenings. And yes, the French boo-boo in the name of our guest quarters was intentional. Somewhere in my skinny past I thought it would be politically correct to use a feminine adjective with a masculine definite article and noun for the name of our lodgings— hence Le *Petite* Paradis—and as proof that my heavenly sweatshop was an adamantly queer one, though Parker has always been too quick to remind me that there was no motive at all behind the misnomer because I was hysterically blind from the fear of being my own boss.

Parker and I have long abandoned any pretense of being in a relationship with each other, and I've all but willed the grandiose, eighteen-foot-ceiling second-floor apartment to him, but we've also accepted, in part because of our wretched, interlocked business situations, that we cannot do without each other, something Hank has also reluctantly had to accept. Somehow I am able to keep Parker's nimble-clawed customers from walking away with the goblets and silverware and Parker is able to smooth over the occasional misunderstanding when one of my more impetuous guests confronts him about not being open for breakfast. Café Surtout has never been open for breakfast and Parker has had no desire to set up shop that early. In fact, Parker prefers to keep his ship running as simply as possible—no motor, no oars, just floating along the current without even a sail; the microwave is used *only* to occasionally help defrost food, not to reheat it; the produce, meat, and fish are bought fresh daily at the local markets; and it wasn't until his third year in business that I was able to convince Parker to accept credit card payments. A couple of years ago I installed coffeemakers in all of the guest rooms, which Hank and I keep stocked daily with fresh chicory- and hazelnut-flavored gourmet coffee packets and filters (which has appeased most of our repeat trade from going off on the no-breakfast business). But even Parker's latest boyfriend, Charlie Ray, who neither works at the restaurant or at the guesthouse (he's a rapidly aging, chain-smoking personal trainer, go figure), is still unnerved when he sleeps over with Parker and Parker refuses to even boil water before noon.

Like many big cities, New Orleans is a melting pot of quirky fools, though I'd always believed—in part, because of our collective queer spirits—our little bent pocket of the Crescent City was more exceptional than most. Parker T. Steinberg came here in the mid-1970s, during the migration of northern Jewish students seeking warmer climates, to attend Tulane's law school, though once he sampled the finest, heart-stopping cooking he had ever tasted in his short and overfed life, he changed professions and never left town. Buddy, fifteen years younger and now in his early thirties, had a similar but condensed experience; a semester at Loyola and a succession of swift affairs, from a Boston priest-in-exile to a local undertaker who had immigrated from Nigeria, had convinced him that his Italian-Catholic heritage could be morphed into a more tolerant though no-less skeptical spiritualism. I'd always considered Buddy something of an enigma: both pious and sexual. Parker had hired him for the front of the café simply for his looks; with his broad nose, black eyes, and a voice deepened by excessive amounts of testosterone, Buddy can double his tips by shyly declining advances and telling his admirers he's already attached and a one-man sorta guy. José, who works with Parker in the kitchen, is something of a hot tamale, too; short, trim, and in his late twenties, he's a dark-haired alpha male with an aggressive Latin swagger. He arrived from a Santa Fe housing project via a sojourn in the Lone Star State as a bar back, leaving town hastily when his girlfriend discovered he also had a boyfriend. Charlie Ray is nothing but friendly local white trash, raised in a trailer park outside of Baton Rouge. Hank, now closer to forty than thirty, is a refugee from a family of ultraconservative Chicago Baptists; overeducated and African-American, he had migrated to New York City first, expecting to be ecstatically embraced as an entertainer, but after an unsuccessful acting and dancing career and too little applause in his daily life, he left the Big Apple for good after one snowstorm too many. For a big-time drinker and sinner like myself, Avery Greene Dalyrymple III, New Orleans was a logical destination; the son and grandson of Holy Roller evangelists, I was fairly certain I could find a few other deviants and delinquents stumbling along Bourbon Street to keep me company.

But all that history and homage doesn't keep the wolf away from the door or the overpampered self-absorbed customers from finding us when they need something, even if it's just to ask directions. Some days are worse than others, of course, but every day is such a challenge that I keep hoping when I roll out of bed that I will have landed on the other side in a parallel universe, one of those Stepford-like stress-free zones where everything is in order and no one is unhappy and my work is so much fun that I have to convince myself that I am not on vacation. But as my luck would have it, trouble always seems to beget more trouble, and trouble made its first appearance one wildly hot June day with the air conditioner in the first-floor Toulouse Suite burning itself up, and snowballed into a shorted fuse that left Parker, in the restaurant's tiny kitchen below, without any electricity and his freshly bought food rapidly spoiling. Buddy tried to repair the air conditioner, cut his finger on a piece of metal, and when the bleeding could not be stopped, rushed off to the emergency room to have it stitched up. The retired schoolteachers next door in the Magnolia Suite had returned from a morning walking tour and the eldest of them, unaccustomed to such intense heat at that early an hour of the day, threw up on the bed and, when she tried to turn her air conditioner up to a higher setting, blew all the remaining working fuses in the main house. José, who shows a little too much curiosity over things going wrong, acted like a deflated beach toy when I dispensed him to collect buckets of ice from a bar on Bourbon Street, while Hank went reluctantly upstairs to clean up the Magnolia vomit, murmuring under his breath that he had not paid his way through four years of college to clean up old ladies' puke. Parker, who can't remember where we keep our toolbox, tried to find a working flashlight beneath the kitchen sink, then tried to find the box of replacement fuses in the pantry closet, then gave up and tried to find me. I stayed in the office and tried to find an inexpensive electrician willing to come immediately, regretting the fact that I was forever pinching pennies and had never just bitten the bullet and taken out one of those high-interest loans and had half the place demolished in order to install central air-conditioning in all of the rooms.

Already, at that hour, I felt unnerved and capable of becoming a mass murderer and decided to have a shot of my favorite liquid gold to steady myself. I don't really consider myself an alcoholic, or even someone with a drinking problem, since I usually try to at least wait until the cocktail hour to begin and always seem to get tipsy right away (which true alcoholics never do, do they?), but since it was already after lunchtime and certain to spiral into a more difficult day, I cracked open the bourbon bottle and had a little nip. That one shot proceeded into another one and another until I was dropping vowels by the mouthful and slurring all of my consonants and cursing everyone and everything in sight, which was when Mack, who lived in one of the second-floor apartments of the old slave quarters and was the friend responsible for bringing Parker and me into this miserable sham of the service industry in the first place, decided he was ready to die. Charlie Ray, who smoked on the inner second-floor courtyard balcony because Parker refused to allow him to smoke inside the apartment, banged the office door open and said to me, "You better come quick. Mack says he's going to jump."

Mack beat us all to the Big Easy, landing at Tulane a few years before Parker. He'd traveled east hoping to outgrow his narrow-minded small-town two-car-garage Texas family and have a few adventures. Mack had the eagerness and affection of a hungry puppy dog; just shy of six feet with wide brown eyes and a dark-haired flat-top, he was the kind of guy whose pebbly stubble of beard across his square jaw never looked cleanly shaved. He was always the older brother to all of us who knew him, the guy who would help someone move his oversized furniture and hastily packed boxes to a cheaper, top-story apartment, the one with a few extra bucks in his beaten-up wallet to lend if you were short for a week or so, the best friend with last-minute advice on what to do about a boyfriend who no longer wanted to be a boyfriend. Mack, now forty-eight, had been sick for almost nineteen years; he'd recovered from his first bout of pneumonia and a combination of drugs had kept the HIV in check for the longest time, but after so many years his virus had grown resistant to the early medications and he had found that the newer combination therapy of drugs was more toxic and only worsening his health. In the last year he'd been in and out of the hospital for blood transfusions and to have a catheter implanted in his chest to allow him to do an IV drip of new meds twice a day. His black stubble was now almost entirely gray, his once-thick head of hair was thinning and balding, and he'd turned into a skeleton with a bladder problem. In recent weeks, he had lost both his mobility and his eternal eagerness and Parker and I had alternated visiting Mack in his upstairs apartment while he went through his new regimen of infusions, helping him to shower or rubbing his leathery skin with moisturizer to keep it from withering into ash and falling completely off his bones. Privately, together, Parker and I had talked about whether it was necessary to find a carepartner or a day nurse who could keep a more watchful eye on Mack when we were both occupied elsewhere with our various chores to keep the place running, but Mack had nixed the idea with the vicious kind of snap I had only heretofore experienced from a dried-out turtle trying to cross Bourbon Street on Mardi Gras. He didn't want anyone "watching over" him, and so we have done our best to respect and accommodate his request. Mack had been Parker's boyfriend first, then mine, and when the pneumonia hospitalized Mack the first time so many years ago, that was when Parker and I had first met. At the time, Mack and I had long since dissolved our own dysfunctional affair, and I was already living in the high-ceiling second-floor apartment and Parker was working as a saucier at a popular hotel restaurant on the other side of Jackson Square. Mack had owned the Creole mansion since the late 1970s when a flush of insurance money from the accidental death of both of his parents had made it possible to buy the building, where he had lived with his first boyfriend Toby.

Mack had never moved out of his second-floor courtyard-view apartment after Toby's death, not even to take over one of the larger and nicer apartments on the lower floor or in the main house when he purchased the connected buildings of the property, preferring instead to rent out these more desirable habitats, which provided him with a decent monthly income. At one point, when Mack was hospitalized for a series of infections, he "sold" the property to myself and Parker—then a relatively stable couple as blindly-in-love gay couples go—for the grand sum of one measly dollar, provided that we would pay all the late taxes due and he could remain rent-free in his apartment for as long as he was alive. At the time, Parker and I had been eager to find our way out of other miserable low-paying jobs and from underneath other exasperating employers, and it seemed like a plausible idea to all of us—starting our own businesses and keeping up with Mack at the same time. Suddenly we had become the King and King of a newly formed dominion with a handsome prince as a benefactor, in as desirable a vacation destination as any poor peasant could wish.

I followed Charlie Ray out of the office door and stood in the middle of the courtyard and looked up at the balconies. "Whadya think you're doing, sweetie?" I hollered up at Mack, who was tottering against the second-floor wooden railing, his T-shirt billowing in the air because there wasn't any weight left to him.

"I can't stand it anymore, Avery," he said.

"Neither can I, baby," I answered him. "Ya want some company?"

He frowned and looked away from me, towards Charlie Ray, bug-eyed and lighting up a cigarette as if he were about to watch an execution.

"Who's he?"

"Charlie Ray," I said. "Parker's boyfriend. You've met him plenty of times."

I felt the sweat dripping down my back and the booze evaporating into a headache. Mack's face went through a variety of motions, as if he were chewing gum and thumbing through a photo album, unable to recall the memory behind a picture, and I yelled up to him, "Want a shot? A good shot of ya favorite bourbon'll do ya good."

This seemed to bring him back into focus. He smiled and said, "Okay."

Charlie Ray, exhaling smoke behind me, cleared his throat with a phlegmy cough and said, "Ya sure that's good for him?"

"Best thing there is," I answered and rushed into the office, grabbed my half-full bottle of liquid hope, and was soon back in the courtyard, heading towards the exterior stairwell which led to the balconies on the upper floors. The stairs were old and wooden and many of the cypress planks had been replaced as they'd rotted away, and it was impossible to muffle the sound of someone walking up or down them—I'd tried carpeting them a few years back but the dampness had created an intolerable smell as the rug and padding rotted away—like the uncleaned locker room of a varsity team with a serious case of athlete's foot—so I had abandoned the carpeting idea in favor of dealing with the occasional complaint from one indignant guest about another more noisy one.

I was rushing up the stairs two at a time, consciously making my progress known with my lumbering thump-thump-thumps so that Mack might hear me approaching, when I saw a cute young black man making his way up the stairs ahead of me. I couldn't tell how old he was, but it appeared he was in his early twenties. He was tall and slender, bushy-haired, with a pretty face in spite of a few acne blisters, and he was wearing a light blue T-shirt and jeans and had a tight puka shell necklace around his throat that gave him a distinctly retro appearance, like he had wandered into town from San Francisco in the 1970s and had never changed clothes. He didn't make a sound as he traveled the stairs above me, moving as if he were floating upwards on an escalator, not taking them step-by-step as I was. At one point when I looked up, he looked down to meet my eyes, as if to make sure I was headed in his direction. I felt a shift in my pulse that wasn't just from climbing the stairs, a worry that made me frown and become suspicious in an obvious B-movie queen fashion. When I reached the second-floor landing, the young man was nowhere in sight, and Mack was leaning over the edge of the railing and my next thought was to get him safely back inside his apartment because he looked like he was about to jump overboard.

"Did you have company?" I asked Mack when he was settled in the chair in his apartment. It was stuffy inside the room and I opened the window hoping to get a breeze going until the electricity was restored.

"Toby was just here," he answered, stretching his neck and eyes up towards me as if he were a baby sparrow waiting to be fed.

Toby had been dead for more than twenty years, but I had no intention of comparing spooky encounters with Mack at that moment. Toby was Mack's first lover, the young man who had invited the twenty-three-year-old Mack home to this apartment one night and fallen so head-over-heels in love with him that he begged him never to leave. Toby had died under puzzling circumstances—the coroner had ruled, in fact, that he had leapt from the second-floor balcony and onto the courtyard below, just as Mack might have been contemplating only a few moments ago. The police easily dismissed the case as a suicide—Toby had displayed a troubling behavior in the days before his jump; he was plagued with insomnia and when he did sleep he was forever caught up in nightmares. Mack had once, in a fit of melancholy, described his boyfriend's behavior in those final days (and evenings) as being as unpredictable as that of a demonic child star threatening to barf. Toby was from a poor black New Orleans family with a long history of its own struggles in the city and, because he was effeminate in both his appearance and manner, it was easy for the police to dismiss his death without a thorough investigation—although he wasn't prissy or campy in the swishy, hyperdramatic ways of the big-haired and fabulously bejeweled African-American drag queens who are forever parading about the Quarter nowadays, but shyly feminine in the sensitive manner of an academic boy afraid of participating in sports with guys twice his size. There was also the admissible and known fact that this gentle young man was openly gay, at a time when it wasn't easily tolerated in the Deep South whether you were white or black, no matter how progressive or perverse the Big Easy considered itself in those days. Mack's masculinity was never questioned, however; he was the butch-looking kind of guy who drove a rusty flat-bed truck around town, the kind of fellow you wouldn't believe could *really* be serious about the kind of boy that Toby was.

Toby was also a frustrated scholar, or a scholar who was frustrated because his intelligence was easily dismissed. He'd been delving into the legends and myths and superstitions of New Orleans, from its Voodoo cults to its superstitions about ghosts and vampires, so many of his friends (and enemies) were quick to label him as loony or psycho or eccentric. Of course no one truly believed in such things: Vampires in the French Quarter? Werewolves in Louisiana? But Toby believed in all of them fervently—or at least believed in the history and legends and myths of them. Mack never mentioned to me if any of this ever personally spooked him or not, but I know he always felt that Toby might have believed he was cursed himself, as silly as it sounds, as if someone—or some *thing*, some kind of force, had been responsible for *pushing* him over the balcony. The police, of course, believed in no such idiocies, and for years Mack carried his grief silently, hoping the passage of time and a series of new boyfriends such as Parker or myself might ease the loss of Toby.

"How can you forget a cutie like that?" I asked Mack, not expecting an answer, just cleaning up some tissues from the floor where he had missed tossing them into his trash pail. Mack's apartment was both functional and sentimental—there was a wind-up alarm clock on the table he had had for years; on his bookshelf were the books he had read and never thrown out, dog-eared, spine-broken paperback copies of *Valley of the Dolls* and *Portnoy's Complaint*, alongside the grease-stained manual for the new refrigerator he had purchased six years ago and the assembly instructions for a window fan he had bought in the 1970s. In front of these were his sentimental objects: the pale beige shells he had collected on his first trip to the beach with Toby and the phallus-shaped candleholder he found in Mexico, as well as his more practical stuff, such as a jar of various screws and bolts and nails and picture hooks and an ashtray holding a small, ceramic marijuana pipe. Toby's old manual typewriter still sat on a tiny desk in the corner where he had last used it some twenty-odd years ago, the newer "electric" one Mack had bought him, packed away in the back of the closet. Throughout the place were reminders of Mack's failing health, from stiffened towels dropped to the floor to the row of vitamin and medicine vials and tubes of ointments and lotions in front of his books.

"He was standing on the bridge just over there, waiting for me," Mack said.

"Who?"

"Toby. Just a minute ago."

"You must have been napping," I said. "And dreamed it up."

"No, he was right here, Avery," Mack said, shaking his head to refute my suggestion. "Waiting for me. We were going to go for a walk together."

"Where to, baby? Where were you going?"

"Over the bridge," Mack said. "He said it was very pretty on the other side."

"He said that to you?"

"Well, no," Mack said. "But I could tell by his face."

"I bet that Toby was a real cutie-pie," I said.

"He was, Avery. He was a real cute guy. I loved him a lot."

"I bet you did, sweetie. I betcha you did."

I made my way through the room straightening up some things— restacking magazines on the coffee table, throwing away the small paper cups Mack used for water to chase his medications, removing socks and underwear from the cracks of the couch cushions—and restoring others, finding the TV remote by the sink and replacing it on the night table beside Mack's bed. I picked up the framed photograph of Mack and Toby standing on their balcony that Mack's sister had taken one day long, long ago—Mack's jaw covered with his dark, day-old black stubble, his arm stretched around Toby's lithe body; Toby's eyes dark and shining, his bushy-haired head tilted against Mack's chest, a puka-shell choker at his neck. I had never met Toby, though I had long ago conjured up an idea of him with the help of this photograph and Mack's anecdotes and remembrances. I'd always thought that Toby would have made a good sort of sorority sister for me to joke around with, maturing out of his natural seriousness into the kind of fella with a cynical sense of humor who seemed more and more absent from my address book. Looking at the photograph of the two of them together, it was clear to me they were lovebirds and I felt certain that the young man with the afro I had seen on the stairs was the ghost of Toby; the face and eyes in the photo were an unmistakable match.

I had never seen a ghost before, sober or shit-faced, or so I had come to believe; my father and grandfather had ejected such sci-fi phenomenon entirely out of my head by reason of it being nothing but secular nonsense or devil-worship, even though the Bible was littered with such ethereal and otherwordly sightings, and the two of them took every opportunity they ever had on this planet to invoke the certainly mystical and mysterious Holy Spirit and use it to heal a troubled soul. I didn't believe in faith healing or miracles—what moron could in this day and age? And the Holy Spirit wasn't a *real* ghost, after all—that sort of leap of faith could be considered heretical. And if the truth be told, I'd grown into the kind of skeptical fool who looked to science and intelligence to rationally explain any sort of extraordinary phenomenon. The only logical explanation I could find for my sighting a ghost in the middle of the afternoon was my own high-level stress and minor intoxication, but since they were both daily occurrences for me, part of my habitual modus operandi, I couldn't really, truly and truthfully, believe that they could be the exact cause of my first ghostly encounter. So no, the ghost must have been real, not imagined, I decided, but I had no idea what to do with that realization. What would a ghost want from me? And Toby, no less? It wasn't as if he could help me find a better boyfriend or clean up the place. I was just an overtired and underfunded blunderer. So I kept moving as I always do when trouble and confusion boil up to the surface; I found a glass in Mack's kitchen cabinet and rinsed it out with water and poured myself another shot of hooch and another, smaller one to offer Mack. *Thank God humans had discovered fermentation,* I thought. *Where would the world be without it?* When I made it back to his chair, Mack had already nodded off, and I tossed my shot down in a flash. Instead of finishing Mack's bourbon off, too, I put it on the desk beside his chair, not so much thinking that Mack would wake and drink it as to offer it as a gift or a token to an unknown spirit—as if to acknowledge to the ghost of Toby, yes, I saw you, I know you are here and you must be watching over Mack for me today, so here, have this one on me and tell me what the hell it is you want from me, if that is *why* you are here. Because the truth of the matter was—I was too busy to deal with ghosts, real *or* imagined.

Back downstairs, things mysteriously sorted themselves out with or without the occasional assistance of human intervention and the afternoon flew by. The heat of the day burned across the courtyard and scorched the bricks; my T-shirt dried out, then grew damp again with sweat and took on the stale smell of a homeless person. Parker returned from the hardware store with new batteries and fuses. The electricity was restored and the inexpensive electrician arrived to repair the air conditioner in the Magnolia Suite and left behind an absurdly high itemized bill. The melting ice was kept handy in case we had another unexpected outage and Buddy returned from the hospital with three stitches in his finger and Parker sent him home for the night. "Can you manage to help out tonight?" Parker asked me when he appeared in the office and I was twisting off the cap of a fresh pint of bourbon.

"Let me put on my happy face, first," I answered, imagining the day stretching out longer and more exhausting before me and wondering how crabby and irritated I would be by the time I had to deal with customers trying to decide between having a mesclun salad or the carrot ginger soup. (It was a clear choice to me; go with the soup, it was simply fabulous, even in the heat.)

"One day you're gonna get sick doing that," Parker said.

"Well then, I hope it keeps me flat on my back for a few hours."

"Seriously, you're starting to worry me. You're starting earlier and earlier."

"Seriously, I shouldn't ever stop. I want to be a full-time drunk when I grow up."

"Maybe you're trying to do too much."

"No, there's too much to try to do so I need to work faster."

"You're going to have a heart attack at this rate," Parker said.

"Thank you for your concern, but I need to get back to work so I can help you out later, when I'm *free*."

Just like in a cheesy TV sitcom, Parker left in a huff and Hank walked into the office and said that Lynette had shown up just in time to cart the vomit-soaked linen and towels away. Lynette and her laundry service was the one luxury Parker and I afforded ourselves; everything in the guesthouse and the café was sent out to be washed—none of us "hired help" wanted to spend our valuable "leisure time" in front of washers and dryers soaking, rinsing, bleaching, folding, and ironing—and Lynette and her lover Talla had inherited Lynette's family business a few years before Parker and I started out in ours. In fact, one of my earliest jobs in the Big Easy was in the Boudreaux washroom uptown: folding, rinsing, soaking, bleaching—a thankless job of cracked skin and burning eyes but for the good spirits of Lynette and her mother and sisters. Hank thrust out his hip, attached his wrist to it, and watched me pour myself another shot of bourbon. I graciously offered him one of his own, hoping it might replace the scowl that had appeared at his lips.

"Are you gonna get soused in front of company?" he asked me.

"Whadya mean?" I asked back.

"You forgot," he said, crossing his arms across his chest and jutting out his lower lip. "I knew you would forget."

What did I forget? I thought. *To turn off the computer, to lock the pantry, to bring more towels up to the Magnolia Suite to replace the vomit-soaked ones? Did I forget to give Mack his medicine? Forget to tell Hank I loved him? Or had I forgotten our anniversary? Or his birthday? Or my birthday? Did I forget how old I was or how old I felt?* I was always forgetting something, but what the hell was I forgetting now? I shrugged my shoulders and opened my palms as if I were a hapless circus clown, certain that whatever it was, I had forgotten it, and that Hank nowadays enjoyed being unhappy with me more than our being happy together.

"Griffin and Felipe are coming over tonight," Hank said. "We've had it planned since last week."

Griffin and Felipe were a couple of young muscle queens who lived in a miniature overdecorated house in the Garden District. They were into a lot of big, heavy things—weightlifting, leather, Mission-style furniture, art deco Tiffany lamps. Felipe was a "Design Consultant," which was an overdecorated way of describing his sagging career as an interior designer, though he had the athletic cockiness of someone who had just scored a touchdown and was ready to have his cock sucked by the drum major as a reward. Hank also had the hots for Felipe; any gay man worth his salt could see the sparks flying between the two of them. They had met at—where else?—the gym, a few weeks before, or at least that was how Hank had explained it to me; for all I knew they could have hooked up in a dark cubicle in the local bathhouse and pleasurably molested each other and now thought they could maintain an ongoing fling in full public view of their significant others.

Regardless of their first meeting, I had no doubt that Hank was hot to impress his newest infatuation and he was hoping our charming though run-down guesthouse atmosphere and Parker's superb cooking could do the trick. I knew it might be a short-lived distraction—I was only an audience of one and could seldom give Hank the kind of consistent rapt and devout attention he wanted and felt he deserved from a lover—and I figured once his passion for Felipe had played itself out in a few weeks (and once Felipe realized that we could not afford to be his new clients), things would be fine between us again. Maybe Hank and Felipe were already hot and heavy into the middle of something, perhaps even a threeway that also included Griffin, because rumor had it—or at least the gossip according to Hank had it—that Griffin could not keep his dick in his pants for more than a few minutes and was often itching to do whomever he desired whenever he could do it and get away with it.

Griffin was the more down-to-earth of the two muscle boys, a high-end sort of carpenter who spent his time refinishing and restoring faux antique furniture. The moment I met Griffin I knew he was the source of any disharmony in his relationship with Felipe. Hank and I had stopped by their undersized-shack-masquerading-as-a-fashionable-address one weekend for a brief round of cocktails after we had done some shopping nearby (the Dauphine Suite was in desperate need of new pillows and I wanted some kind of scatter rug to throw over a coffee stain on the carpet in the Magnolia Suite). It was clear to me that Griffin was the one capable of snaring the most attention from outside partners, which was why Felipe might have been so eager to show off Hank to his lover. Hank, for all my roaming eyes and lack of attention towards him on days like today, was still as cute and sexy as the day *I* had met him two years before at that aforementioned dark cubicle of our local bathhouse.

Whereas Felipe was short and thickly built like a high school football player, Griffin, with his shaved head, ice blue eyes, and dark goatee, had the lean, chiseled look of a rock star waiting to be worshipped and adored by his geeky fans. Deep down, Felipe might have resented the fact that Griffin got all the attention wherever they went. To me, Felipe was as nondescript as any ole gay-boy gym bunny with thickly muscled body parts, but the chance of seeing Griffin again in his tight leather pants had been enough for me to agree with Hank's wish to be, well, a more social, rather than sexual, couple to another more sexual, rather than social, couple of muscle queens—even though it had now slipped my mind.

I tossed back another shot of firewater and said, "Buddy's out tonight," thinking that might please Hank a bit, knowing there wouldn't be too much eye candy around to distract his new beau. But he was only annoyed.

"What about Charlie Ray helping Parker out?" Hank asked.

"Charlie Ray has the immunity card, you know that."

"He could still pitch in every now and then," Hank said, the hand back again at the disjointed hip. "Why does he get special treatment?"

"He doesn't get special treatment," I answered. "They have a different arrangement from us. I'll fix up a table in the courtyard and you can eat with Felipe and Griffin out there. I'll come out and chat when it's slow in here."

When it's slow? I thought, and put the glass down and considered pouring myself another before I moved to the next task at hand. *When is it ever slow around here, even when I'm not subbing as a waiter?*

Hank was now visibly perturbed, I could tell by his tight lips and the frown lines that were digging into his forehead. "I'm going to the gym for a while," he said, as if to pay me back for something awful I had just done to him.

He knew this could tick me off because there was always too much work to do for any of us to take a break, and for about three seconds it did. Then, as he was about to leave the office, I said, in my most sweet, passive-aggressive manner, "Have a good workout, honey." By the time he had puffed up his chest and made his frown deeper, there was a prying customer rapping his knuckles at the door, one of the two fossilized gentlemen staying in the Royal Suite, asking where he could catch the Charles Street streetcar and how much money it would set him back.

I spent the rest of the afternoon clearing away some of the rubbish in the courtyard, tossing out waterlogged paper cups, napkins, weeds, and even a bright yellow Café du Monde coffee tin that Buddy had filled with cracked shells and twisted pipe cleaners and placed as a Voodoo charm near the courtyard fountain. In the last few months Buddy had become involved with a caramel-skinned tour guide named Dwayne, an expatriate yoga instructor-cum-graduate student from California who had stumbled upon his African slave ship roots while researching a paper for his master's degree. Dwayne had given up his teaching job and yoga practice to exhume the forgotten histories of the Quarter and along the way embraced its creepy gothic fables of ghosts and vampires and brightly decked-out Voodoo queens as part of his heritage, just as Toby had done decades before. Dwayne was a sharp and clever gumshoe, however; tall and lanky, he wore his hair in dreadlocks tied together behind his head, sported a few obvious piercings in his ear and eyebrow, and led his tours around the Quarter wearing a black floor-length cape. Dwayne and Buddy made a striking couple, oversized and cartoonish, like Ichabod Crane dating Clark Kent, and it was hard not to seek out little glimpses of intimacy between them. Even Parker, who usually kept his sexual fantasies to himself even when he was in the deepest throes of passion, had expounded on the what-ifs of Buddy and Dwayne's sex life, wondering out loud to me more than a few times about what roles and positions they must assume in bed. In matters of the occult, though, I had come to believe that Buddy was something of a gullible, big-muscled pawn, submissively placing the growing number of charms and tokens and spiritual offerings in and around the café and guesthouse according to his cunning swami boyfriend's specific instructions. Buddy might once have been a pious and devout Catholic, but he was easily spooked by what he had learned about, and had come to believe in of the powers of Voodoo and the ancestral orishá. I could find his elaborately constructed charms and art installations (such as a pink spray-painted baseball cap lined with white pigeon feathers) anywhere and unexpectedly, beneath the computer in the office, in the bathroom cabinets in the guest rooms, on the windowsill in the café's kitchen.

That afternoon while sorting through the clean laundry, I found a light blue painted stone covered with yellow plastic beads in the small walk-in closet of a pantry behind the stairwell and next to the tiny restrooms we maintained for restaurant guests. The pantry was the place where we kept odd supplies under lock and key for both businesses, the guesthouse and the restaurant, such as soap, shampoo, candles, dishes, cloth napkins, and Parker's stock of better booze for the bar. The stone reminded me a little too much of a plant I had neglected a few months before that had yellowed from neglect and then died overnight, after I had drowned it with too much water thinking the more fluids I gave it, the healthier it would become. I knew I would have to bring this to Parker's attention, and I stopped and carried the stone to the kitchen to confront him, but my admonition fell away when I remembered Hank's extra dinner guests that we would also have to feed in the courtyard. So instead, I sampled Parker's special of the night (Catfish Medallions Au Gratinée: *yum yum, yum*) and complimented him on it ("Sweetie, this is as divine as you are!"), then took a bowl of broth, some soft bread, overboiled broccoli, and chocolate pudding on a tray up to Mack's apartment. Mack seldom made it through much of the food Parker fixed for him, but we knew it was better than anything he could get at a hospice or under other circumstances. Mack's days were now mostly spent in his chair or his bed, watching TV, napping, reading a magazine or a book, sometimes writing or drawing in a journal; on good days he liked to surf the 'net with the laptop Parker had given him several Christmases ago, downloading dirty pics he liked to show to one of us later. We were all grateful that we had not yet entered that hateful realm of morphine drips and adult diapers, so there was never any displeasure over ungluing dried potatoes from the keyboard or picking up a spilled dish of carrots. Mack was still in his chair, dozing, the TV tuned to a talk show, the bourbon I had left him earlier untouched. I closed the window and turned the air conditioner back on, slugged back the liquor, and wiped a wet washcloth across Mack's face. He stirred lightly and acknowledged my presence and the tray of food. I offered to help him to the bathroom, in case he needed to make the trip, but he waved me away with a soft flutter of his hand and reached for the TV remote.

Outside, on the balcony, I stopped and looked down at the courtyard below, and a fleeting thought of jumping washed over me. Mack was not doing well; he was becoming worse, not better, and I knew he might need to be hospitalized again soon, that things might not turn around for him, that we could be headed towards more intensive care. For years Mack had been our guiding spirit, our jack-of-all-trades, helping Parker out on a busy night in the café, carting the laundry bags out to Lynette's truck for me in the afternoons. He was the one who knew how the sump pump worked, how to relight the water heater, how to patch the roof when it leaked. Even when he had become progressively ill he could always give us an answer to those inexplicable things that baffled the rest of us—how to get the door lock of the Burgundy Suite to work better or how to keep the shelves in the pantry from sagging. Had he been well he could easily have repaired the air conditioner that day for us and swiftly restored a calm to all our disorder.

Soon my anxieties over Mack progressed into every other worry I could summon up: the guesthouse was beginning to look shabbier, the rooms needed repainting, water stains were growing larger, the carpets were unraveling and the linens were so thin from constant washing and bleaching that they could shred at any moment from the puncture of a painted fingernail. I was convinced that the old slave quarters were literally sinking into the ground; every day little pieces of mortar sand were scattered across the courtyard waiting to be swept away and one day they would have to be replaced or our house of too-carefully-balanced credit cards and old bricks would come tumbling down on top of us. I hated having to nickel-and-dime everything because it made me feel like a miserly obese Scrooge, but it was the only way we were going to survive in this place—we would never get the electrical wiring upgraded, never get central air-conditioning installed, never get the brickwork repointed. Parker's restaurant seldom showed a profit because he was always choosing the better (and more pricey) cuts of meat and exotic vegetables and spices without passing the price on to the customer and every month we were borrowing from one account to pay off the next. There seemed to be no relief in sight, only more work and more work and more work and more work and I knew there would come an evening when the fat old hamster in the wheel would just run out of steam and keel over. As I leaned over the balcony railing I noticed a movement in the plants below, a rustle of leaves which meant that some kind of unwanted animal had probably found its way into the courtyard. We were occasionally visited by one of the neighboring cats, particularly if Buddy had set out a Voodoo concoction made of dried chicken bones he had salvaged from the café's garbage, and they were easy to detect and shoo way, but only last week I had noticed an exterminator at the end of the block trying to rid one of the other houses on the street of something larger and more sinister, which meant that the varmints could have migrated here. I made a mental note that I should put out some traps and poison after closing up the restaurant that night, and completely forgot about the notion of wanting to jump and end it all because once again there was so much to do too quickly.

Back in the kitchen, I offered to help Parker with the food prep, but he shooed me away and said to make sure I had everything I needed to keep the bar running smoothly, which I took to mean that it was now open season for me to have another drink, or at least the legitimate, Academy-sanctioned expensive one of the night, this time from the better stock that we kept at the bar. I had barely got my buzz going again when the first customers of the evening arrived, a newly-wed and clearly already-overfed pneumatic couple that I sat by the window, and before I had even sobered up, I was dealing with a party of seven who individually asked three-thousand questions about the ingredients of each appetizer and entrée, to which I blithely ad-libbed answers in my most haughty and waiterly manner. ("Why yes, the okra is organic!")

Things went smoothly enough after that. Fallen forks were replaced, water goblets refilled, a salad was remade without red onions for a woman wearing an expensive-looking diamond ring and a formfitting tube top, the querulous table of seven ordered a second round of drinks, and a necklace made of beer bottle caps was discovered behind the good whiskey, no doubt a charm Buddy had placed there that was intended to keep me away from the bottle; José even had time to wash a few oily dishes and pans before the next influx of gluttonous customers arrived. Hank showed up at the door with Griffin and Felipe and, because I was busy trying to understand the orders from a whispering party of three, I waved him towards the alleyway, which meant I would join him in a few minutes. I slipped the table order to Parker, fixed the muffled threesome their drinks, then took a set of menus out the back door and into the alleyway, where I discovered that José had already placed water glasses and a basket of breadsticks on the courtyard table. Charlie Ray had sniffed out the party—or maybe Parker had told him about it to get back at me for having to cook extra nonpaying meals—and he stood smoking beside beefy-boy Felipe, his eyes cruising Felipe's torso as if he was ready to roll over on his back and lift his legs in the air, much to the visible dismay of Hank.

I mustered up all of my remaining charm, smiled and extended my hand to Felipe and said, "I hope you don't mind dining al fresco tonight." The courtyard at this darkening hour was magnificently impressive, the candlelight on the table, the long flickering arms of the plants and pattern of bricks lit with soft, theatrical spots of green light that Hank had installed in a moment of inspired obligation, the dim-yellowish glow of table lamps through the sheer curtains of the balcony windows, the dark outlines of the wooden spokes of the balcony railings and the sound of the bubbling water of the fountain. The place where we kept the main courtyard table was always a good twenty degrees cooler than the heat of the street at this time of year and the clear night skies above and the hint of a full moon rising gave the area exactly the sort of lavishly romantic impression Hank had hoped it would make.

Felipe limply held my fingers, as if he had expended all his energy on the circuit machines at the gym, air-kissed my cheeks in mock Eurotrash fashion, and complimented the courtyard. He was wearing a tight-fitting white T-shirt that showed off his nipples and hinted at a tattoo around his left oversized bicep. Behind him, Griffin moved into view and leaned in and kissed me dryly on the lips. I tried not to swoon and turn googly-eyed but there was all of sudden a lot more blood rushing around my body than I thought I owned; Griffin was shirtless except for a black leather vest held together by a few thin cords of leather string. His upper left arm was covered with a black-and-blue-ink tattoo, the body of a wolf stretching towards his shoulder, a weave of thorns and paw prints left in its wake. I felt my throat go dry and my jaw drop open and for a moment I contemplated suggesting that we simply switch boyfriends for a while; I would willingly give Felipe the sour-faced Hank for as long as he wanted him as long as I got the pleasure of the divinely decadent Griffin in return, even if only for a few milliseconds.

"Can I bring out some drinks for everyone?" I asked, not so much to be a polite host, but to shift my focus away from wanting to stare at (and adore) the you-betcha-I'm-a-hottie-in-bed-too Griffin.

Martinis were the drink of choice for all except Griffin, who wanted a light beer. Instead of trying to navigate the brick passageway with individual glasses, I made a pitcher and poured the martinis when I returned a few minutes later to the table where they were all now seated (including the smoky caboose Charlie Ray, who had lit another cigarette). José arrived a few seconds later with a cold beer for Griffin and more breadsticks and I tried to talk about Parker's specials for the night in a way that sounded like it wasn't the spiel of a breathless, harassed waiter; I purposely stood next to where Griffin was seated so I wouldn't have to look at him and lose my mind and the mini-iota of self-respect I still had left, but when I had finished my monologue, Griffin wrapped his arm through my legs and around one of my thighs, tilted his head up towards me and asked in a gravelly whisper, "But what do you recommend, Sir?"

The flagrant sexuality unnerved me and it took a few beats before I responded with a grin and said, "I always go for the hot and spicy dish."

"That sounds like the right choice to me," Griffin answered. "I'll leave myself in your hands." The impression of his arm around my leg had not been without its consequences. I could feel my blood pressure rise, sweat form across my brow, and my cock fatten with delight. I shifted myself so that his arm would fall away and I could place the ashtray that was in the center of the table in front of Charlie Ray's place. Hank shot me a distressed look, all glaring eyes and parallel brow lines; I knew he was upset with Charlie Ray crashing the dinner party and usurping Felipe's attention, but Charlie Ray would also buffer whatever extra work Parker might have to do to feed this group. Charlie Ray, with his spiky black hair and long spidery eyelashes, was about the same age as Hank and the muscle boys, but instead of a buff bod he had a lean, exotic, trashy look about him, as if he had just pulled himself out from the bottom of a twelve-man orgy. Charlie Ray, in fact, had an insatiable sexual appetite, or at least that was how Parker had described it and I had no reason to disbelieve the fact (or explore it further). Charlie Ray had been through a string of broken hearts (others, of course, certainly not his own) before he landed in Parker's lap and I knew he would probably only stay around as long as he could do so without being sucked into the maddening and dizzying chores of the place. In my opinion, he had already overstayed his welcome, a fact that I knew Hank was also thinking of at that exact moment.

I chatted up the more exotic items of Parker's menu, took their orders, and raced back to the restaurant where the breathy threesome was eager to look at the dessert menu. I got lost in finding a chilled bottle of Chardonnay for a party of two, then suddenly adding up the checks for the whispering party and the raucous table of four behind them, and when I made my way back out to the courtyard, our brawny foursome had already finished

their soups and salads and José was clearing their plates. Out of the corner
of my eye I saw the leaves of a plant rustle and hoped it was just a breeze
blowing through and not an immigrant family of rodents looking for the
next place to call home, or God forbid, a snake that might have wandered
out of the gutter. I cast my eyes suspiciously around looking for something
else unnatural to catch my attention, like the ghost of Toby wandering back
down the staircase yellow-eyed and zombie-armed and ready to disrupt
the dinner party and be a nuisance, but there was nothing but my own
nervousness ready to trick me.

"Hank was just telling us about your ghosts," Felipe said.

"My ghosts?" I answered, a bit taken off guard. At first I thought he
had read my mind. I hadn't confessed to anyone that I had sighted the
ghost of Toby earlier in the day, so of course I was a bit unnerved. Then
I remembered he must be referring to *our* ghosts—the ghostly legends of
Café Surtout and Le Petite Paradis. A few years ago, during a particularly
slim tourist season, Parker had concocted the story of Angelle, a nineteenth-
century slave girl who was charged with having murdered her lover—the
last of the Dubuisson family line—and brought to trial as a mean-spirited
Voodoo priestess, in order for the café and the guesthouse to get some free
publicity and be mentioned by the weirdly-costumed walking tour guides
schlepping through the Quarter. Parker's story had traveled from one tour
guide to the next, each of them creating his own specific details until one
day an officious newspaper reporter with horn-rims and an out-of-date
Sixties flip arrived at my office, ready to debunk it all. But because she
could neither prove that the Dubuisson heir had *not* been murdered nor
that his slave Angelle *had* been a Voodoo priestess, the reporter had only
succeeded in perpetuating our myth. Parker and I had never admitted the
impish fabrication to anyone, not even to our new business-slash-sexual
partners; in fact, as the years went by, Parker continued to elaborate on

and embellish the details of the story to his inquisitive customers and I occasionally joined in with the ruse. Ever since Hank and I had become involved with each other, however, I had been hesitant about bringing up the story out of concern for any racial sensitivity Hank might harbor over their being slave and master and living together disharmoniously on our property. But clearly it was Hank who had told these puzzling scandals to our guests, perhaps with an ease he never exhibited to me about it, so now I fell into another spiel, this one brief and awkwardly told, about Pierre Dubuisson's first lover, Angelle's older brother Aaron, whom Pierre murdered and buried beneath the courtyard, the details of which always interested our gay guests. "Aaron thought he could blackmail Pierre into winning his freedom," I said, not looking at Hank or soliciting his reaction. "But instead, Pierre tossed him over the top-floor balcony while they were arguing. Angelle, who was only eleven years old at the time, witnessed this, but did not tell her parents or her masters, afraid that she would also be beaten. Years later, when she became Pierre Dubuisson's mistress herself, she is said to have placed a spell on him so that he could not love anyone else but her, and that ended his interest in a host of other boy-toys. But when he announced that he was marrying another woman, she poisoned him. The records of the time show that Pierre Dubuisson died of yellow fever, not poison, and the ghost of Angelle is seen wandering into the guest rooms now and then, trying to find someone who will believe that she is not a vengeful spirit, only a girl who wanted to be in love."

"So she's a good ghost?" Felipe asked.

"More an enigma, I should think," I answered, feeling a bit coy myself. "Sometimes charitable, sometimes intrusive."

"There must be a reason why she appears," Griffin said.

"Why should there be a reason?" Charlie Ray asked.

"Nothing happens by accident," Griffin answered.

"Ah, so you're a philosopher," I said to Griffin, catching his eyes and feeling suddenly young and flirty as well as exhaustingly drunk, as if the groom had suddenly fallen into my arms in a toilet stall at his wedding party and confessed he was making a big mistake with his new bride and I was the reason.

"All order must have a reason," he added.

"And all disorder needs to be organized," I smiled, scooping up the empty bread basket beside him.

While I was refilling water goblets around the table, Hank, who had clearly had more drinks than he could manage, began mangling a short anecdote of a guest who had once seen a strange man in "old-timey clothing" leaving her room while she was stepping out of her shower. She called the police but since nothing from her room was missing, or had been moved, Parker had actually had the audacity to tell the officers it was the ghost of Pierre Dubuisson trying to anger Angelle into removing the spell from his soul.

"The apprehension must be terrifying," Felipe said, consolingly placing a hand atop Hank's wrist. "Living with ghosts who could appear at any moment."

"You don't notice them too much," Hank said, as demurely as he knew how from all his practice in acting classes. "You get rather used to them being about."

"So you've seen them?" I asked him, wandering back to the conversation at the table. "You've actually seen them, yourself?

"No, not really," he answered, shooting me a dirty look, as if I had caught him wearing someone else's skimpy costume and confronted his authority on the subject of our revenants. "But there is certainly something *unusual* about this place."

When Hank started to tell our buffed, low-body-fat guests about the disturbing wails of a baby that guests occasionally heard while they were staying in the Dauphine Suite (we never had babies staying in the guesthouse and, as far as I knew, except for a few thousand childish-acting adults, there wasn't a single infant living anywhere on this block or the next), I sheepishly excused myself to rush back to the kitchen to help José bring the entrées to the table. Felipe and Hank had been sensible enough to order the evening's specials (Felipe the Catfish; Hank the equally appetizing Crab-Stuffed Pork Chops). Griffin had opted for the café's hottest and spiciest dish, which that night (other than himself) was the Shrimp and Sausage over Grits. Charlie Ray had ordered true to his roots—a rare hamburger with ketchup and yellow mustard. I opened a bottle of wine for the table, poured glasses for everyone except Griffin, who again wrapped his arm around my thigh and begged in his gravelly voice for another beer. When everyone had enough pepper and cheese and water and Griffin had a fresh, cold beer, I retreated to the dining room just in time to seat a preppily-dressed party of two.

I made a few more visits to the courtyard to check on the meal, open another bottle of wine, and offer the dessert menu and coffee, while inside the customers continued to arrive until Parker stuck his head out of the kitchen and announced it was time to lock the front door. As the last tipsy and bloated customers began to make their way out of the restaurant, I removed the soiled tablecloths and napkins and folded them into the laundry bag in the kitchen. Through the back doorway I heard Parker outside in the courtyard, talking with the dinner party, his sarcastic rebuttal, "Why everything has a special ingredient!" making me smile; no doubt he was being elusive about revealing the ingredients he used in one of the specials of the night. I unlocked the pantry between the restrooms to get fresh tablecloths and noticed a quick movement on the floor. I was certain that whatever serpent or rodent I had detected roaming beneath the leaves of the courtyard plants had now furtively made its way into the pantry, and as I shifted the box on the floor with my foot, hoping to scare it back outside, I noticed a set of ice blue eyes. Startled, I stepped back as a white-haired dog growled and opened its slobbery jaws, its pale blue eyes turned a fiery red, and it scampered up the wall in the most improbable way and disappeared through the ceiling just as it revealed with a snarl the full size of its wolf-like fangs to me. The rush of fear and confusion and blood to my brain caused a momentary black-out of my vision. I didn't collapse to the ground; instead, I stood still and took a deep breath to calm myself, since my pulse was racing as if it were an agitated squirrel doing laps around my chest. *What was a dog doing in the pantry? How in the hell had it gotten inside here?* As my vision returned I saw tiny glowing orbs of light swirling around my ankles and rising up in the same path the wolf-dog had taken up the wall and into the ceiling, until they too disappeared in the most improbable and astonishing way. As I continued to regulate my breathing to calm myself, I cursed the fact that I had had too much to drink and was now *seeing* things—dogs, wolves, disco lights, *ghosts*. My heart sounded in my ears as if I were racing up the old cypress stairs to the floors above. This—this now—this was certainly not a ghost but an *illusion*—a trick of my feeble, overworked, inebriated mind. Maybe there had been something *else* in my drink? Could someone be out for me? Ready to slip me a mickey or a tab of LSD?

I looked again at the floor and the wall and saw nothing but white plaster and dirty bricks. I shuffled my feet in a silly little dance, expecting something else to leap out at me, but there was nothing but the grainy scrape of the rubber soles of my sneakers against the floor. Just as I convinced myself that I was hallucinating and this was all a great big mistake and misunderstanding of some sort and not some unbroadcast episode of the *Twilight Zone*, I detected someone standing in the doorway behind me. Startled, I turned and saw Griffin checking out my backside with his tattooed arm up against the door frame and the other hand tucked half into his jeans pocket.

"You're not trying to avoid us?" he asked me, his eyes as astonishingly blue as the imaginary ones I had just conjured up on the menacing animal-in-question-with-fangs.

"Not at all," I answered, pretending I was not only sober, but also not concerned that the wolf-dog I had just seen would make a return appearance. "Just finishing up some stuff."

That was when I felt all my blood rush right down into my cock. Griffin stepped inside the pantry and the door fell shut behind him. He slipped his hand out of his pants pocket and brushed it against the crotch of my pants. My hands instinctively slipped inside his vest, rubbing against the bristly cropped hair of his chest. His hand kneaded my crotch while he nuzzled his neck against mine and alternately licked and bit my flesh, the sensations of pain and pleasure making me both smile and wince. His other hand made its way into my pants and beneath my boxers and he fondled the shaft of my cock first, then worked his fingertips down to my balls, cupping them in his palm as if to gage their heat. I fingered his nipple, felt the cold steel bar that pierced it, while he widened his mouth and swallowed my chin as if he were about to eat me.

Then, he slid to his knees and took my cock in his mouth. I leaned against the pantry shelves as he clutched my ass cheeks and moved me deeper into his throat. I felt a youthfulness flame and rise up in my chest as my lungs swelled with air and my cock grew harder. I had a sense of becoming light, not weightless, but bright and glowing, a mystical elevation which reminded me of why I so much enjoyed that first drink of the day. I forgot all about my illusions (or disillusions). There was nothing worth doing other than what I was doing now, or, rather, what Griffin was doing to me now. Every problem was suddenly a nonproblem. Troubles belonged to somebody else in another place. I had entered the *Twilight Zone*. The twilight zone of my needy libido. Griffin seemed to grow abstract and more profound as he engulfed me, or, rather, swallowed my erection, as if he were merging my lightness with a mysterious purpose. He brought me to the point of orgasm, pulled away to taunt me as a cool stream of air hit my wet cock, and then his mouth was back again and warmly swallowing me. I tried to postpone my orgasm for as long as I could enjoy the sensation of him at my crotch, my eyes studying the design of the tattoo of thorns that disappeared into the dark hair of his forearm. Then I pushed his mouth away from my cock and shot onto the floor, immediately aware that I now had something else to clean up—a puddle of my own sperm.

Griffin smirked and eased himself out of the pantry and the door fell shut behind him. I zippered myself up. My heart was thumping against my rib cage and my throat was dry and ready for another drink. *What the hell,* I thought, exhausted and released and suddenly tension free, and I took one of the cloth napkins, wiped up the floor with it, and shoved it into the back of my pants pocket. As I stepped out of the pantry and relocked the door, I noticed someone making his way up the stairwell, a dark-skinned hand floating along the banister. I looked up and saw the young bushy-haired Toby again looking down at me, his expression indicating, *Time to follow me. Follow me up the stairs. Now.* My pulse leaped, started doing laps again at an abnormal pace, and I followed the apparition up the staircase, once more two at a time, stopping to catch my breath and look around for him as I reached the top floor. For the first time that day I was truly worried about my health—my heart was beating too hard and I felt certain if I didn't slow down and relax I would most certainly risk a stroke. The ghost of Toby was nowhere in sight and below me in the courtyard I could see Griffin rejoining the dinner party. I felt as if I had climbed a mountain, my chest struggling as if my breath had been weakened by a higher, thinner altitude. Cautiously, slowly, I made my way down to Mack's door, knowing, just knowing, what it was I would find.

Inside Mack's apartment, the TV was still going and I turned it off with the remote control. Mack's eyes were open, but his breathing had stopped. I felt his wrist for a pulse, but the skin was clammy and cold, and I knew he was beyond resuscitation. I took my fingertips and closed his eyelids and sat for a moment on the edge of his chair to give him a final moment of respect. Mack was dead and I had not told him good-bye. He had been the glue that held us together; even when he became sick he was the reason we did the things we did and I knew that it would not be the same without him; all of our feelings would be different, changed, our tiny little kingdom missing its fabled, fabulous prince. I wanted to stop and cry, but there was still a lot of work ahead for me, so guilt soured my stomach and my self-worth took a tumble into self-pity, and I sat holding Mack's cold hand, rubbing his flesh as if I could rekindle his soul. His heart had finally given up, or maybe his heart had finally determined it was time to join Toby and spare the rest of us the unpleasant path we were headed on in the months ahead. I looked around the room to make certain that there was nothing in disarray, nothing to be discovered later that should not be, and then left the apartment.

Downstairs, Parker was back in the kitchen and José was tending to the last set of customers, a startling handsome young couple, both dressed in black. I wiped down the bar area, emptied the ice bucket, and was carrying glasses to the kitchen when Hank stepped inside, arched his eyebrows as if daring me to try and prevent what came next, and said he was headed with the muscle boys to a bar on Bourbon Street.

I said good-bye to Griffin and Felipe outside the main door of the restaurant, Felipe air-kissing me his thanks, Griffin grasping his hand at my shoulder and saying he hoped we could get together another time. Even that small breath of him aroused me, my cock straining again inside my pants, and I nodded and smiled and waved like a phony bobble-head souvenir as the four of them made their way towards Bourbon street, Charlie Ray sending a puff of smoke into the moonlit street just as I turned away. Watching them leave, I felt an emptiness because I had kept Mack's death a secret from them, not wanting to be a high-crisis drama queen and alter their evening plans, or God forbid, keep Hank from finding a little bit of happiness. To balance this, of course, I rudely disappointed a pair of bespectacled young tourists who wanted to eat a late dinner at the café, and relocked the front door, vulgarly flipped the Closed sign towards the window, and yanked down the shades. Parker was at the sink washing a pan when I turned off the faucets and brusquely told him to stop cleaning. "I'll finish up here with José," I said to him, deflecting my eyes to oily, watery stains at the waistline of his once bleached-white chef's smock. "You might want to pay your respects upstairs before I call it in."

It took him a few seconds to understand what I was telling him. Then his big eyes welled up with tears and he let out a soft, "Oh no." Parker was a hefty-sized man with a cheery disposition, even when he was annoyed and irritated, and it bothered me to watch him become upset with this news. Mack had always been Parker's confidant and I could always count on one of them to find out the mood of the other. Parker didn't allow me to witness too much of his despair, however; he hugged me with a long hard squeeze, as if I had just told him I was moving out of town and I would never see him again, and then he left the kitchen. I heard the stairs creak and shift as he made his way timidly up to Mack's apartment.

I found José and sent him home, telling him it had been a long day and if he wanted, he could come in late the following day for helping me cover Buddy's shift. I washed dishes for a while, let others soak while I put out fresh tablecloths, then went and cleared the remaining dishes and glasses from the courtyard table. It was after midnight when I called the police to report Mack's death and two baby-faced officers who had been on Bourbon Street were standing in the courtyard in a matter of minutes. Parker was still with Mack, his face all flushed and blotchy from crying; he was wearing his prayer shawl around his shoulders and his yarmulke was atop his balding head of short, graying hair and when I noticed the prayer book in his hand, I felt all at once like a heretic and a heathen myself who was always being questioned about his disbelief. My father and grandfather had hammered their Bible quotes into my brain day after day of my childhood so that by the time I left home, I wanted no more of it. God was no longer a part of my daily life, except for a plea in the most exasperating circumstances. But the truth was that I had never lost my belief in God, really; no, I always felt as if I had just put Him in the back of my closet, like a pair of expensive pants that no longer fit because I had eaten too many Oreo cookies and mint chocolate chip ice cream and no longer cared to lose the weight to wear them again but could not see myself parting from them because they were so expensive and once beautiful. What picked me up out of bed each morning was not faith in a God (or a Goddess or some genderless New Age Higher Power) but the need to work to pay the bills, to keep the little cluster of us together and going and out of harm's way. Work was both my faith and fate, and it was often what made me aware of both the presence and absence of the God I had been raised believing in. But Parker, I knew, was not a devout man either. Like the rest of us he had found himself with a loss and was grappling to reach an understanding about death.

Parker and I answered the officers' questions about the cause and probable time of Mack's death, and I told them that I would take care of all of the funeral arrangements and would call Mack's family the following day. The morticians arrived, two thirtyish guys with long, oily hair and pointy sideburns, and they zippered Mack into a black plastic body bag and carried him out of the apartment on a stretcher. I offered the officers coffee or dessert before they left, which they gladly accepted, seating themselves at the courtyard table, where only minutes ago it seemed, Hank and his dinner party were tossing their superstitious laughter against the bricks. They were both young and hungry, not on the parish force more than two years apiece, and Parker kept them entertained about the secret ingredients in his pecan pie ("The more booze the better flavor, I always say."), while I continued cleaning the last set of pans in the sink. Finally, when everyone had left, the restaurant cleaned and locked up, I sat in the courtyard with Parker while he drank a glass of red wine and smoked his daily cigarette, the only one he allowed himself to indulge in.

"I wish I had known he was so close," Parker said. "There's so much I wanted to tell him."

"Like what?"

"Little things," Parker said. "How the sauce tasted tonight. How the sausage dried up too fast. That sort of thing. He always liked hearing the details, so I saved them up for him."

He tapped a few ashes at his side, and I did my best not to frown and look where they had landed against the bricks. "I hope he's comfortable now. At rest."

"Mack was never uncomfortable," I answered. "He always wanted to be here. With us. It's what kept him going. He was happy."

"I meant now," Parker said. "I hope he's at rest now. In heaven or wherever we end up when we die."

"You don't really believe in all that, do you?" I asked him. "Life after death? Immortality of the soul? Angels or eternal damnation?"

"Of course I don't," he answered. "I'm too skeptical."

"And probably oversentimental."

"But I would like to imagine him at rest," Parker said. "I want him to be at a place where he is not suffering."

"There's no such thing as suffering after death," I said. "The body dies. The soul does not suffer."

"But don't you wonder where it goes?" Parker asked. "The soul. After death?"

"I'm sure we spend more time dead than alive, so I would like to think that it's a painless place. Or experience."

"All I know is I miss him already," Parker said, and cleared his throat.

I knew that if I turned my head and looked over at Parker's face, I would catch the tears welling up again in his eyes, and I didn't want to begin a contest to see who could cry the loudest and hardest.

"We can sell now if you want," he added. He knew the businesses were wearing me down and, at the bottom of things, we both knew that Mack was the one who had kept me going. I could never have abandoned him, no matter how often I wanted out of this insane, no-profit backbreaking business, and I could not desert Parker and his café unless he was the first to cave in.

"Who would want this place?" I asked first, and then, after a few seconds, "And what would I do?"

Parker T. Steinberg, I knew, would only move on to another restaurant. Cooking was his joy, his pleasure, his talent, his passion, and owning his own restaurant had always been the path he had seemed destined to take, working his way up through the thankless chain of restaurant jobs, from dishwasher to line cook to chef. But I had no practical, marketable skills other than folding and cleaning and I had not an ounce of desire to do that somewhere else.

"I could buy you out," he offered.

"With what?" I answered laughing. "I'm keeping you afloat."

Had we been a couple romantically in love this would have certainly provoked a fight, but as the brotherly companions we had become—hell, each other's family, really—Parker simply sighed and accepted my statement with resignation and said, "I could manage things better." He stubbed the cigarette out in the ashtray and took his hands and drew my head towards him. He kissed me somewhere in my hair, his smoky stew of tobacco, garlic, and onion odors falling around me. "Think about it," he said, and left me at the table with the empty wineglass and the smoldering ashtray. He took the stairs slowly again, this time as if he had aged a hundred years since finishing cooking and cleaning and grieving, and his heavy weight made the stairs shift and creak as he made his way to his second-floor balcony door. I waved him goodnight, cleaned up the table, and then, back inside the office I shut down the computer, checked the reservation book, and ran the hot water for a bath.

So where do we go next? I thought, pouring myself another glass of bourbon, feeling it sting my stomach as if it were the first of the day. *Is death termination or transition? Or is there simply nothing out there at all but a big blank space of nothing? A twilight zone of emptiness.* I undressed and threw my clothes into a corner of the bathroom and slipped into the tub, where I soaked until the skin on my fingers began to shrivel and I thought I heard someone calling my name, but it was only the wake and waves of my random movements through the water and the splashing sounds echoing across the tile walls. If there was something, if there was an afterlife, solitude was probably not very likely. It must be a very crowded place, the dead easily outnumbering the living. Years and years and years of people dying. Many more dead people than the ones still on earth.

Dry and wearing my robe, I thought about calling Mack's sister in Texas, but knew it would only be troublesome to spread bad news at such a late hour. Instead, I lay in bed, listening to the movements around me, water running through the pipes, the shifting of the floorboards upstairs, thinking it was most likely some drunken guest headed back to bed from the toilet. I picked up a book to read, thought I heard a baby crying and strained to hear the way the voice broke, imagining it was not a child but the boyish, high-pitched sobs of Parker in his bed, crying, miserable over the fact that Mack was gone, though there was no practical way I could have heard him through the spaces that separated us now. Then, I found myself thinking of Toby and Mack, what it must have been like for Mack the night Toby had died. Had he broken down and cried, sobbed, moaned, beaten his fists against his brow, felt the same kind of crushing pressure in his chest that I felt now, unable to release it? No, Mack might have never shown his discomfort or his pain over this, too—he just wasn't that kind of guy. He was a man's man. He would have held it all inside. I had never met Toby—he had died long before I arrived on the scene—so how could I have possibly seen his ghost twice that day when I didn't even know firsthand what he looked like? If I really believed in ghosts then I would lose my mind for sure. Stress and drinking had caused all my illusions—something inside me must have sensed Mack's final hours and conjured up Toby and the pantry hallucinations as mental ways of coping with it. The mind's rejection of truth. *Denial.* My illogical logic led me next to thinking about Mack and how we had met at a dinner party given by a couple of graduate students who had long ago moved elsewhere; I had no idea of how to reach them now to tell them he was gone. In my memory Mack had never been a sickly man, though the night we met he had a cough he couldn't seem to shake, and a few months later it would take a bitter turn for the worse. Mack was always the strong and determined one; he had helped me paint the guest rooms; he built the shelving in the copper-topped bar that Parker found for the café. He had gotten the drawers of the bureau in the Royal Suite to open without sticking. We had thrown him a surprise birthday party the first month we were open.

None of us had believed that Mack would ever die; we had assumed his immortality the way defiant young men enlisting do their own when they are off to war, thinking more of foreign lands and new adventures than of battle and possible death. *Immortality.* The soul will spend more time alive than the aging, physical body could ever know. I was having trouble separating the soul of the man from the still, lifeless, final body I had watched the morticians remove from his apartment. Where was he now? *Nowhere,* I thought, *except missing in action from where he is desperately wanted.*

The words of the book blurred and I put it aside and switched off the lamp, feeling the emptiness of my missing Mack. When Mack had returned the last time from the hospital, I had been afraid of leaving him alone in his apartment. That night I had stayed with him, leaving Hank downstairs, sleeping beside Mack in his bed for what would be one of our last and most intimate moments together. All I did was embrace him, hold him from behind, my arms snaking around the furry bag of bones he had become. Though he seemed to sleep safely and comfortably in my arms, I was wracked with worry and unable to relax, fearful of becoming entwined in the intravenous tubing and yanking the newly implanted catheter out of his chest.

In the darkness of the room, the soft hum of the air conditioner came into focus and I turned onto my opposite side, worried that the chill of the draft would leave me with a sore throat in the morning and out of commission to prevent the place from falling apart. I felt my stomach grumbling and my heart beating in my chest and knew I was luckier than many gay men of my generation; so far, I'd been able to keep myself moderately healthy through the years of perplexing relationships and arduous affairs, remaining HIV-negative from one dysfunctional partner to the next, the biggest battle so far between high cholesterol and elevated blood pressure and a tendency to overdrink when things became hectic. Again, I fell into another thought of Mack; how, when we slept together as a couple, he had embraced me, just as Parker had, and Hank would have done now if he were here, and then I tried to find some comfort in the fact that wherever Mack was now, whatever afterlife he had landed in if there was any kind of afterlife, at least he might have been reunited with Toby. For all of us who followed in Toby's footsteps, it was clear that he had been the love of Mack's life.

Then I was asleep before I knew it, lost in a dream where I kept chasing after Toby up an unending flight of stairs. The frustration momentarily woke me; I brought the darkness of the bedroom into focus, and closed my eyes again, but instead of falling back asleep I made up a list of things I would need to do in the morning: call relatives, order flowers, buy plastic beverage cups to use at the wake. Soon, however, I fell into another dream, or, rather, willed myself into remembering Griffin before I fell asleep, the stubbly touch of his chest, the clutch of muscle at his shoulder, the snaking thorns of his tattoo, the fattening of my own cock. Then I was chasing him, as I had done with Toby, but the stairs had given way to the crumbling bricks of courtyards and blackened streets and decaying passageways. I followed him to one street that I was certain was on the other side of Jackson Square, but when I looked around for a landmark to anchor myself, I realized I was running again, this time with something chasing me—an animal, forcing me to flee. The white fur of the dog came into focus and then the wolf-like snarl of teeth. This time fear lifted my head off the pillow and I thought about getting out of bed to drink some water. But exhaustion pushed my eyelids closed and I was dreaming again: this time I was falling through the darkness until I willed myself to stop falling and I was standing at the courtyard fountain trying to lift out a nervous, deranged goldfish to save it from something else that was in the water, trying to attack it. A face floated into view, Griffin's again, and the fish seemed to swim calmly, then disappear altogether as I began to fall through the water—now air—towards Griffin's face, into the darkness of his mouth. The roughness of the floor of his tongue where I landed seemed to split apart and pulse in a steady rhythm, changing into a pair of beating wings on either side of my body.

I woke up again with what I had thought was the tension of an erection but was really a burning sensation playing in my chest—heartburn from all the food and booze of the day and night. I lay there willing it to go away and when it did, rolled over on my side and tried to return to sleep, thinking, instead, of how much I missed Mack, how much I missed Parker, and how much I was now missing Hank.

Two

The most daunting challenge about getting older is finding new ways to feel young. Sex is always a rejuvenating tonic—but even when it pervades and absorbs the consciousness throughout the entire day, the truth of the matter is the actual physical event of sex only accounts for a few minutes of activity and then what do you have? Usually just the desire to do it again. I've been lucky to have a stirring fantasy life and a steady string of boyfriends, lovers, and playmates with healthy sexual appetites, so I've never had to put myself on the constant prowl for sexual partners to get off with and keep myself feeling young. That's left me with a lot of energy to direct elsewhere, which on every day since Parker and I have started our businesses, has been aimed at bedspreads, linens, trash baskets, and ring around the tub. I suppose love and pride accounted for a lot of my complacency with these thankless, bone-numbing chores those first few years we were together, but what once felt as if I were the undisputed monarch of my own worthless castle, now felt as if I were trapped in a fairy tale waiting for a buzz-cut, military-trained Prince Charming to arrive and force a tiny, narrow glass slipper on my big fat toe. My discrete tête-à-tête with Griffin in the pantry had unlocked a hopeless fantasy of being rescued from beneath a pile of moldering laundry.

The following morning began with a phone call from the funeral home, which set my circulation throbbing at too rapid a pace for the rest of the day, the noise of my own bloodstream so earsplitting I could barely detect the lady on the other end of the phone informing me what viewing room

Mack would be laid out in. Even in my groggy state, I found enough good sense to remind her that there was to be no open casket, per Mack's wishes, and she rustled through the paperwork and assured me that everything would be as I had arranged it the evening before.

Launching myself successfully out of bed was another matter entirely; Hank was AWOL, his side of the bed flat and undisturbed except for where I had hysterically flung my legs and arms throughout the night from one nightmare to the next, hoping to find him like a cherished teddy bear and draw him closer to my chest for security. I knew that this was clearly the beginning of the end of us and the recognition of the fact made the ache in my back from the position I had been sleeping in seem worse than it might have actually been. As I waited for the hot water to work its way through the rusty, patched-up pipes and out the bathroom faucet, I studied my face in the mirror. It was an interesting face, no doubt about it, full of fortysomething complications: a high hairline and broad forehead, a strong jaw, but baggy eyes and floppy skin starting to form a double chin at my neck. I'd always been blessed with looking a bit younger than my true age, though exhaustion always seemed to work its black magic and make my chunky features seem weak and anemic. Early in our courtship Mack had said my face looked like it was always working even when I wasn't doing anything of importance. Then, I took that to mean that I appeared alive, curious, and inquisitive, but by the time Parker and I had been business partners for a little more than five minutes, I knew Mack had meant I looked analytical and worried. Looking at my tired old face in the mirror, I could not find an ounce of whatever might have lured Griffin towards me the night before, though the memory of the elaborate tattoo on his shoulder and the clutch of his arms at my ass made me grow hard and randy again, as if I were still a virile, young stud capable of landing a shirtless role in a music video. I thought about jerking off because it might have been a good dose of exercise to lift my spirits, but decided I needed to keep an edge about myself to make it through the long day ahead. This made me remember the mornings when I was a teenager and I would wake up early so that I could sneak into the bathroom and study myself intently in the mirror to witness myself changing, awed by the hair growing beneath my arms, the stubble breaking through at my chin, the wiry shrub building at my groin. Now, I twisted myself sideways, pulled in my gut and imagined I was a porn star being called to the set. When the illusion cracked, I rinsed my face with water, choosing to keep the grayish stubble of my beard going for a day or so because I hadn't the energy—or enthusiasm—to shave it away.

In the kitchen, I fixed a cup of instant coffee, not wanting to fool around with the spitting and choking multicup coffeemaker since Hank was not around to drink more than his share, then booted up the out-of-date virus-prone PC in the office and set about looking for the list of names Mack had made for me almost a decade ago—the list of who to call on the day I would need to call them. The list wasn't in the tray where I thought it would be on the side of my desk, but I found a copy I had made and hidden in the back of my address book, the creases so deep and permanent in the paper that I needed to rest my elbow at the edge of the page to be able to read the names and phone numbers. I set about placing calls to local friends first, listening to my voice, so emotional and unrehearsed as I began, grow hoarse and phony as I became used to revealing the sad news about Mack's death, as if I were cold-calling a customer to change long-distance carriers. By the time I reached Mack's brother-in-law Stuart in Texas, I had mastered a distance between the task at hand and the morbid, depressing fact of what I was really doing. I asked Stuart if he would pass along the news to Mack's sister (because I didn't feel like commiserating with a woman I didn't much like), and said that I would have a room available at the guesthouse for their family to stay in. Stuart wasn't interested in getting off the phone so quickly, wanting to know the details of the night before, what time Mack had died, what his last day had been like, if he had said any last words, and if a priest had visited, and I had to squeeze my stomach muscles to keep from allowing my suppressed grief to rise up my windpipe and tumble out into a teary confession of how much I was truly going to miss Mack. After I had given all of the trivia to Stuart that I could remember and wanted to reveal in a phone call, he said, as if to conclude our conversation, "I suppose we can sell most the furniture we don't take back with us. Celia's had her eye on that old armoire in the café for years. It's still there, isn't it?"

Whatever sorrow I had been experiencing quickly became indignation. Celia was Stuart's wife and Mack's sister, and from the tone of Stuart's voice, I took it that he believed Mack still owned the land and building and thereby the businesses and contents and inventory of our shabby guesthouse and always-in-the-red café, and I didn't hesitate in setting him straight. "Yes, that armoire cost Parker an arm and a leg and we had to hire specialty movers at a double peak rate to get it into place," I said. "And you know that Mack was only a tenant here, Stuart. Parker and I bought the building from him more than a decade ago."

I took the ensuing silence to be Stuart's grasping for a devious and underhanded strategy to counteract my statement. "I don't remember him telling us this," Stuart said. "I hope you have all the paperwork in order."

I assured him that I did, but when I hung up the phone I let out an exasperated groan; Parker and I had our business papers and licenses in working order out of the daily necessity of it, but I had no recollection that we had transferred the property deed and, if we had, where in the hell it was located in this mess of a place. I was just about to call Parker in his apartment, knowing I would probably wake him up in as rude a fashion as I had started the day, when he appeared at the office door. "I'm not opening the café today," he said, leaning all of his weight against the doorknob and making me wonder whether the wood or brass knob or door hinges would be the first to break from the pressure. His hair was all lumpy and his eyes puffy, which led me to believe that he had come to my door directly from getting out of bed and had not had a very settled night himself.

"But we have a full house," I said, putting the tender strain in my voice I used when I really wanted something to go my way. "I'm putting up Mack's sister and her family—Celia and the two kids and that husband of hers. They'll be here before you know it, trying to clean the place out of everything we own. And people will be dropping by all day and wanting something to eat. So ya have to cook something, Parker, sweetie. At least hors d'oeuvres or snacks. Those kids are sure to be hungry when they get here."

"Kids?" he echoed back. "You want me to cook for children?"

"You were a child once."

"And I had no appreciation for food," Parker said. "I was a lousy child."

You still are, I thought, trying to hold in my annoyance. Why was Parker choosing today, of all days, to be stubborn and pretend to have a nervous breakdown? *I* was the one who was always exhausted here. *Me, me, me*—Avery Greene Dalyrymple III—overwrought and overworked, nineteen or more hours every day, every week, every month, holidays included with no vacation and no overtime pay. My next thought was that I wanted a drink, but I tried to hold myself together—I hadn't even finished my first cup of coffee. "You still have to pay José and Buddy," I said, hoping this financial impairment might change his mind. "You just can't close up shop and send them home without paying them. They're employees. They show up expecting to earn money and get it at the end of the week. You just can't have them walk in here and tell them they're not making any money today."

"Add it to what I owe you," he said.

"You don't owe me anything," I answered, reaching for the bottle of bourbon and adding a splash to my coffee cup. "We're in this together."

The *together* seemed to hang in the air waiting for Parker to acknowledge it and accept it. When he didn't, when it fell flat on the floor with a big, fat plop, I said, "Oh, all right, *you* keep everyone happy and entertained and *I'll* cook."

I thought this would easily make Parker change his mind; my cooking was as notoriously bad as his was infamously good. I had once created a broccoli soufflé that was so hard and salty it wouldn't dissolve in the sink, so when Parker didn't disagree with my latest suggestion, I knew he clearly had no intention of cooking *anything whatsoever* that day. "All right," he said, after an acceptable pause to consider the idea. "Show me what I need to do."

"You can start by stripping the linen off of the bed in the Burgundy Suite when that young couple checks out. It's sure to be a mess and Hank's not here to do it."

Parker arched his eyebrow at my news and I added, "I didn't chase him outta here. He didn't show up last night."

"Was Charlie Ray with him?" Parker asked.

"He's missing, too?"

Parker didn't need to answer me. I could tell the answer by his slouchy body posture and disposition. So this was what was going on. He wasn't depressed because of Mack's death; he was depressed over Mack *and* Charlie Ray's abandoning him for a night. But just to be an evil diva and rub salt deeper into the wound, I said, "I thought you were in love this time."

"I *was,*" he said. "Am. *Still.*"

"So this has happened before, I take it," I said. I know I should have left the discussion alone, but I wanted to see if Parker was as miserable and disappointed in his affair as I had recently become in mine.

"Don't start jumping on me," Parker said in the slow, high-pitched whine he only used when he was really exhausted. "I had a miserable night. One lousy nightmare after another."

"You shouldn't eat so late at night."

"And you shouldn't drink before breakfast."

"I'm agitated. And suffering."

"You know you make the better martyr," Parker said. "You'll need to go to the bank. Deposit last night's take."

"I'll add it to my list of things to do to keep *both* places running."

"Now you're mad," Parker said. "I didn't show up to fight. I just don't want to cook today. My heart's not in it."

I knew I needed to cut him some slack; if anyone knew how hard Parker worked, I did. "I sent flowers to the funeral home," I said. "From both of us."

"Just tell me what I owe you."

"I'll figure something out," I answered, and this seemed to appease him more than if I said I would pick up the tab on my own.

I spent the rest of the morning inventorying the contents of the cabinets and refrigerators in the café, making a list of what food I would need to feed Mack's avaricious relatives and the other assorted guests and freeloaders who might drop by throughout the next few days knowing we'd have an open house and an impromptu buffet, while Parker sat on his generously-padded tush in the office and played computer games until the checkouts began shortly before noon. He seemed overwhelmed before the hard work even began, not even totaling up a bill properly for the elderly ladies who had stayed in the Magnolia Suite, and I stopped my explorations in the kitchen to help him strip the guest beds and change the linens. When Buddy showed up with his bandaged hand I told him about Mack's passing and, after we had exchanged an awkward embrace of condolence and he had composed himself, I told him that the kitchen would only be feeding special guests that evening but that he and José would still be paid their usual earnings, and sent him off to buy hamburgers, hot dogs, sausages, buns, chips, dip, and assorted raw vegetables. Before he left, he gave me a curious and melancholy expression and I said, "You got a better idea?"

"There's no customers, Mister D? Really?"

"Just family and friends," I said. "We'll set up the portable grill and a cold buffet in the courtyard and some extra tables. Is there someone you'd like to invite?"

My offer seemed to take him by surprise. Buddy had worked at the café for almost two years and even though I considered him an integral part of the working components of the place, I had seldom pried into his social life, relishing, instead, imagining whatever sexual details of him seemed to waft through my overtaxed mind. Buddy'd always wanted to keep his private life as distant as I did, though I was more unsuccessful with my own. "You're one of the family, after all," I said, trying to dispense with my usual officiousness because he seemed to be on the verge of tears. Buddy had often spent time with Mack even when he clearly did not have to do so; some afternoons he would run up with a plate of food or check to make sure he was maintaining his fluids, and then stay to watch reruns of *Dark Shadows* or *The Twilight Zone* or a creature feature on video, and I wanted Buddy to know that I was aware and thankful for all of this. I knew from my conversations with Mack that Buddy talked a lot about his boyfriend

Dwayne and I relished those hints of sexual details I could garner even secondhand. I also knew that Dwayne was chomping at the bit to scour our property for any supernatural hot spots and roaming poltergeists he could uncover, and Buddy confirmed the fact by saying that he'd like to ask Dwayne to join him that evening.

"I doubt he'll meet any of our resident spooks tonight," I said. "But you're both welcome to decorate the courtyard with anything that might help."

"Really, Mister D?" he answered, tensing his neck and blinking his eyes several times, a habit I had noticed he had when he was nervous. Or suspicious. Or overeager. Then he stopped and his dark eyes grew large and moist again when he remembered the purpose of the gathering.

"Within reason, of course. A black crepe is fine, but no phony tombstones or fake blood or bleached skulls. We have children coming and the adults will be drinking."

"No skulls?"

"No skulls."

"If they're frightened by them, there must be a reason."

"A skull is scary. Trust me on that one."

"Okay. No skulls."

While Buddy was away shopping, I took the time to enjoy a proper drink from the better stock of the bar and fantasize a few seconds about sex. My curiosity over Buddy's sex life always seemed to ignite a string of what-ifs and I had not been able to shake the memory of Griffin from my mind all morning. For a moment I considered abandoning all my future chores to find a place to escape by myself and masturbate him in and out of my system. Or at least use the technique of masturbation to ease my own tension and relieve myself momentarily of grief, knowing that sex was the one thing besides booze that was capable of distracting me from matters at hand. But before I could put that plan into action Parker had left off changing linens and towels to go to the funeral home and José had arrived and was already anxiously shifting back and forth on the balls of his feet wanting to know what was going on, because it was clear to him that there was more than the usual disorder to the place. I told him about Mack and the change in the day's routine and asked him to help me move some tables and chairs to the courtyard.

"You can afford to do this?" he asked. José always had his ear cocked for any kind of news, seeming particularly curious whether Parker and I were making a profit or might be going under at the end of his shift, and I often felt I had to conceal both the best and the worst of our financial facts from him. Parker had mentioned only last week that he had never expected José to last as long as he had in the kitchen, acquiescing to the whims of two worn-out *faygelehs*. José had also made no bones about wanting to get enough business experience so that he could own his own place and all of us knew he was ready to do it if and when he found the necessary capital.

"Of course," I answered. "Mack was our patron saint."

"So he was a partner, after all?"

"Not legally," I answered. "But spiritually, *yes.*"

I seemed to detect a slight sense of fear rising in José. "So he was helping you out?"

"He was always generous to us. It won't be the same without him, but we'll manage. Work a little harder, I suppose, here or there, polish the old silverware a little brighter instead of putting it up on eBay so we can buy a new set."

My rah-rah speech didn't seem to offer him any relief, so I sent him away to inventory the wine at the bar we could use for the wake, a job I had been considering doing for my own pleasure over the last few days in order to see what new (and expensive) bottles Parker had acquired, but had never gotten around to doing so. There was still one last room to clean and make up and I pushed our housekeeping cart to the Orleans Suite, where I bagged up the dirty towels, scoured the tub and toilet, wiped down the sink, laid out fresh towels, and put new linens on the bed. Finished, and finally alone, I stopped in front of the large bathroom mirror to let a recollection of Griffin make me hard. Oddly, since I had encountered Griffin, I was also thinking more sexually of Hank—the texture of the skin of his hips and thighs where his body went from soft flesh to rough hair, the way his mouth twitched when he was thinking and holding back his words, the thick bundle of hard muscles that tensed up around his shoulders and triceps when he was annoyed. I was certain that no one knew him as I had known him and, as I was fondling myself with my hand shoved into the crotch of my shorts, lost in a reverie of stroking Hank, the color of the blue ink against Griffin's dark hairy forearm washed across my memory. Just as I was orchestrating a potential threesome in my mind, I was interrupted by Lynette shouting outside in the courtyard, clipping the three syllables of my first name into one long Aaaaa-eeeee. I quickly tucked my privates privately away and hauled the laundry bag outside, meeting her beside the office door.

She kissed me on the cheek and wrapped her arms around my back, her tart, hard-working smell rising up out of her clothes. "It must seem empty here to you, now," she added after we had exchanged a few recollections and sympathies over losing Mack. She had heard the news of his passing before she had arrived and I could tell her of the fact, the gay N'awlins telephone tree quickly disclosing one piece of gossip after another as if it were a news flash arriving on a ticker tape. Mack was a part of the local lore because he had lived in the Big Easy for more than three decades; his path had crossed with most of the other longtimers of the queer and activist communities, and he'd been a big brother to many.

Lynette was a fit, slender, and mannish-looking sort of woman, her skin the color of bittersweet chocolate, her hair buzzed close to the scalp, and she had a penchant for wearing large, oversized dangling earrings that looked like they could double as gothic weapons of torture or barbaric hunting tools. Her personality, however, was as demure and raucous as that of any Southern debutante; she proudly lifted a joint out of the pocket of the vest she wore over her work shirt and shorts and offered it to me with another remark of condolence. I waved the gesture away, saying, "Better not, I'll start seeing things again."

"What things?" she asked me, widening her eyes and placing the joint at her dry, cracked lips, then fishing out a lighter from another of her vest pockets, and lighting it.

I had made it thus far through the day without any sightings or hallucinations and so had come to believe that my previous day's visions were merely creations of my mega-burdened sanity and not really real at all, so I found no reason not to confess my frivolous visions to Lynette. Lynette was one of the few close old friends I had in the Quarter. When we had worked together at her family's laundry we had always stopped for a break such as this, Lynette pulling out a joint and lighting up, me confessing something about an emotionally unavailable guy I wanted to know better who might be avoiding me so I couldn't get to know him better. Lynette was always full of appropriate dismay or joy, easily reflecting the way I felt—or *should* feel about something. The heat of the day was overwhelming and the sun was bright and blinding by now, and we walked to sit on the shady lip of the fountain in the courtyard and looked away from each other towards the large, gold-and-black psychotic fish. Lynette took a deep drag of the joint and passed it to me, and this time I readily accepted. I held it in front of my lips and said, before taking a deep toke myself, "Did you ever know Toby?"

"Toby?" she echoed back. "Mack's Toby? Only in passing. My cousin worked with him for a short while when he was at the grill on Bourbon, before he quit. Before he went loony, that is."

"I saw him yesterday."

"Lorda mercy, don't tell me," she said, shaking her head back and forth as if something had been dislodged and she wanted to hear it rattle, the long, gold earrings she had on swinging and rocking as if they were pendulums of a grandfather's clock trying to balance themselves out during an earthquake. Though she was suitably alarmed as I had hoped, Lynette was also as superstitious as they come—she carried both rosary beads and Voodoo charms courtesy of her girlfriend, Talla.

"Right here. At the steps. The ghost of him. He was here to tell me that Mack was leaving me. Or that Mack was joining him. One or the other."

"Lorda mercy, don't say it's true," she said, easily spooked and crossing herself, her upper body rocking back and forth as if she were a rabbinical student hunched over the Torah in search of divine truth. "You saw him?"

"Plain as day," I said, looking out at the sun-drenched courtyard around us. "But I got to the top of the stairs and he was gone. But I saw something else I can't explain."

I hadn't smoked a joint in almost a year and a half and I did not feel even a remote buzz. José was still in the courtyard, circling us and squinting and moving his hand up to shade his eyes, to better watch us smoking and hoping to read our lips. He had finished moving chairs and dressing the tables, and I waved him over and offered him a hit, which he gratefully accepted.

"You haven't seen any dogs around here?" I asked him when he tipped his head back and exhaled into the air.

He bent his head slowly down and looked at me, shaking his head with bugged-out suspicious eyes. "No big rats or mice? Possums or snakes?"

"Dragonflies," he said. "Some big ones. And lizards. Tiny. Nothing big, though." He took another drag, standing slightly to the side of us, as though not to eavesdrop on our conversation, but able to hear every word of it.

"I was in the pantry last night and there was a dog," I said to Lynette, but loud enough for José to hear—he might as well know that I could be losing it, just in case somebody needed to pick up the slack around here. "Or a wolf, maybe. I'm not sure. But he scampered up the wall as if his paws were suction cups and he disappeared right before my eyes. It was the weirdest thing. I don't believe it was a hallucination, or anything, but something like that just can't *vanish*."

"A wolf?" Lynette said, loud and startled enough to draw José back into our conversation. "You saw a wolf? And he just up and disappeared?"

"If it was a real wolf, it wouldn't have disappeared through the wall," José said.

"The ceiling, actually. It went through the ceiling."

"The ceiling?" Lynette said, making the sign of the cross again and bobbing a bit faster, but steady, like she was an indispensable part of some kind of Rube Goldberg contraption.

"A wolf ghost?" José asked.

"No, not a ghost. A wolf. But I guess not a real one."

"You got some evil spirits coming out at this place," she said. "You gotta be careful what you doin'. A death in the house always unsettles things. Could be that Angelle's doing. She could be stirring up a lot of things because there's a crack in the spirit world with Mack going."

I held my tongue, not blabbering the fact that Angelle had been an invention of Parker's years ago when, well, we were both slender and hopeful and full of a pregnant imagination, eager to bilk as many spooked-up tourists as we could hoodwink into spending the night at our joint.

"Bet that Voodoo queen can summon up all sorts of things," she said. "I suppose the spirit of one could do it too. I'll tell Talla to stop by. She can feel when things are outta whack in a place. She'll know right away what's goin' on here."

Talla was Lynette's bosomy girlfriend and business partner, a heavyset orange-blonde daughter of Cuban émigrés. Talla had been raised half Catholic and half Santería in Miami, self-educating herself in Wicca and witchcraft when she arrived in the Big Easy in order to make a few extra bucks by reading tea leaves or tarot cards at a card table she set up in Jackson Square on the weekends. Though her interest in the occult always seemed sincere to me, her psychic abilities were a bit on the phony side—in my opinion, she couldn't tell a Jack of Hearts from the Ace of Wands, and I resented the fact that she was always so willing to tell her friends' fortunes and futures for a new wad of bills she could use to pad her cleavage. I'd always thought that it was all right to hustle the tourists wandering around the Quarter, because that was business, after all, but it was never right to do it with your friends, never the ones who could phone you up the next day and say that whatever you had predicted had not happened at all and was nothing but hoodoo nonsense and money down the drain.

"It's not necessary," I told Lynette, waving off a final hit of the joint. "I must have been tired. Or nervous. Hank brought friends by last night and I felt bad I couldn't spend more time with them."

"Angelle always wanted to take over this house," José said, behind us. "Maybe she was trying to scare you away."

Lynette and I both turned and looked at him. "How do you know this?" I asked José.

"Dwayne talks about it right in front of the café," he said. "Part of what he tells the tour groups."

"I didn't know you were so friendly with Dwayne, too," I said, suddenly suspicious that the increased number of Voodoo charms and spooky art installations that I was finding in the courtyard could be José's doing, not just Buddy's. Dwayne often stopped by the café for a drink at the end of Buddy's shift and questioned Parker about the history of the building, and José was always coming out of the kitchen to listen in before he set about his least favorite task of washing up the greasy pots and pans. The thought occurred to me that it was time to complain to Parker that his ridiculous myth had spiraled completely out of our control and that there were now too many other players expanding on the sad saga of Angelle and it had to come to an end. It was, well, affecting the way we ran our businesses.

"She wasn't a witch," I said next. "Or a Voodoo queen or a spiritual high priestess. She was just a put-upon young girl, like all young girls are. So let's just stop trying to rewrite history."

As I said this a crack of thunder rumbled above us and we all looked skyward with uneasy laughter. This was followed by a double flash of lightening, then a heavy drop of rain landed at my feet, followed by others flopping in succession in the fountain, on my shoulder, at my earlobe, and then crashing wildly around us, *plop-plop-plop* and into a full-fledged rainstorm. Lynette sprang up and waved good-bye, making her way through the alleyway pushing her laundry cart towards her waiting truck. José and I began trying to salvage the clean tablecloths from the courtyard tables, then we both retreated to the door of the café as water began to stream along the slope of the roof and into and over the gutters to puddle in the courtyard. The downpour lasted for a good twenty minutes, enough time for me to fix myself another drink.

"I bet we could get a ghost tour to stop here for lunches," José said, when I followed him into the kitchen of the café.

"Sure, and think how much harder we would all have to work to keep up the extra business."

"We could hire assistants," he said, trying to catch my eyes.

I almost revealed that we could barely afford the ones we had before I realized that José could be setting another trap for me in hopes that I might disclose our shaky monetary situation. Instead, I answered, "Well, I hope I get to pick out a hot, young one when we're ready to do that."

Finally, the rain stopped and José took towels and dried down the chairs and benches, while I mopped at the puddles, steam rising around us from the unexpected collision of the moisture and the heat into a thick fog which settled into my clothing and annoyingly pulled it away from my skin. I had reached the area by the fountain and noticed the butt of the joint we had smoked lying between the cracks of the brick. I leaned down and picked it up and held it in my palm and, just as I was about to walk away, noticed a cloth napkin on the bricks. Oddly, it was both soiled and dry, and when I lifted it off the ground I remembered last night shoving it into the back pocket of the pants that I had on again today. Instead of using it to wipe the sweat away from my forehead, I wiped my brow on the side of my shirtsleeve and tucked the napkin away again in my back pocket. But just as I was about to get lost in another memory of Griffin, my eyes glanced into the water of the fountain, thinking I should check it for debris or see how badly it needed to be cleaned or if the storm had finally finished off our panicky fish. I watched one of the goldfish dart into the path of my reflection, and, as I started to count them all to make sure no one had absconded with one of them as a souvenir or side dish, I noticed a reflection of what appeared to be a woman standing on the railing of the balcony above and behind me. There was an almost soundless noise at my ear as something brushed my temple, like the soft flick made by a lightbulb when it suddenly burns out. I turned around and saw something—a bird? a bat?—flying off the balcony rail and over the rooftops, but there was no woman around anywhere to be seen.

At first, I felt more suspicious than frightened, as if I had detected an intruder but had not yet recognized the danger of it. Then, as my mind grasped the possibility of another supernatural encounter, it seemed to summon up the accompanying fear of having witnessed it. When I looked back again at the water of the fountain the face of a young black woman wearing a dark scarf over her hair swam into view, her eyes open and blinking at me, as if she had been sleeping underwater and I had awoken her. I felt a crushing presence against my chest, as if I were drowning, and a dizziness swam around my brain pushing me close to blackness. For a few seconds I wondered what kind of danger I could possibly be in because I could not believe what I was seeing, then the waves of the water seemed to contort the woman's face into an evil, ominous expression, as if she were laughing at me. I stepped back from the fountain agitated and unnerved and lost my balance on the edge of one of the bricks, but caught myself with the handle of the mop before I fell. When I stepped up to the fountain and looked back once more into the water—to convince myself I hadn't seen something and that I was merely hallucinating again—this time from the pot—the face had disappeared. I looked up quickly, with a startled panic in my chest, hoping I could find someone to confess my newest hallucination to, and noticed Mack's family heading down the alleyway and into the courtyard.

"You just missed the rain," I said, shrugging off my fear and offering my hand for Stuart to shake, amazed that they had made the drive from

Texas in record time. *They must smell money somewhere*, I thought, then tried to push the thought away because there wasn't any kind of money to be found anywhere in this sinkhole, and if there were, José had probably discovered it first. Stuart still possessed a tall, goofy, yuppie appearance, with his thick-lensed eyeglasses and lightly graying hair, and he seemed more businesslike than a family member using his best manners through a tragedy, as though his wife had told him he had to be the bad cop to her good one. Celia was thin and nervous looking with her dark curly hair pulled away from the heat of her neck. Of the few times I had met her before, I had never seen any indication of Mack's collegial spirit as part of her own DNA, nor did her disposition seem at all pleasant or easy going now. Nonetheless, I lightly embraced Celia; I hadn't seen her and her family in almost two years—since she had visited when Mack went into the hospital for some unexpected tests. I complimented her on looking well (though she seemed almost as flummoxed as I was) and then I leaned down and shook the hands of the two squirming boys, Sean, eight, and Noah, six, both of whom had inherited their parents thin features and dark hair.

The boys ran across the courtyard to the lip of the fountain to look at the fish and I waited apprehensively for one of them to yell back about the dark lady under the water who was making them feel sick. When neither of them did, teasing and testing each other with punches and slaps instead, I turned to their parents, offered my condolences again, and escorted them towards the office. I could tell that Celia and Stuart were ready to talk business, but I was unnerved by how much of Mack's face I had detected in the young Noah, something familiar around the eyes, and I could only focus on getting the family as quickly away from me and settled into their room as I could.

I helped carry their luggage up to the Magnolia Suite, which Parker had respectfully tidied up and provided with cots the boys could use if they didn't want to sleep on the convertible sofa, quietly grateful that I had given them the room with a balcony that faced Dumaine Street and not the courtyard, where the boy's squealing and squalling would certainly have annoyed me and every other respectful guest. Before I could get away, Stuart asked me some quick questions about parking and the safety of his car while Celia tried to get her hyperactive boys to settle down. Unfortunately, Celia caught hold of my wrist just as I reached for the doorknob. "Avery, was it a painful death? Was Mack suffering?"

I shook my head no, but could not find any words of comfort or compassion, and to restrain our suddenly rising emotions, we both averted our eyes to the large floral painting on the wall, done by the same artist who had created the cloud portraits for the café.

"I've forgotten how exquisite the paintings are here," Celia said next, with a shaky tone to her voice. "This one must be worth a fortune."

"It is," I answered her. "We're lucky to have it on consignment from the artist. Parker and I could never afford something that valuable. The insurance we pay just to keep it on the wall is a bit ridiculous."

She gave me a sour, unconvinced look and said, "Why would an artist want you to keep it here for him?"

"Because we tell all of our paying customers that they can buy another one just like it at his gallery around the corner."

Back downstairs, Buddy arrived with the food and black crepe and while he unloaded the bags and stocked the shelves of the café kitchen and decorated the courtyard, I asked José if he would accompany Mack's family to the funeral home and sit them with Parker. He seemed uncomfortable with the task, even though it meant taking a break and getting out of the café, and so I said, "I know it's an unusual day. They'll be a lot of people here tonight, coming over from the funeral home. I don't want you working all night. Is there someone you want to invite?"

He asked if he might bring over his boyfriend, a Bengali musician who worked in one of the clubs on Bourbon Street, named Kaku (which I was told, at one point during my introduction to him a few weeks before, meant something similar to "younger uncle" or "small brother"). Kaku had never spent time in a tenement or a temple in Bangladesh or anywhere else in India, for that matter; he had been born in a suburb of Berlin and raised in a three-story home in Chapel Hill, the son of a tenured microbiologist who taught at UNC, and he had landed in New Orleans under some kind of a scientific pretext, though he'd abandoned it for more sinful pleasures like the rest of us other lost souls. His name always felt too silly to me to say out loud without adding a chuckle after it because it made me think of "Cuckoo," not "Honored Younger Brother," so I was always referring to him with José as Your Boyfriend or Your Pal or in some other variable manner to show my respect. In person, Kaku was a rather serious young man, however: thin, with wire-rimmed glasses over his brown eyes, and long, elegant-looking fingers that strummed and tapped various musical instruments (and other things, as I often delightedly imagined). Some days, out of sheer exhaustion and boredom, I even summoned up fantasies of José's love life, imagining his rapid seduction of his long-legged, nimble-fingered beau with such ferocity that I often feared I was turning myself into a dirty old man, fixated on pornography.

I told José that of course it would be fine for his Honorable Vegan Mate to make an appearance, and to make sure we had enough vegetables to keep him happy, and then he disappeared upstairs to find Celia and her boys. When I looked up a few seconds later from the grocery bag, Hank, my sour-faced errant lover, was standing in the doorway of the café.

"We need to talk," he said.

"*Now?*" I answered him. "Can it wait till later?"

"I want to get it off my chest now," he said.

Hank was always willing to be confrontational whenever it was necessary (and sometimes when it wasn't); there was always something that needed to be discussed and needed to be discussed right away. But whatever he had to say—whatever was always on his chest or his mind—was usually just the tip of the iceberg. There was a deeper, unspoken subtext to our relationship that seldom reared its head but was always there, behind our every discussion. Hank did not like the fact that we lived together in what used to be the location of the slave quarters of the house, even though it had been a residential building longer than it had been used for its original intent. The real truth was that Hank hated having to work for me because of our sexual relationship—but then he didn't want to have to work for anyone, really, because he felt it made him subservient—and I hated having to tell Hank to do things around the place because it gave our personal relationship an unequal balance. Even more, I always felt that Hank should show some initiative and find things to do around the place without my having to tell him about it, that he might *want* to help out with the work because it would help our personal relationship work out better, which he never, never could seem to do. Of course I was conscious that there was an ethical business problem to our even being in a relationship and working together, but I was also aware that I had been trying to make Hank fill the widening void that had been left with Mack being housebound and unable to help out with all the unthought-of chores and Hank just wasn't that sort of guy. Lately, I had been trying the approach of keeping my mouth shut about his lack of motivation, doing all the work I could on my own, which only made me harbor a deeper resentment towards Hank's employment and presence.

I asked Buddy to start making the ground beef into patties we could cook on the grill. I took two glasses and the bottle of bourbon—the café's best—and followed Hank to one of the courtyard tables. Instead of sitting in a chair, which still had a bit of dampness to it, I placed the glasses and the bottle on the table and stood with my hands behind my back, waiting, well, for the next big pile of shit to hit the fan.

"I'm sorry about Mack," he began.

"I'm sorry, too," I said, keeping myself still and tense. "He was one of the great people of my life. But I think there's something else on your mind."

"I know it's bad timing," he said, "but I think it's time we call it quits."

"I know you're not happy with things the way they are," I answered.

"It's too much," he said. "There's never time for us."

He turned his eyes to the ground, away from mine. I could not dispute him on this fact and I reached out and poured a glass of bourbon and offered it to him. Hank was close to ten years younger than me and I was aware that because of that I always felt younger in his presence, even when I found him discouraged or discouraging, like now. When he shook his head no to my offer of a drink, I took a sip from the glass myself. The bourbon was good and strong, shooting right down to my stomach and directly into my bloodstream.

Hank had not yet abandoned his boyish dreams of success. Like some of us, he always seemed to be on the lookout for a stranger who would arrive and carry him off bareback into the sunset, promising him both fame and fortune, in his case a starring role in which he could be a quadruple threat—actor, singer, dancer, *and* director. So the truth of the matter was that it wasn't that I couldn't find time for us, it was that he was looking for something better for himself. I knew he was disappointed to have found himself working as, well, a *maid*, and because of that there was both a bitterness and a resentment every time I broached the subject of him auditioning for one of the clubs or tourist revues that popped up around the Quarter or on the riverboats. I had tried to be an encouraging and inspiring lover, but was always shot down, like a clay pigeon cracking in midflight.

"You just don't want to feel anything," he said.

"That's not true," I answered. It was true that I did not feel for Hank the intensity I had felt for Mack or Parker or perhaps even for a guy I had met at the baths when I was twenty years younger, but I felt *something* for him nonetheless; it had just become harder for me to show it—and, well, it was tangled up in all this other crap. "Let's not throw the blame all in one place. Maybe you just don't feel the same way you did before. When we first met."

Hank had pursued me hard the night I first saw him at the bathhouse, and, afterwards, he was always there for me in a supportive way, or at least he had been. Parker and I had opted for younger lovers at about the same time, feeling a need for something that we were not finding with each other. My sex life with Hank was still in relatively good shape—we could count on each other a few times a week in that regard, and I knew that that was not the reason he was breaking up. I knew him well enough to know that if I had reached out my hand to him at this very moment, stroked his cheek fondly with one hand, pressed him into a kiss and fondled his crotch, all would be well and we might be on our way—at least—to an immediate sexual reconciliation. A good romp in the sack would have done us both some good, but I didn't initiate that gesture because I thought it would have only been a temporary solution and not a proper resolution to our ongoing problems. Instead, Hank reached out his hand for a glass and I poured him a generous shot. "Where will you go?" I asked him.

"I don't know."

"Well, you don't have to disappear right away," I said. "If you want to keep your job, I have no problem with that. You know I need the help and will have to find someone if you want to quit. Either way, if you're not uncomfortable with the idea of hanging around here you can stay in Mack's apartment for a while until you find another place. I *do* like having you around, you know, and not just because you're working for me."

He nodded and seemed grateful that I had not fired him and tossed him out into the street in an angry snit, but depressed that he had found himself in a position where he still felt trapped, living only two floors above the place where his bliss had soured. Across the courtyard, I noticed the leaves of a plant shake as if a breeze—or an animal—had made their way through them. I poured myself another glass and then asked him, "Did you at least have some fun last night?"

"Who invited Charlie Ray?" he asked, with irritation in his voice.

I knew not to pry any further. It was clear that Felipe and Charlie Ray must have hooked up in the way that Hank had hoped that he and Felipe would and this was certainly a contributing factor to Hank's dispirited mood. Across the courtyard the leaves rustled again and I stopped Hank's story about the strippers at the bar they had walked to to ask him, "Have you seen any dogs in the courtyard the last few days?"

"Dogs? You mean like that mutt Charlie Ray?"

"No, real dogs. Animals. Dogs or wolves or rats or snakes?"

"Snakes?"

"Or bats?" I asked next. "You haven't seen any bats, have you?"

"You're drinking too much," he said.

"I don't drink *enough*."

"You're going to make yourself sick."

"Thank you so much for your concern—*all of a sudden*."

"If you're starting to see things."

"I'm not seeing things. I asked if you had seen a dog in the courtyard. I thought I saw one last night."

"Nope," he said. "Not a thing. *Except a skunk.*"

"I didn't know you were the jealous type," I said.

"I'm not jealous," he answered. "Just disappointed."

"Aren't we all, dear," I said. "Mack's key is on the hook beside the computer. Don't get too comfortable up there yet. His sister is ready to claim whatever she can that's not nailed down."

But Hank didn't seem entirely finished with expressing his thoughts. "I wanted things to work out, you know."

"I know."

I spent the rest of the afternoon in the kitchen with Buddy and José, spicing up pounds of hamburger, sausage, and hot dogs, and the task seemed to calm me—I was always in a better mood when I was occupied with a mindless task, just not overwhelmed by many. Hank moved some things up to Mack's apartment, and I felt his misery when my eyes caught sight of him and it swirled and tumbled into my stomach until I realized that I would miss aspects of him I had never appropriately expressed my gratitude for. Then I had to move on, forget him again when I got caught up in a delivery of flowers someone had mistakenly sent to the café instead of the funeral home, and then I had to explain to our few paying guests about the evening's rather unusual gathering in the courtyard.

When it was dusk, I went around and lit the candles on the tables and the little altars Buddy had hastily concocted for the occasion and turned on the colored spotlights. Buddy had made arrangements of things around candles that reminded him of Mack's energy, from a strange, knotted piece of rubber IV tubing to a cutout of the channel grid from a page of an old *TV Guide*, to aide his spirit in entering the land of the dead. Customers had always softened their horrified glares when I explained to them that what they thought was trash that had been left on their room's nightstand or on their bathroom shelves were really offerings to our resident Voodoo deities. Once, Buddy had even nailed a dusty, black-painted sneaker to the back wall of the closet in the Royal Suite that had frightened a newly-wed couple into wanting to immediately check-out when they discovered it and I had rashly concocted a story that it was good-luck omen intended to inspire their marriage to become a long and joyous adventure.

As I was walking towards the back kitchen entrance, I noticed someone running shoeless across the bricks and towards the pantry door—it appeared to be a young black man, well-built, in a light-colored vest-shirt and similar colored calf-length pants and my first thought, even with the odd costume, was that it was Hank coming back downstairs to retrieve something. I knew at once that it wasn't the ghost of Toby—the young man's physique was so physically different—larger and more muscular than the wispy boy Mack had been in love with. When I reached the stairwell I didn't see anyone; I checked the pantry door and it was still locked. I retrieved the key from the side of the kitchen door and unlocked the pantry and flipped on the overhead light. This time I was steady and suspicious enough to expect to find a phantom wolf snarling and rushing at me. Or even something else, something equally frightening. Instead, there was nothing but a soft humming sound that seemed to turn itself into a high-pitched wail, like the air being squeezed out of a helium-filled balloon. But the wail had an eerie human component to it, as if it were rising out of pain.

I thought it might be a noise from the light and I stepped onto the bottom plank of shelving to make myself taller, worried, however, that I was sending too much weight onto the thin piece of wood where I had placed my shoe. As I drew my ear closer to the light, the pitch became softer, as if it had moved further away. Now it seemed to be coming from beneath the floorboards, and I wondered what was under the floor of this small room—Parker and I had never done a major renovation to any part of the buildings and this area was between the main wing of the house and the old slave quarters behind it; the pantry was literally a shed-like bridge between the two buildings. I looked down at the floor and heard the sound grow louder, the wailing rise in volume, pitch, and despair. Next, the planking rippled, as if it were a wave of water washing towards shore, a traveling buckle as it receded and returned. As it moved again across the room I swore I saw two large, dark, weather-beaten hands reach up between the cracks and try to rip the old cypress boards up. Then the rippling and wailing stopped, and I could hear nothing except my heart thumping at my throat.

I was just reaching towards the shelf where we kept the hammer, crowbar, and other assorted hardware and tools, ready to defend myself against the next wave of waving floorboards, when Parker stuck his head inside the pantry and asked, "Everything okay in here?"

"Yep," I answered, giving him a big fat lying grin, but thankful for his arrival and interruption. "Managing fine."

"There's a bunch of hungry people in the courtyard, you know."

"Can't have that, can we?" I answered, pushing him outside, flipping out the light, and locking the pantry door behind us.

I was both relieved and worried that I was being drawn away from another idiotic hallucination because there was more work at hand, something else that needed my attention. There were about twenty ill-humored people now in the courtyard who had arrived from the funeral home, all standing around like aristocrats waiting for someone to serve them food and cocktails. I started pouring glasses of white wine into plastic beverage cups and passing them around, while Buddy brought out the trays of condiments and bread, and José soon had the platters of cooked hamburgers, sausages, and hot dogs ready. Kaku, José's musician friend, had arrived and offered to put on a CD of his band he had brought—"jazz-lite," was how he described it—and I showed him how the courtyard's stereo system worked and soon there were little pockets of people eating and talking to a soft accompaniment of rackety, unpredictable music. Buddy had lit sandalwood incense because it had been Mack's favorite and the smell of it hovered in all of the contained spaces of the courtyard, an earthy reminder of the man we were all missing. Celia tried to corner me into going over Mack's finances and the furnishings of his apartment, but luckily Noah and Sean were in cranky moods and she soon disappeared to take them to bed. That did not keep Stuart from scouting out Parker, however. I saw them talking at a table but refused to intercede when Parker turned and glared at me. When things seemed to be running smoothly enough, I left the courtyard and unlocked the pantry door.

I had the first floorboard up in a matter of minutes—I had spent the interval at the party mentally locating the hammer on the pantry shelf, prying the nails up with my imagination, and seeing myself lift the boards away and stack them in the corner, so that when it actually came time to do it, it seemed as if I knew what I would find beneath them. Of course, what I found was nothing but bricks and dirt. Old caked and packed muddy-brown Louisiana dirt. Nothing there to scare or unnerve me. But I had become a man with a mission and I used the serving spoon I had brought into the pantry with me and began to dig the bricks away in the area where I had seen the grasping phantom hands, then wondered what had become of the hand trowel I had bought last spring when I had decided to repot some hanging plants, but dismissed the impulse to stop and search for it, continuing to dig with the serving spoon. My pulse had accelerated, sweat had dampened my scalp and the back of my neck, and I fought off the urge to have a conversation with myself about what I was doing being intensely ridiculous, instead mentally chanting in my brain, "I'm not going crazy, I'm not going crazy." Behind me, I heard the noise of the party continuing and I knew that as long as the food and the music and the booze held out, no one would really miss me, and that maybe Parker would get up off his sorry, gloomy ass and take over hosting for a few minutes and help me out with the too-too-heavy burden of always having to take charge of things.

Soon I was perspiring heavily beneath my arms and I had to stop and wipe the sweat from my eyes, using the stained cloth napkin I'd pulled from my back pocket, and the sharp smell of dried sperm sent a rush of memories of my night before in the pantry. That was when I spotted a glint of silver in the hole where I had cleared the bricks away and been digging into the dirt—something metallic catching the gleam of the overhead light. A buried treasure, I was sure of it, and I began to dig faster to find out what it was.

I was so excited that I was discovering a lost treasure that the spoon bent from the pressure of my grip, so I reached my hands down and started digging with my fingers, feeling the dirt lodging beneath my nails but loosening the dirt around something that seemed to have a thin, polished handle. As the soil moved through my fingers, small pinpricks of light began to rise up out of the dirt like carbonated bubbles in a glass of champagne, though their movements seemed to be more patterned than random, swirling around the object as more of it became revealed to me. The tiny lights behaved like alien beings driving mini–flying saucers, an intelligence emitting along with the energy of their light, spinning around my feet and arms as if to sniff out who I was and what I was doing and why I was doing it. They gave me more of a sense of awe than fear and it gave my task a lightness and excitement to see the lights growing and traveling around me, as if I were dancing in an abandoned disco with a giant sound system playing my favorite Donna Summer song. Then the lights began to rise up through the floorboards in other areas of the pantry, traveling towards the object I was after, as if they were trying to detect what was beneath the ground, too, creating, in effect, a whirling halo of light around my body and my hands.

In a few more minutes I was holding a pocketknife in my hands—no more than eight inches from the bottom of the handle to the tip of the blade. The handle was made of white bone, polished and speckled with imperfections and stains from the brown dirt. I wiped off the knife as best as I could, finding a carving of some kind of plant or flower on both sides of the handle. I dug out the caked soil from the design, cleaned off the blade, the swirling lights around me now growing more faint as the metal of the blade became cleaner and brighter. I had no idea what the knife was doing in the ground beneath the pantry floor and if I had been smarter, or perhaps not so drunk, I would have immediately realized that I had disturbed something ancient and priceless and hallowed that I should have left alone. But I was still fearless and excited by the prospect of uncovering a valuable treasure that could save us all from potential bankruptcy. The spine and the top of the blade were both chipped, or I thought they were chipped. As I cleaned more dirt off of the knife, I found that designs had been chiseled into the steel here, too, in what looked to be a random though beautiful pattern of waves, yet the same pattern that had rippled through the planks a moment ago. The blade had not corroded at all and on the side of it were engraved the initials *A.D.* Even though the initials were the same as my own, I knew the knife had never belonged to me. I was sure that this knife had something to do with the original owners of the house—perhaps Antoine Dubuisson or even our enigmatic Angelle. I certainly had no memory of having owned a knife like this or burying one myself beneath the pantry floorboards, but I had surely lost a few thousand brain cells in the last two days, not to mention a few million since we had started our hectic businesses. And if I hadn't done it, who had? And why? Why was it hidden away in the ground between the buildings? I refused to be scared because I had uncovered it. Instead, I found the spring on the side of the handle and bent the knife closed and gave the handle a last polish before putting it in my pocket and patting away my sweat to make myself more presentable.

Outside on the courtyard, Parker was talking with José's friend Kaku, telling him about his favorite ingredients to add to a stew no doubt, or why Kaku should stop being a vegetarian. Parker always expected everyone to share his bottomless appetite and palate. When I approached them, Parker turned to me and said, "I'm sure that Avery could benefit from more daily fiber, too."

"I doubt it," I answered back. "Too much gas already."

"Smaller meals are the best," Kaku said, "particularly if you don't get enough exercise."

"Avery gets plenty of exercise lifting bottles, don't you, sweetie?" Parker said.

"I really enjoy swinging around cast iron frying pans," I said with a polite nod to Kaku. "Strengthens and tones the grip while forcing the body to maintain its balance." Next, I apologized to Kaku for interrupting them and told him that I needed to take Parker away to privately discuss some specific business problem that needed our immediate attention. Parker gave me a frown—in his mind, nothing ever needed immediate attention unless it was food burning on the stove or he wanted me to save *him* from something utterly intolerable and Kaku was suitable enough eye candy for Parker to be annoyed with me for interrupting his conversation. On our own, however, Parker was already poised for attack. "Why are you trying to spook everyone?"

"I told Buddy he could put out a few things around the place."

"No, telling José you're seeing ghosts and imaginary dogs."

"I think it was a wolf," I corrected him. "And you're the one who started this whole ghost thing."

"What are you talking about?"

"Where did you get that story?" I asked him.

"What story?"

"Angelle. You told me you made it up."

"Well, I did. Sort of."

"Whadya mean, sort of?"

"Mack told it to me."

"Mack?"

"Yep. When we first met. He told me it was part of the history of the house. It was part of some big project Toby had been working on for years."

"*He* never told me this," I said. "And *you* never told me this."

"It was just a story. It never occurred to me to tell you until we decided to go into business together, but I knew that if I told you then, it would spook you and you would back out, because you were looking for any kind of reason not to open the guesthouse, remember? After we had been open for a while, I knew nothing would make you back out of it because we were in so deep, so I thought it was safe to talk about it. Only I told you I made it up."

"So it's a true story?"

"Mack told me that Toby had told him about it," Parker said. "That's all I know. He was writing something about it. About the history of the house. You don't really believe it, do you?"

"Toby?" I said. "Toby knew about this?"

"I suppose he did."

"So we have ghosts? *Real* ghosts?" I shot back at him. I was just about to show Parker the knife that I still had in my pants pocket, but first I wanted a drink. Another drink. I felt a desperate urge for the burning fire of a good, strong, ultraexpensive, high-end fifty-year-old whiskey to coat my throat and bottom out in my stomach and flush up into my brain, so, well, I could think things through better and not seem so flustered. As I was making my way across the courtyard towards the table that Buddy had set up for drinks, I felt a thump at my chest, as if someone was squeezing my heart. I could feel the sweat watering my armpits and more breaking out across my brow and this time I recognized it was partly from fear. It occurred to me that I had finally pushed myself too far and an impending heart attack was soon to be the result. A pain shot through my neck and my left arm began to hurt, as if the muscle had been clenched by the fangs of a wolf. I started coughing—I'd read somewhere that that was the best thing to do in a situation like that—to keep the heart active and pumping. But with each cough my vision went black, then black and starry, until I began struggle for breath and swivel my head around in alarm. That was when I noticed Griffin in a corner of the courtyard and this was followed by another thump and a clutch in my chest, followed by another wave of blackness and the rumbling sound of thunder.

I had the sensation that I was falling to the ground but when I looked down, expecting to feel the blow of the bricks as my knees hit them, I realized I was still standing and I was straining and waiting to hear the next crack of thunder in what seemed to be the absence of sound. Around me the party in the courtyard was suspended, everyone motionless, as if someone had pressed the PAUSE button on a DVD. José was frozen in place holding a tray of hot dogs, Kaku was sitting nearby, his finger in his mouth where he had hoped to discretely lick away the barbecue sauce he had just secretly tasted. Buddy was somewhere between sitting and standing, and Parker had a hand against his neck, which meant he had not enjoyed our conversation. Even the rattlesome music of the stereo had stopped, though I was now conscious of hearing my breathing, my chest rising and falling, my arm moving into my pants pocket and my fingers fidgeting with the pocket knife I had just discovered. But the only other movement around me that I could detect was Griffin traveling towards me in an odd sort of floating way, as if he were gliding over the bricks on a motorized skateboard. Tonight he was dressed in a white vest with fringe and white leather pants, as if he were headed to an ABBA reunion concert, and, as he got closer, I noticed that his tattoo was different than the one he had the evening before, though nonetheless elaborate. On his arm where the wolf of the prior night had been was now a bird—a dove or an eagle, maybe— with outstretched wings, flying towards his shoulder. Below, instead of the paw prints and thorns of before, were the outlines of two snakes, one light, the other dark, entwined and threading themselves into a similar braided design. My first question was to ask him how he did it. Change tattoos overnight. Only it came out as another cough.

"Don't be alarmed," Griffin said to me. "You'll be all right in a moment. Things will resume as they were."

"You saved me?" I asked, testing the sound of my voice with what seemed to be another cough, but this time wasn't.

"From yourself?"

"Then why?" I asked him. "Why have things stopped?"

"This is all of your own doing," he said. "Your will has stopped them."

"*My* will? Why would I do that?"

"Because you're confused and you need time to think things through."

"I always need time to think things through. That doesn't mean I can stop time to make it happen."

"But you did this time, didn't you?"

"But why did it hurt?" I asked him. "Was I having a heart attack?"

"Your brain had to find a way to accept the pause," he said. "And this is what it came up with. Sort of adolescent sci-fi fantasy formula, if you ask me. Stop-motion therapy with a bit of pain and drama. I've only taken a form I felt you would accept."

"Then you're…"

"No, not at all. At least not in the theology that you know. Or have been taught. You mortals have it all wrong, you know. I'm merely the outward representation of an internal manifestation of your mind."

"Which is what?'

"Let's say your conscience," he said. "Or your intelligence. Not everyone would see me as you see me now."

"So no one knows you're here."

"I'm not really here," he said, waving his hands towards his feet, where his boots were also white leather, to match the rest of his outfit. "Only here." He pointed towards my skull and tapped it with his fingernail. "I must have really made an impression last night."

"Worked for me," I said. "Does this mean that I can't expect a repeat performance?"

"No," he answered. "That wasn't me. That was *him*."

"So we're not going to have sex, then?"

"No. Not us. Not now."

I tried to contain my disappointment, or, rather, certainly not let the external representation of my internal conscious being see it. "Then what is it I need to know?" I asked. "What's happening? Why have I done this to myself?"

"Let's not get too rhetorical," he said. "I can't provide you with any answers. Only insights into things you already know. But it seems clear to me—or the me that you have imagined me to be—that there are some souls around this place that feel that they are not finished here. On earth."

"But it's a made-up story," I said. "And there's no such thing as ghosts. Or purgatory. Or limbo. Or alternate worlds."

"So you don't believe in them?"

"I can't believe in them." I said. "I have too many people relying on me." I waved my hand to the stonelike figures around me. "These people can have breakdowns. I *can't*. I'm too busy."

"So instead of seeing ghosts, you are creating them to be representations of your internal moods. They are only acting as you wish them to."

"Meaning?"

"Meaning that there is a lot of residual psychic energy floating around this place," he said. "It happens at old buildings like this, places where there have been struggles, death, worries, hard work, lots and lots of history. And this energy is only taking the form that you allow it to take. You are shaping it. It's not shaping itself. You'll understand this when the time comes to know it."

"How do you know this if you are really me and I don't know this," I asked him.

"But you do," he said. "The knowledge of life is stored in your unconscious mind. You've always known this since the flame of being created your consciousness. It's sort of like DNA and genes and chromosomes. What makes you human and an individual at the same time. This imprinted unconscious memory is who you are and who you will be."

While he had been talking I had been feeling the handle of the knife in my pocket. I withdrew it and held it in my outstretched palm for him to see. "But this is real," I said. "I didn't make this up. I could hurt myself with this."

"It is a fact of history," he said. "Yes. No doubt about that. And it will serve whatever tangible or imaginary use you decide to give it in your task."

"My task?"

"We all arrive with a purpose. It is why we are here."

"You're not talking about something difficult and Biblical, are you? Like building an ark?"

"You have been drinking too much," he said. "And by the way your family here—your family of friends, lovers, and employees—is quite worried about your overindulgence."

"You're not telling me to stop, are you? Is that what this is all about?"

"You must do what will aid you in your task."

"And that is…?"

"That is something you must discover yourself. Let's just remember how the saying goes, 'If you want to get something done, give it to a busy man.'"

I was just about to ask him if the *A.D.* that was engraved on the blade of the knife was for Antoine or Angelle Dubuisson when I felt a pain shooting up my thighs as my knees hit the ground and the knife fell against the bricks in front of me. There was a flash of lightening and around me the party was moving again; the sound returned first—a burning cough in my chest—followed by the motion and tug of someone lifting me up by the arms.

"Are you all right?" Buddy asked. I had fallen to the ground near where he and Dwayne were seated.

"Yes, yes, yes, of course," I said, with a bit of irritation to my voice. "Just trying to do too many things at once."

But I was also perceptively shaken and I tried to think it all through as I dusted off my knees. Had I just had a minor stroke or had I, in fact, stopped time and gained enlightenment from my subconscious? Was I supposed to have a drink or stop altogether?

Dwayne had shed his black cape for the evening and was dressed in a black T-shirt and tight-fitting black pants, showing off the size of the equipment at his crotch that was certainly what was keeping Buddy happy and interested in a relationship. As he stood and tried to help me regain my balance, I tried not to stare at the impression of his larger than normal genital endowment against his inner thigh, but my eyes kept floating between my imagined size of him and the heft of the knife that was still in my hand and the memory of summoning up an image of Griffin only seconds before. Finally, I moved my hand out towards Buddy, and said, "I've been meaning to show this to you and Dwayne."

Buddy took the knife out of my hand and Dwayne took it from Buddy, rotating it in what little light there was left in the courtyard. He brushed the dirt off the casing, and I expected him to say something as snide as I would have under different circumstances, something like I should have cleaned it up before giving it to him to look at, but instead he said in his overeducated way, "It certainly looks authentic enough."

He rubbed his fingers along the handle, thumbed the spring and brought out the blade, studying the chiseled side and the engraved initials. "It's not a Vendetta. The design is not right."

"Vendetta?" I asked him.

"They were popular in the seventeen-hundreds," he said. "Used to defend Corsica and imitated throughout Europe. There was a Moor's head on the handle, not this—this looks to be a flower. No, probably a plant. A lotus design. They were popular with French knife makers. Around Thiers in the 1800s. This tiny mark here, right at the bottom of the blade, is probably a signature of some kind. Early sort of trademark symbol. You should have it appraised. It might be worth something, even though the handle is clearly bone, not ivory."

I looked again at the knife, wondering how Dwayne knew such details, thinking that maybe I was being gaslighted—that this was a plant, a setup to make me think I was crazy and swear to give up the sauce. "I discovered it beneath the floorboards of the pantry some time ago," I slightly lied. "When one of the planks was loose and I was trying to repair it. Look at the engraved initials. *A.D.* Whadya make of them?"

I'd always expected Dwayne to unmask our hoodoo ruse one day, but he was the type of man who took every clue, even the silliest ones, seriously. And he seriously wanted to find a ghost to believe in. One that he could really *see.*

"It could easily have been something the Dubuisson family owned," he said. "Something a merchant might have given them as a gift, in return for favors, something Mrs. Dubuisson might have even wanted."

"It does have a feminine look about it," Buddy said. "A lady's knife."

"But what about Angelle?" I said. "Could it have been hers?"

"I doubt that a slave girl could have afforded something like this," he said. "Or even have been allowed to possess something this dangerous."

"Perhaps her brother?" I asked. "Aaron?"

"Pierre could have given something like this to Aaron," Buddy said, with a series of nervous blinks. "Out of affection."

"No," Dwayne said, brushing his dreadlocks over his shoulder and bringing the knife up closer to his eyes. "I doubt that Pierre would have made that kind of attention so obviously known with a gift. And to a slave? Maybe it belonged to Antoine Dubuisson. That would make sense."

"You don't think it has any special meaning, do you?" I asked. "Any special powers?"

"Special powers?" Dwayne asked me. There was amusement in his voice, as if he knew how ridiculous I must have sounded even to myself.

"Or a curse?" I asked. "Would witches put a spell on a knife?"

"I sincerely doubt that a Voodoo mambo would put a spell on a knife," Dwayne said, trying not to sound haughty or make me feel foolish (which I already felt). "On a person, maybe. But a knife? No, I don't think so."

"You're both giving Voodoo a bad rap," Buddy added. "It's not about dark power."

José had been circling the edges of our discussion, curious about what I had given Dwayne to inspect. Now he broke in and asked me, "How did you find the knife?"

"Whadya mean?" I asked him.

"Was the blade stuck in the ground?" José now had hold of the pocketknife and I could see him trying to calculate its worth—in a way that Dwayne had not.

"Why, yes. It was," I answered him.

"Not flat on the ground?"

"No, it was stuck into the earth."

"The fifolet," José said, his eyes growing wide. Beside him, Dwayne and Buddy both sighed and bobbed their heads as if the Master of the Universe had finally revealed the secret to getting to the highest level of a video game. I looked at them as if they were three clowns watching a dog perform the tricks they had taught him, but they also seemed to regard the knife as a special prize and, for a moment, I began calculating the ways I could spend the fortune it was sure to bring me. Then it dawned on me that I was truly in the midst of a conspiracy, a mutiny in which José was the likely ringmaster—sailors attempting to steer the sinking ship into port and court-martial the skipper! This was all part of a plan to toss me into bed and take over running the guesthouse, I saw in a flash of paranoia.

Well, let them have it. I've had enough of it. Then, of course, my possessiveness kicked in.

"Meaning?" I asked, unable to hide my rising aggravation.

"To cut out the spell," Buddy said. "The fifolet spin around the knife and stop. It means something ominous is about to happen. Or they're going to block the path to danger."

"What ever is a fifolet?" I said next. My tone had become a shrill mix of exasperation and irritation.

"An old legend," Dwayne said, "brought by the French colonists. A phenomenon like ignis fatuus, corpse candles, ghost lights—things like that. They were tiny fireballs that would escape up through the swampy ground if bodies were decomposing beneath. If you put the blade of a knife into a stump of a tree or straight down into the soil of the earth, the fireballs would be drawn to it. In the morning there would be blood on the blade."

"Blood on the blade?"

"Did you see it?" Buddy asked me. "Did you find it with blood?"

"Have you all lost your minds?" I asked them. "You don't believe this nonsense, do you?" Of course I didn't tell them that only moments ago in the pantry I had been surrounded by fireballs, tiny swirling lights that simply vanished when I took possession of the knife. Or that I had just had a conversation with my Higher Power disguised as my Internal Psyche. I certainly didn't want to appear crazy since I already felt foolish in front of them for initiating such a ridiculous conversation—and then trying to believe in it.

"The fifolet were considered to be souls who had escaped purgatory," Dwayne said. "Or babies that died before they were baptized."

"Babies?" I said. "Now we're getting really gruesome."

"But the pirates thought that if you followed the lights, it would lead you to a hidden treasure," José said. "Jean Lafitte's treasure."

"*Jean Lafitte's treasure?*" I echoed back, wiping the blade of the knife in the napkin and folding it up into the handle casing. *Wouldn't that solve a lot of problems around here,* I thought, but said instead, "This is all nonsense. You have all been drinking too much. Or not enough. Can I get anyone another drink?"

They all nodded no, and none of them said that I had had enough, so perhaps a revolt was not at hand, but before I left them, Dwayne said, "I'll be glad to look through my notes for something like this." According to Buddy, Dwayne had copious case notes on the supernatural phenomena that had occurred at each of the buildings he stopped at on his walking ghost tour through the French Quarter. As I walked away, I recalled that Dwayne had sat with Parker a few months before in the café, asking him about the legends of our ghosts, which was the way he had first met Buddy. Perhaps Dwayne knew more about the history of this place than I did, if Parker had been keeping his trap shut with me all this time. But fifolet? Souls escaping from purgatory? Jean Lafitte's treasure? I *was* going crazy because everyone around me was crazier than I was. I was certain of it now. I was the co-captain of a ship of fools. I wanted another drink and I couldn't get to it quick enough.

While the party continued, I went back to the pantry, swept up the dirt, and replaced the bricks and floorboards as carefully as I could. Examining my finished handiwork, I just knew that I would have to hire a carpenter to repair it properly and began calculating the expected (and sure to be exasperating) costs. In the kitchen of the café, I washed the knife off in the sink, momentarily frightened as the brown dirt turned a bloody red in the water. *Blood on the blade?* It was all too foolish and absurd. *It was just dirt. The same dirt that was in every crack and pore and crevice of this messy ruin.* I dried off the knife again, nonetheless examining the towel I used for any sign of blood and was satisfied to see that it was only dirt after all and that I had only imagined a gruesome mess. Then I walked across the courtyard to the office where I intended to keep the knife until I discovered another use for it. I could not find a place for it; it seemed too ominous on the nightstand, too important on the mantelpiece, and everywhere I placed it, it seemed to draw me back to it. I finally settled for placing it inside the refrigerator, regarding it now as some sort of talisman to keep me from wanting to have something to eat (but certainly not preventing me having another drink).

By the time I had returned to the party with a fresh drink in my hand, it was beginning to break up; José was leading Kaku through a two-step dance that obviously had special meaning to both of them and I began bagging up the discarded paper plates and plastic glasses and bringing them to the trash. Parker was now talking with Buddy and Dwayne and I realized that neither Hank nor Charlie Ray had made an appearance tonight. At this point I doubted that Charlie Ray would ever return; to me, he had always seemed to be just marking time with Parker and I felt a sympathetic pang towards my weary old partner. Hank had remained upstairs in Mack's apartment throughout the wake and it hurt me that he felt he had to stay away; I remembered at one point during the evening I had looked up at the balcony windows and deeply missed them both.

When José and Kaku progressed to a public display of affection, French kissing and fondling each other as they danced, I broke them up and told them it was time to close up shop unless they wanted me to film what was next. In a way their behavior reminded me of my early years with Parker, when we would fondle and dance and stick our tongues down each other's throat at the slightest hint of happiness. I also knew that José's drive to succeed reminded me a bit of my own, so I wasn't surprised when he approached me before leaving and said, "We could throw a press luncheon saying we've discovered a new clue to Jean Lafitte's treasure."

"We can leave the media out of it," I answered him.

"We could all be rich and famous and on cable TV."

"Infamous, I think would be the proper term," I said. "And probably in jail when they discover we're lying."

"Not lying," José said. "Just hoping. Hoping to succeed."

Yes, he was a little bit too much like myself, I thought, or at least when I was his age. *Hoping to succeed.*

"We can help out however you need us," Kaku said. "We won't let them close you down."

Yes, everyone had been drinking and talking a little too much tonight. *Close us down? Who was going to close us down?* What kind of trouble was Kaku thinking of? Did he mean that Celia, the ghost of Angelle, or the pirate Lafitte would be doing us in? I didn't stop to try and solve that puzzle—it was all speculation within a day of speculation. Instead, I walked them to the alleyway entrance where Parker had been standing talking to Buddy and Dwayne and I said my goodnights, leaving the circle of them to tie up the last bags of garbage.

Back inside the office, I looked through the mail, mostly bills, poured myself another drink, and ran the water for the tub. Studying myself in the mirror, I realized I looked extremely haggard with the gray stubble of beard now fully visible across my tired, puffy face, but I still hadn't the energy or enthusiasm to shave it away. As I soaked and drank in the tub, I considered that there were too many tangible factors not to believe in ghosts or supernatural phenomenon—too much was happening that I couldn't discount. There was the ghost of Toby. The dark lady in the fountain. The young man in the courtyard and the waving floor planks of the pantry, not to mention the lightning bugs of lost babies. Or trapped souls. But why would a soul want to hang around this place? And why now, after all the years we had lived here did they have to show up? Heaven and hell were just human creations. Human interpretation. A state of mind. Maybe everyone before us had gotten it all wrong. Maybe souls never departed earth's atmosphere, just lived on in eternity outside the perspective of time and vision. Maybe ghosts of the living were like humidity, rising and falling according to the whims of Mother Nature, Father Sun, and the orbit of Planet Earth. Or maybe all we needed was a little more fiber in our diet to make sure that we did not disturb anyone else in another life.

I had no idea what to do about any of it. Suddenly I was thankful to realize that Talla, Lynette's girlfriend, had not shown up that evening all fluttery and concerned. She would have been certain to have intervened with an arm-flailing spell or a suddenly discovered tarot card and made everyone nervous and stressed, not just me. Things were really not unmanageable, just, well, *confused*. I was thankful just for the knowledge and silliness of the legends and myths that Dwayne and the boys had told me that night. But fifolet? Fireballs of lost souls? Jean Lafitte's lost treasure? I laughed at that last one, grateful that I had not entirely lost my sense of humor despite the loss of both Mack and Hank.

In bed, I waited to fall asleep, expecting a thump at my chest and my inner creation of Griffin as my consciousness to return and give me some further insight (or at least entertainment), but when he didn't—when I failed to summon this Higher Power cum Internal Psyche—I turned out the lamp and fell into a light dream where I was conscious of trying to get a stain out of the floor of this room. Something dark and sweaty had left an oily imprint in the shape of a curled body in a corner, legs tucked up near to what appeared to be the waist and shoulders. I scrubbed and scrubbed but the shadow would not disappear.

A light rapping on the office door window woke me a few minutes later, and I thought it must be Hank, penitent and wanting to come back and give it another try. I rushed into the other room and pulled back the sheer curtains and looked out at the courtyard. Parker was standing at the door when I unlocked it and pushed it open. He was in his sleeping outfit—not really pajamas, but a combination of clothes he wore when he had difficulty sleeping in air conditioner weather—a long-sleeved T-shirt and boxer shorts.

"I can't sleep," he said, the way a small boy would admit it to a parent.

"Parker T. Steinberg, you're not scared, are you?" I asked him.

Parker was the kind of guy who didn't want anyone to tell him how to do his job or live his life. He didn't want any help in the kitchen or in the office. Personally, he was also self-sufficient—he bought his own shaving cream, chose his brand of toothpaste, bought the right size of underwear for himself, and didn't want anyone nagging him that the rent was due at the first of the month. But as long as I had known Parker he had never liked to sleep alone.

"Of course not," he said. "I was worried about you being lonely, what with Hank upstairs and all."

"Well, then," I said, "come in."

He padded his way through the office, around the desk with the computer, and into the room in the back. Parker and I had never slept together in this bed or in this room, but he instinctively slipped into the right side of the bed, the side he always slept on, and I slipped into the other. He didn't want to talk—Parker was never a bedtime talker—never much of a chatterer any time of the day, really—but he wanted to snuggle because this was the easiest way for him to fall asleep.

I wanted to make a snide remark about how he must be exhausted from doing nothing all day, but I didn't want to start a fight, at least not right before bedtime, and then there he was all about me, his big furry body wrapped around me, and wafts of the familiar smells and breaths I had always enjoyed and felt secure with.

Parker fell asleep easily, but I was wide awake, trying to sort out a lot of things, particularly why I had allowed someone like Griffin to make such a big impression on both my conscious and unconscious states. This gave way to worries about the future—there was a whole period of eight days next month that were not booked for any of the guest rooms and I suddenly saw it as our likely path to bankruptcy. When I got tired of trying to calculate the day's losses from the restaurant being closed, the extra food purchases for the evening, and the rent-free nights for Mack's family, I closed my eyes and fell into a dream about sleeping in Parker's arms. I dreamed he shifted himself, began kissing and fondling me the way he always had, slipping his hand to my crotch first and making me hard. Next, his mouth opened and he pressed his lips and hot breath against my neck, ready to give me a hickey. Soon, I had swiveled around and was on top of him, rubbing our bodies against each other. I reached for him beneath me and he was hard too, then I pushed myself up so that I straddled his thighs and could grasp both of us at the same time.

I woke with an erection, my hand clutching both of our cocks. As consciousness returned to me, I was aware of something beyond us, some kind of being watching us together in bed. Parker's head was pitched back against the pillow as if he was still in his dream but awake enough to enjoy my stroking him. I could feel the being circling us, as brightly and intently as the fireballs had done in the pantry. Was it Mack or Toby? The ghost of Angelle? Or something more sinister, a wolf-like dog ready to attack?

Parker dug his hands deeper into the mattress and rocked his hips and his orgasm came first, and mine easily followed. He didn't wake while I left the bed and found a towel, dried myself off first, then brought it back to the bed and wiped it across his stomach, leaving the towel spread across his bare crotch as if to protect him from our voyeur.

We snuggled into each other again, but broke apart just after sleep returned, both of us feverish and restless, rearranging our pillows. Sometime late in the night (or early in the morning), Parker woke sweating from a dream.

"Are you awake?" he asked me.

I was only in a light sleep, and I said, "What's wrong?"

"I was dreaming that I was falling and couldn't stop," he said. "The same dream I had last night. When I tried to scream so that someone could hear me, I couldn't make a sound. Someone had stolen my voice."

"Who stole your voice?" I asked. As I tried to concentrate on what he was saying, I felt a heavy urge to surrender to sleep. But then I sensed a movement in the room that was neither Parker nor myself. Our voyeur was back. I was certain of it. And I was sure it wasn't Mack or Toby.

"I'm not sure," he answered. "It was dark."

I pulled his head to my chest and patted his back, my eyes trained on the blackness of the room. He stayed there for a while, sweating, till he fell back asleep. The warmer Parker felt against my skin, the more I worried about something happening to us, and just as I had convinced myself that all was well, nothing was wrong and I was only going crazy, I closed my eyes to fall asleep, only to hear, in the far-off recesses of my mind, a baby crying, the gag and cough and sputter of a tiny voice that disappeared in a bright flash of light beneath my eyelids.

Three

As a preacher's son, I grew up with a skeptic's eye for my father and grandfather's narrow-minded Bible-thumping religion, as distrustful of its pleading prayers and shouted passages from the Good Book as my father was of the magical spells and babbling enchantments of gnarly warlocks and gray-bearded wizards. The older I grew, the less hope I invested in any alternative faith, believing more in the nature of science and the science of nature than in any kind of psychic phenomenon, miracles, or messages from the dead. None of this has ever stopped me from uttering a small prayer in a moment of crisis or to potentially banish an inconvenience, however; a quick "please God, save me from this fate," which was exactly what I said when Celia was rapping her rings against the office window before I had finished spiking my first cup of coffee of the day. Parker, my comatose and retired partner, was still asleep in the back room and I closed the door between the rooms so that I could talk with her privately in the office.

"I'm sorry to bother you so early," Celia said. "But Stuart took the boys out for breakfast. I thought it might be a good time for me to start looking through some of Mack's things."

"I have someone staying up there," I answered. "But let me call him and see if he's up."

I knew I would wake Hank up; he was seldom an early riser, particularly when he wasn't in the mood to work (which was most days), but I called the phone in Mack's apartment, exactly two stories above where

I stood in the office. I heard it ringing upstairs through the floorboards and the empty morning air rustling with the vibrating sound. I knew that if Hank woke I would hear him stir, hear the floorboards shift and creak as he made his way across the apartment to where Mack had kept the phone on the table near the front window. The phone rang six times until the answering machine picked up, and Mack's voice's started with a message. My stomach tumbled at the familiar sound of him, the cadences and patterns and words Mack had always used. I tried not to show my dismay to Celia, tried to subdue my next fretful prayer to God, and pulled my ear away from the receiver and hung up the phone, not wanting to leave a message that Hank might or might not hear. Maybe I had misjudged Hank's presence all along, and instead of being *in* for the entire evening, he had been *out* and had never returned. I felt the loss of him, then the loss of Mack, then my annoyance with Celia for bringing them both back into my consciousness so early in the morning. I found my main set of keys in the desk drawer and told Celia I would go upstairs and make certain Hank was not still asleep in the apartment so that she could look around. She followed me up the stairs and at Mack's front door, waited behind me as I knocked.

I heard no movement inside the apartment, no one approaching the door, so I unlocked it with my key and stepped inside. There was no one in the front room where Mack kept the television and a table and chairs, but in the back room I found Hank sitting up in the bed, a book in his lap. He was still dressed as I had last seen him the day before, in jeans and a T-shirt, and his skin had an oily, clammy sheen to it as if he had been sweating through the night. He had a dazed, far-off look in his eyes, as if he were stoned or had been sleeping with his eyelids open, and he had taken no notice of my entry and made no move to greet me, though his eyes had followed my approach towards the bed and he knew I was there.

Celia had followed me into the apartment and into the back room, and I turned to her and said, "Wait a minute outside, please," which she kindly (and surprisingly) did.

"Hank?" I said, jostling his leg. "Everything okay?" I'd lived through some of Hank's dark, depressive moods, but this seemed to be something odder than what I might have expected.

He lifted his eyes and looked at me and said, "Did you know all this stuff?"

"What stuff?" I asked.

"All this," he said, lifting the edges of the small book he held in his lap. I picked it up and saw that the pages were full of handwriting, the black ink soaking into the stiff fabric of the cream-colored paper in patches and blotches—the book was some sort of old diary or journal, an artifact he must have discovered while rummaging through Mack's bookcase for nighttime reading. "Hank, Mack's sister is here. She wants to look around the apartment. Why don't you come downstairs to the office for a while. Have some coffee with me."

I tried to keep my rising annoyance in check, not to let it be visible to Celia, because it really *was* too early in the morning for a sensible adult to be awake and moving about. Why was it that everyone in my life was so catatonic these days? And why weren't they sharing their drug of choice with me? *I* was the one who needed something to relax. *Me, me, me. I* was the one watching the backs of all these potential mental patients.

Hank took the journal out of my hands, slowly walked through the rooms and passed by Celia without even acknowledging her. He was a zombie, his eyes glazed over in thought, his body stiff and emotionless, as if all the energy of his life and humor had been shocked right out of his bloodstream. It occurred to me that maybe he had taken an antidepressant, or that he had gone to one of the clubs and someone had slipped him a bump of something on a dance floor that hadn't yet worn off, but whatever was going on with Hank certainly didn't feel like it was something he had expected to occur. I nodded to Celia and said, "It's okay. Look around at whatever you want."

I followed Hank outside to the balcony, where he stopped and clutched the journal to his chest. I was about to pump Hank for more details on his reading material and his odd state when Stuart and the boys rushed into the courtyard below. Stuart saw me on the balcony upstairs and yelled, "I forgot my cellphone. I've got to talk to my office this morning. Is Celia up there?"

Ungraciously, I rolled my eyes and nodded that she was and before I knew it, he had said to the boys, "Go wait upstairs with your mom."

Hank seemed oblivious to this interchange, even unaware of the booming sound of the boys as they made their way up the two flights of steps. I thought about admonishing them, yelling at them to be quiet and behave like gentlemen because there were a few paying guests who might still be trying to sleep at this early hour, but I knew they wouldn't respect my wishes because their parents certainly didn't, and my loud, irritated voice would only add to the decibel level now rocketing through the courtyard.

I tried to slow them down on the balcony by standing directly in front of their path, but they took greater joy in rushing around me and inside Mack's apartment to find their mother, their voices a mix of high-pitched squeals and laughs and taunts. I heard Celia blithely telling them to settle down and asking where their father was, but they continued running in circles like they had already exceeded their acceptable daily sugar levels and were now emphatically hyperactive.

It's hard to explain what happened next; it all transpired so suddenly and yet seemed to play as if it were acted out in slow motion. Hank had turned his back on the boys, had braced one hand on the wooden balcony railing while the other still clutched the journal, as if to steady himself because he felt ill. Sean ran out of the apartment first and deflected to the left to avoid crashing directly into my stocky legs, followed by Noah who decided to go in the other direction, between where I stood and where Hank was against the railing. Hank was not as oblivious to the boys' activity as I thought he was. He shifted his posture to allow Noah to squeeze between us and as he did so, he must have pressed his full weight against the spokes of the railing. The wood creaked first, then creaked again as the old nails splintered away from the flooring of the balcony. Hank came to as he was falling—I saw whatever had been lost inside his mind come alive again as his startled eyes widened with the realization that he was falling over the collapsing railing.

Instinctively, my hands flew out by my side to keep the young boys in place, the aging crone attempting to protect the younger generation. The boys stopped to watch Hank fall in slow motion off the balcony. First, he lost his balance, his shoeless feet shifting and finding no ledge to stop them, then his foot rotated because there was nothing there to prevent it and his body began a revolution that followed the motion through the air. As I held the gape-mouthed boys beside me, I saw Hank disappear, first, as if he were going up, not down, and then falling out of my sight. Light seemed to brighten for a moment as if it were blinding me and then all sound fell away until I heard Hank's high cry and then low groan of pain as his body hit the bricks of the courtyard below, followed by the flap-*deflap-deflap-plap-plap* of the splintered wood bouncing against the bricks.

I pushed the boys against the wall of the building and said, sternly, "Stay there," and ran towards the stairs. The next few seconds were thunderous, cataclysmic, with true panic setting in, the loss of both faith and control as I felt a punch to my heart and a struggle to keep breathing. I invoked another prayer as I lurched my own weary body into motion: *Please God, please, please, please, let him be okay.*

The steps downward seemed endless and repetitive, even as I lunged over three and four of them at a time, my heavy feet now sending thudding *boom-boom-booms* out into the enclosure. As the courtyard came into sight, I noticed Hank's body lying on the bricks, but as I moved closer to him it seemed the body was of somebody else, dressed like the specter of the young black man I had seen the night before—in a soiled beige colored shirt and calf-length pants. He was lying on his side in the area in front of the office doorway and as I made my way to him I could tell he was still breathing. I was only momentarily confused because I knew I must again be hallucinating. Only when I was down on my knees beside the body, feeling for the pulse at his arm, did the details of Hank's face swim back into place.

"Hang on, Hank," I spoke towards his exposed ear, "I'm calling an ambulance."

As I stood up, I sensed that we were not alone and I turned my head quickly to acknowledge whomever was there before I rushed inside the office to call for emergency services. A man was standing at the back entrance of the main house, and at first I thought it was Stuart, because of his tall, odd, elegant look, but as I went inside the office the features of his appearance began to register in my mind—the man had been attired in a white ruffled shirt, a waistcoat, and royal blue pants, and the expression on his face had been one of both anguish and relief. The image of him faded from my mind as I concentrated to give the operator the proper street address of the guesthouse. Behind me I made a conscious note that the door of the back room was still closed, which meant that Parker was still in bed and asleep and out of commission. It didn't occur to me that I needed to rouse him—I was too distracted with getting help for Hank first, and I was certain Parker could hear my imitation of a highly-strung wailing Banshee as I described the accident to the operator and that he would come out at any second and ask what was the matter and offer to help. As I held the receiver in one hand, my other instinctively reached for an emergency pint of cheap whiskey I kept in my bottom desk drawer when I could find nothing else better to drink and I slipped it inside a pocket of the sweatpants I had put on when getting out of bed earlier. Only then did I realize that I had not even had a chance to clean myself up—now unshaved for two days running, I had not even had an opportunity to wash the sleepy grime from my face. I must look like a prison guard after a double shift and a riot and I grabbed my wallet from the shelf of the desk where I kept it and shoved it into my other pocket and rushed back outside.

Upstairs on the balcony, Celia had pushed the boys inside Mack's apartment and when I was back out on the courtyard, she warily bent over the remaining railing and asked if Hank was all right.

"Of course, he's not all right," I snapped back at her. Hank had lost consciousness, though his breathing continued, but I had no idea of whatever other internal or physical damages he might have sustained. I tried not to openly display my panic again, tried not to imagine Hank dying the day after Mack had, and I took his hand and grasped it within my own and began talking in a mostly gibberish way, certain that he was going to die, telling him that everything would be all right and that I loved him and needed him here to help me make a go of things, remembering that somewhere I had heard that hearing was the last sensation to go before a person died—so I wasn't about to shut up.

Stuart returned to the courtyard just as two ambulance workers were rushing through the alleyway. I explained Hank's tumble from the second floor to the tallest guy, while the other worker, a short, heavyset woman who looked like she had started eating doughnuts nonstop before she learned to chew, casually checked Hank's pulse and breathing as if she was ready to perform a postmortem. I kicked the splintered pieces of the balcony railing that had fallen into the courtyard against the walls and, as the ambulance workers tossed Hank onto the stretcher as if he were a lifeless aquatic specimen that had washed up onshore, I walked over to Stuart and told him in a clipped, manic voice that if there was anything the family needed that day to check in at the office with Parker. I had no idea if Celia was aware that what had happened might have been because of the boys, not really certain myself if Noah had caused Hank to fall or if something—some other force or will or, God forbid, *spirit*, had used the opportunity to push him off the balcony.

Or had I caused this? Had my own mental breakdown over the last few days contributed to this accident? "There are no accidents," my father used to say to me. "God has a design for each of us." Was this part of my task? What Griffin had prepared me for? Had I summoned God in the pantry or had he summoned me? And where was he now that I needed him to watch over Hank? What could he possibly be doing relaxing at a beach in Hawaii or witnessing the baptism of a cranky, colicky six-week-old infant when He was needed here, right now, *pronto!*

Please God, please, please, please, let him be okay, I mindlessly chanted in the back of the ambulance, trying to block out the relentless sound of the siren bleeding through the tin frame of the van. I was gripping the book that Hank had been holding when he fell. Somehow as I reached for his hand, I also clutched at the journal. *What an idiot thing to be doing,* I thought, *clinging to something with such hope.* It was already a hot day, the back of the ambulance stuffy and uncomfortable. From where I was seated I could only see out of a portion of the grease-smeared rear window and I pitched my body back and forth, trying to absorb the shocks of the ride and not be nauseous, glimpsing pink-skinned, sun-blistered tourists behind us crossing the street to reach the shade but stopping to look back at the ambulance pulling out of sight. I gave the taller ambulance worker Hank's name, address, and other details as we reached the outskirts of the Quarter and moved into the thicker traffic of Canal. I tried not to blame myself for the accident, but at the bottom of my thoughts was the realization that I was responsible because I had made Hank my responsibility. It was my fault for ignoring Hank. My fault for not being a better lover—or a better boss. For sending him upstairs to Mack's apartment. For suggesting that he stay and not leave. It was all my miserable, selfish fault because I was so overworked and unfocused. I should have had the railing checked years before—if the stairs could weather and splinter and fall apart, why hadn't I realized the balconies and the railings could do the same?

As the ambulance sped along I tried to remember good things about us, moments when things had worked with Hank, when we'd both been happy and in love, though they seemed harder to find, lost in the memory of one argument after the next, one disappointment after another. There were the touristy things we did together the first months we were dating— the swamp tour, a trip to the casino, a drive down Plantation Road. But each time I had been worried about leaving the guesthouse in Parker's unsteady hands and I had confessed as much to Hank. Hank had shown an early resentment at the way the business asserted its pull on my time and attitude. When he moved in and began to help out, Hank never had the easiness about the place that Mack had. He resented customers asking him about stripper bars and boat rides, was offended if someone offered him a tip, or a compliment. The first night we met at the bathhouse I had complimented his smile. He was thin and exotic looking with a short white towel wrapped around his waist. "What you after?" he snapped back at me, not a shred of humor in his voice. "Whatever I can get," I had chuckled, trying to be easy going. I was escaping work for the night, escaping responsibility, escaping aging—I, too, was in a towel, but feeling decidedly unsexy and needy, heavy and bloated, conscious of the graying hair on my chest.

Hank was surprisingly enthusiastic in bed, eager and playful in a way he wasn't outside of it. In bed he could smile and caress and compliment— kiss and hug and sometimes even dream about the future. This good twin of himself wanted to party and fuck and experiment with whatever toys he happened to find in one boutique or another. I'd often wondered why he left that part of himself behind, unable to carry it around with him through the day. He made me realize that there are often many sides to the same person, different situations turn us into different people.

If I were a better Christian, or the kind of Christian my father had trained me to be, I would have healed Hank before the ambulance workers even arrived, pressed my hands against Hank's head and heart and invoked the magical presence of the Holy Spirit with a shout of "Help me, Jesus! Bring us hope!" God would have appeared exactly as my father had orchestrated it in front of his elated congregation and Hank would have coughed and gasped and fluttered his eyelids open and miraculously risen up, unscathed and unharmed and seized by the restorative power of the belief in God. But there was no kind of God like that, no matter how many times I had seen my father and grandfather shout, "He has been healed by the power of the Lord God Almighty." God was not a showman and there was no such thing as an ordained miracle. The notion was as ridiculous to me as believing in ghosts.

At the hospital, Hank was rushed into a hallway and I was left in a lobby to wait and silently drive myself mad. Alone now for the first time in what seemed like years, I started panicking, wondering how I was going to handle Hank being crippled or Hank being disabled or Hank being a vegetable or Hank being dead. All those years I had looked after Mack counted for nothing—I had no compassion or understanding whatsoever for what lay ahead for us; I only saw a path of doctors' visits and therapy and medication and slow, slow heartbreak, and again I found myself praying to be released from this misery, to have Hank watched over, to have my life restored to the miserable, mega-burdened balance it had been at only a few days before. "The plans I have for you are plans to prosper you and not to harm you," I remembered God promising Jeremiah from my Sunday school Bible class. "Plans to give you hope and a future." *Did I need to pray more? Harder? How could I get Jeremiah's special treatment too?*

I tried to reach Parker on the phone, but he did not answer the office line. There was no answer in his apartment, no answer, either, when I tried Mack's apartment and not even Celia picked up, and my anxiety escalated into the frenzy of a haunted teenage scream queen in a slasher flick as I tried the number of the café and waited and waited as the phone went unanswered. No one was looking after the place—I was certain that tiresome, bitching customers were turning on their spigots and finding only cold water, that time-sensitive requests for reservations were going unnoticed and spewing to the floor from the fax, curling up and hiding beneath the desk where I would never find them, that our appalled guests were leaving in disgust and not paying their bills because no one would come to the office door after they had knocked for almost fifteen seconds.

I wasn't about to leave Hank alone at the hospital until I knew that his status was stable and that he would survive—so I tried to accept the fact that I was stuck with myself, stuck with my memories and aches and anticipations and nightmare scenarios. Okay, so God had put me here. What must I do? What must I see? What part must I play? Or should I just sit and rejoice with my newest bout of suffering. Suffering produced endurance and endurance produced character and character produced hope and hope could not disappoint as long as you continued to hope. Right? *Right?*

This was not my first crack-up. Every time Mack had gone into the hospital I had become ballistic. It wasn't just that each time I became a divided soul torn between two places—needing to work at the guesthouse and to keep vigil at the hospital—it was that hospitals frightened me, cast me into the unknown and conjured up a hateful suspicion. I became a spook myself—scary, vicious, demanding, exactly the kind of person everyone wanted to avoid. I would have rather dealt with a rowdy booking of frat boys during Mardi Gras week than to wait in a hospital corridor for someone to tell me the results of a blood test or a biopsy or X ray.

So I sat again in the waiting room, neurotically twisting my fingers around each other, watching other arrivals enter through the pneumatic doors: a mother rushed inside holding her little boy's hand, bloodied and wrapped in a towel that was turning from pink to scarlet as I watched; a hard-breathing pregnant woman took a seat beside me and grasped her belly as her unstrung husband went to the receptionist and tapped on the countertop for her attention; then, a pair of ambulance workers pushed a bloody body across the room and through a set of swinging doors. I tried to get lost within their lives and misery and worries instead of feeling trapped within my own, but I reached a moment when I had to look away from it all, and I instinctively opened the book that I had held against my lap for so long as a new source of distraction. The pages of black handwriting blurred before me and I randomly thumbed through them. At first I thought they had been written in a foreign language, the letters were so thin and slanted they were almost indecipherable, then words and phrases such as "unopened barrels," "shipment from Mobile," and "by special order" floated into my consciousness alongside columns of numbers and an inventory of stock items such as "satin ribbon," "leather gloves," and "canvas tenting." *Thank God my eyesight has not yet deteriorated,* I thought briefly, trying to bring back my sense of humor. *Thank God I'm not some nearly blind old fart always reaching for a pair of glasses.* Then I stopped at a page and simply began reading:

June 5, 1822

What sad fate awaits us even in a house like this where slavery still prevails alongside compassion? Since I have left France and returned to Dumaine Street to partake in the great American mercantile system by joining Papa's business as his partner, Papa has relented and opened his ledgers to my inspection and I am now fully aware how impoverished our family truly is. Our income is scarcely sufficient of late to cover our expenses and he is right that we should consider selling our slaves, now a growing burden to our income (or lack thereof). How Papa must have managed and done without and saved and scraped to send me away for an education, how much he must have sacrificed himself, how Mama must have gone without for so many years, just so that I could study abroad. Quel dommage! I am truly ashamed. Now I am indebted even further to Papa because I know these facts; how can I even consider striking out on my own after finding how much I truly owe him for all that I have?

Into all this moral disaster Aaron has become my sole friend, my true companion, my natural half, full of the same ancestral blood and passions as I have inherited and this is what draws us close. Our night visits are kept secret from the rest of the household, though I know that many are already suspicious of our personal sentiments towards each other. How I have missed him while I was away—in our private time he refreshes my soul; we recall our boyhood years together—our games, our studies, our gentle reproaches and fond endearments to each other. His body has become hardened and stronger, weakened and toughened by the straps and whips and yoke, whereas mine has slackened from too long hours spent at a desk instead of beside him in the storeroom. His passion for Freedom as of late has stirred up his animosity and inevitably we spend much time whispering on what is to become of him—and us. I cannot entirely shake away my growing shame while I am with him, not because of how I have come to feel for him, but how I am unable to reveal Papa's desire to sell him and the others to catch up with debts. I had promised him many times, since our boyhood, that when Papa fully passes along the trade to me, when things are prosperous for our family, I will free him and all in the household when it is my turn to preside, but he is too impatient and not at all humble and certain as I am of the years that have already passed between us, saying that Antoine must understand the dilemma at hand—himself the son of a white man and a slave woman, raised to be free by my Grandpapa, trained and educated to inherit the Dubuisson trade.

What has become of us? Our family? Les gens de couleur libres. Children of slaves owning slaves themselves. Is there nothing that society has taught any thread of my ancestors or have they been too caught up in the need to impress the rest of society? What is hateful is to see the puffed-up vanity of the Creole women in Papa's store, the haughty airs of the free men whose credit has proved worthless over time. I see Angelle watching them from the corner of the store, mimicking the way they inspect our goods as if what we sell is not good enough quality for their hands even though they cannot afford it, and I see the desire in Angelle's eyes to have all that they would have, though what they have is nothing, really, nothing except their bloated impressions of themselves. I say prayers of thanks that Mama did not live to see this state of things in either the store

or our home, to see the household divided by the attentions
Papa gives Angelle and not Aaron. In all respects Aaron has as
much right to the fortunes of the Dubuisson trade as Antoine
does, both of them sired by Grandpapa Christian, yet born
of different wombs and generations apart, Papa born first of
Jeanine, the family slave now long dead, and Aaron twenty-eight
years later, the son of Evangeline, her niece. If Grandpapa raised
Antoine a free man, why did he not do the same for Aaron?
Had Christian Dubuisson lived, survived the dreaded fever of
this place, would he have allowed Aaron the fate that father
has determined for him? Papa always resented Aaron's birth,
resented Grandpapa's nocturnal needs, yet Angelle's arrival was
celebrated in the household twelve years later when we were
both just boys. Grandpapa kept no secret of the fact that he
had sired such a beautiful baby girl at his old age, adoring her
as much as he disregarded Aaron. Angelle will be a beautiful
woman some day and I know that Papa has his eye on her. He
has not kept it secret that he intends to send her abroad when
the time comes, and she is fast approaching those days, though
how he intends to pay for this folly I cannot understand, even
if it is to sell Aaron and Manny and Grady and, perhaps, even
to accomplish it, Evangeline, who now shares his bed since
Mama's death, just as she did with Grandpapa Christian. What
would Grandpapa make of that? His son, bedding his last
mistress, lusting after his half-sister—but then who am I to
judge him, really, I, myself, in love with Aaron—my half-uncle
by blood? And what of the fact that we must keep this love
hidden—from the family, from society, perhaps even from the
good and benevolent Lord himself. Am I as wretched as the
rest of this family? Are we cursed to keep our secrets and flaunt
our shame?

At night Aaron has often whispered to me that Grandpapa
had promised Evangeline that both her children would be free

some day, that Aaron would in time gain his Liberty, and I know that this is the fueling point of his temper of late. Father only sees trouble in Aaron: the slow work, the missing inventory, the impudence of talking back to the Master of the house. I fear that Aaron will run away one day and have a fate far worse at work in the fields or in the swamplands than what could happen if he stayed and remained a part of our family. Animosity breathes animosity and if Aaron would only not be so difficult, I feel certain Father would recognize his kin and the value of Freedom and Liberty to all humans.

A young nurse with an olive complexion and a thick lower lip arrived at the lobby and called my name and I closed the book and hurried towards her. She told me that Hank's injuries were not critical, that his shoulder was dislocated and his arm was broken in two places. He was awake and responding well and it did not seem as if his spinal cord was injured or that his head had suffered any injuries other than the scrapes and bruises from hitting the bricks, but they wanted to admit him for observation and additional tests. I was mumbling little prayers of thanks as I followed her through a series of corridors to where Hank was lying in a bed surrounded by curtains, his eyes open, nervous and alert. I could tell he was fighting to stay awake and he only acknowledged me with something that sounded like, "There you are."

"I just gave him something that will help him sleep," another nurse said, more to the heavy-lipped nurse I had followed through the corridor than to me, and by the time it had registered to me that they were silently communicating some kind of fact to each other, Hank had closed his eyes. "We'll move him up to a room shortly," the first nurse said, not looking at me but at a monitor screen beside Hank's bed.

I sat and waited again, this time in a chair beside Hank's trolley-like bed, checking his face every few seconds for a sign of pain or awakening, my own mind continually chanting, *Why? Why? Why? Was this an accident? Part of a plan? Is this my task? Or is my task now complete?* I still didn't want to leave him just yet, even though I was aware that he was not in the critical danger zone I had hysterically imagined for him. This seemed part of something larger that I didn't quite understand yet, connected in some way to Mack's death, the ghosts, and the book I clutched against my chest. I'd see Hank get settled in his room, make sure things were going fine for him, and then proceed directly to the cemetery where Mack was to be buried that afternoon, hoping, against hope, really, that all was well and taken care of back at the guesthouse and the café. If I gave myself a goal, a plan, perhaps that would create logic within all this chaos.

I remembered the pint of whiskey in my pocket and I discretely brought it out and took a long swig. So maybe God had at least given me the foresight to reach for my own medication. If, as my father said, nothing was an accident then it wasn't accidental that I wanted a drink and had been inspired—or called by the Holy Spirit—to travel with my own cheap stock. The rush of the alcohol along my throat and into the ulcerous walls of my intestines brought both energy and comfort, warming my chest and clearing my mind. All thoughts of prayers had stopped and I no longer felt like I needed to scream to vent my frustration or awaken God to the fact that I needed his *immediate help.* I took a deep breath, counted backwards, and looked down at the journal in my lap. So Hank had found Pierre Dubuisson's journal among Mack's books—why hadn't I known of this book before? Is this what had upset Hank? Made him so shocked that he appeared comatose? Slaves owning slaves, a piece of forgotten history. It was certainly shocking enough. Or had the strong and intimate bond between two men disturbed him? Master and slave as relatives and lovers? A hint of incest? A brotherhood both pure and corrupt? Or was it the obvious intimacy and love between two men that had disturbed him, what he felt he had been unable to achieve in his own relationships? I found the place where I had stopped and began to read an entry dated June 7, 1822.

My heart is blackened and I can find no way free of my sorrow. Aaron was caught today trying to sell the knife I had given to him, brought back from my time on the continent, carried safely in my baggage during my two month passage. A merchant near the docks accused him of being a thief. He was beaten on the site and a policeman dragged him back to the store where he was taken into the back courtyard, humiliated in front of the family and the household, and flogged by Papa for stealing an item mon Père could not even identify as his own. Manny was forced to clean Aaron with salt water and shackle him up with chains to prevent him from escaping. I tried to stop it, telling Papa that I had given Aaron the knife, that I had found it in a store in the rue de la Bretonaise, had had a jeweler engrave the initials on the blade, but Papa said I had no right presenting such a thing to a slave and that whatever the cost I had paid for such a thing, it had surely been accomplished only with what money he had provided me for my time abroad.

Papa did not see the beauty of the knife, the craftsmanship nor the detail of the design, only its potential danger—and his violent reaction towards Aaron is only a continued acknowledgment of his fear of him. Papa refused to believe my facts and I was forced to present him with another case, telling him that Aaron had every right to be a free man like Papa was, born from the loins of the same free kin of Dubuisson as himself. How did it look to the household, Papa treating Aaron like this? What kind of example was he setting?

Papa called me impudent, told me that I had only garnered nonsense abroad, not any practical wisdom or education, and it had only been a waste of time and income to send me to France because I had failed to learn anything practical. His rage grew and instead of lashing out at me, he directed it further at Aaron, shackling him to a courback, the iron yoke riveted to his neck. Aaron was denied both food and water and kept outside in the courtyard overnight, not even in a covered space.

How can the laws of this land allow such things to happen? This treatment is only certain to bring harm, not remorse or change. This city is full of such daily and revolting treatments against the Negroes—whose ancestors' blood is mingled within my own. This is certainly not a New World, only a continuation of the Old Evil Ways. I understand Papa acts as others do in this city, but how can I tolerate such behavior from anyone? How can this injustice be changed? Stopped? We are all borne of one race, of one divine Being, descended from the Adam who was cast out of Eden. Already in the Northern and Western states good minds are preaching the Emancipation of the Negro but here, here in my beloved home, personal interest brings an immediate and formidable opposition. Only last month antagonists fell upon a sympathizer in Bourbon Street, covered him in blows and went off telling him that if he started up with such nonsense again, someone would teach him better respect for American Values. American Values? Whatever could this be?

This evening, I slipped down to the kitchen, found bread and water while the household was asleep, and brought food to Aaron, washed and treated his wounds the best I could. He was hardly conscious and I had to lift the jug of water to his lips and help him swallow. I held his hand and prayed that he would grow stronger, that his spirit would not be hurt, that he would not become evil. I tried to believe that he was not a broken man, or that Papa had whipped away his passion to survive.

I must press Evangeline to intercede in this inhumanity,
tell her that since she shares Papa's bed she must find a way to
spare Aaron's inevitable decline. But her reaction today was one
of quiet resolve, as if this were something she had expected to
happen, and she understood the dual pain she must now feel,
watching her lover beat and subdue her son. Aaron must not
die this way. How will we look to others? How will we look to
ourselves when time manages to slip further from us?

I stopped reading when Hank was wheeled away for another test. A
wide-hipped, big-bosomed nurse gave me the number of the room on the
fourth floor where he would be brought about an hour later. I went to the
floor and sat in a waiting area that overlooked the entrance to the hospital
and a hot, black-tarred parking lot, filled with banged-up used cars and
vans. I sat for a few minutes, blinking my eyes at the heat outside, then
bent down to the journal, thumbing randomly through the pages though
my anxiety prevented me from settling down to read. Instead, I went to
the pay phone near the elevator bank and called the office, the café, and
Mack's apartment again, but there was still no answer from anyone, no one
was picking up the phones, and in my mind everything was continuing to
fall apart. Checkout time had come and gone. Check-in time was rapidly
approaching. Time was moving faster in a place where I was not. I felt my
neck muscles tense, the nerves and tendons as taut as if they were stretched
by a rack. I could see the hours, days, weeks, and months passing in large
pockets of space with each second-hand tick of the clock on the wall. I was
simply waiting, waiting, waiting.

This was why I seldom left the guesthouse anymore: paranoia. Why I
had never taken a real out-of-town vacation in almost six years: worry that
no one else was doing his job. I was micromanaging a staff of one and he
was missing in action, confined to a hospital bed waiting for tests. Back in

the visitors' area, I took another sip from the pint of whiskey and glanced nervously at my watch to avoid staring at the clock on the wall, hoping that Parker had left for the funeral home. For a while I sat in the sunshine of the window, breathing, meditating, praying, remembering passages from the Bible my father had misinterpreted in his sermons, sipping from the pint of whiskey that I was slowly draining, wondering why I had never invested in a cellphone for either myself or Parker; why hadn't I spent more money to avoid aggravation? Next, I drifted into thinking of other resolutions and goals to pursue—I'd take out a high-interest loan from a prissy bank queen, or ask around for the name of a scratchy-speaking loan shark in the Mafia who could torch the place if we defaulted—anything to get the place in better working order and avoid any lawsuits from other guests further down the road. I'd have the railings in the slave quarters redone and tested, the pointing of the brick upgraded; the gutters desperately needed cleaning, the café needed a fresh coat of paint and maybe a new sink or a second one in the kitchen. How could I even dream of installing central air-conditioning when there was so much more to do to the place first? Then, I reached a moment when I needed to stop such thinking and planning, and my eyes dropped towards the journal and I continued to read.

June 18, 1822

Aaron's health has not improved after two days of rest and it seems certain that Papa will sell him before the month is gone. What rankles Papa more, however, than Aaron's inability to work in the storeroom, is the hoodoo which has set itself upon the house like a plague. Three days ago Papa woke to discover a black paper bag beneath his pillow, filled with dust and dirt and chips of bone, a hex intended to cause him harm, placed there by someone in the household who wanted to see him ill.

Papa interrogated all about the contents and the access to his room at night, and suspicion rose highest against Evangeline, though she denied any such doing and seemed wounded by the suggestion of it. Papa was not at all worried about the powers or spells emanating from such a cursed placement—he believes in nothing of the Voudou. He was more angered that those he has entrusted can no longer be thought of in that manner, his private room invaded and abused, everything now causing his suspicion and questions. Of course it has created a chill in his relations with Evangeline. Everyone in the city knows of her practices of the Voudou, kept hidden and underground from Papa's sight but well regarded by her société. Papa has kept the household as strictly Catholic as Grandpapa Christian had, every slave baptized and given Christian names since their acquisition. He distrusts the hoodoo and mam'bo just as Grandpapa did. Christian, a boyhood refugee from Hayti's slave wars, raised Papa full of skepticism and disregard for any religion except the pure one of Jesus and the Holy Saints. Myself, I am loathe to disparage any religion, new or ancient, if it be that sort of thing that offers comfort to those who seek it. We are now a part of a country where tolerance must be inclusive of all things strange and uncertain, and I find it peculiar that men of intelligence and understanding lose all rationality when confronted with a bag of powder and harsh smells. Where is their faith in God? In the justice and compassion of mankind?

Perhaps our family history deepens Papa's cruel treatment of Aaron. Aaron, himself, has not kept secret his belief in the faith of his ancestors. Evangeline has often bragged of Aaron's joyous spirit at the gatherings in Congo Square, the tams tams and chantings causing a magic transformation to her son, his dancing a whirl of dark limbs and white teeth, and she must have whispered such things at night to Papa. I, too, have witnessed Aaron's change at such gatherings, but such bliss is not a stranger

to me; I see it often when we are in each other's embrace and I
have felt, as well, its restorative powers, as powerful as any kind
of religion mankind can create for itself. Papa's mistreatment
of Aaron has become so well known in the district that this
morning the front stoop of the store was dusted with brown
chalk crosses. Throughout the day more trinkets and small bags
were discovered meanly placed about the store for him to find.
I know that these spells are meant to aide in Aaron's health and
acceptance as much as to cause Papa's fear, but each subsequent
gris-gris only harms Angelle more than anyone. She has much
more future to be lost than any of us.

Evangeline has made her hopes deeply known to Papa. Last
evening she again spoke to Papa about Aaron, begging him to
let her son have time to heal and find his strength and remain
in the household, pleading that he had no desire to rebel but
only wished to belong to the family. Papa treated her harshly,
banishing her from his bedroom over disputing his reasoning,
but this morning he called her into his office and presented
her with an ultimatum when another bag of powder had been
discovered beneath his bed. Papa told her that Aaron would be
spared, kept in the family, but in doing so, both of her children
would be raised and treated as slaves. Aaron could remain but
at the cost of Angelle's Freedom.

Evangeline held her tongue, cried instead of protesting, the
ruin of Angelle a shock to her. Both of her children now to live
as slaves? How could Papa act in this manner to her? And to
them? I only found this out when I came upon her crying in the
kitchen and made her confess this new turn of shame upon our
family's once good name.

Angelle, of course, did not understand this decision when
it was accepted and laid out before her. She, herself, fell into a
malady of wailing against her mother's breast. This treatment by
Papa has caused everyone considerable distress; such practices

as this are condemned in this city—a free offspring of slaves becoming a slave again. No such thing has happened in our family before.

So it is no surprise that Evangeline's countenance has changed, her stare at father harsh and unforgiving and silent, reticently silent, as a slave's must be in matters of opinion to their Master. Into this void all things ominous have risen to the surface, offerings and trinkets and gris-gris forever being discovered about the place. After dark the household undergoes a radical conversion as the candles are lit and shadows draw across the rooms and apprehension rises to the surface. Outside in the courtyard, Grady and Manny whisper even in my presence, and I am worried that the whole place might be set afire if not by them, then by others.

Today I beseeched Papa to change his decisions, if just for the sake of restoring balance to the household and settling the rumblings which seem to grow louder by the minute. His reasoning is unyielding; in fact, if troubles persist like this, he told me, then Aaron will be sold nonetheless and Angelle not far behind him. What was here will be restored, he said, by the decisions of the Master of the house, not by the slaves, the ungrateful replaced by those who need Work, not Freedom.

This turn of news took Evangeline to bed. She fell into a fever this evening, attended by a mam'bo who stole her way quietly through our courtyard. From the terrace of my room I could see the candles burning in the lower windows of the slave's quarters and now there is fear for her health, as well. Papa will surely punish her if she falters with her chores tomorrow and Angelle is not strong or old enough to replace her where she is most needed, particularly in the kitchen. Tonight the household will surely not sleep, the days ahead full of more trouble.

I stopped again when Hank was wheeled down the hallway and I followed two nurses into the room where he had been placed. Hank was still unconscious and I asked one of the nurses what tests had been performed and what results, if any, were now known, but she deflected my concern by saying that the doctor would be down shortly to talk with me. When she left the room, I finished the pint of whiskey and waited for a buzz to reach my brain, thinking now of this strange sequence of events I had been part of—sighting the ghosts, finding the knife, reading the journal, praying to God for a miracle to keep Hank alive and well. So Parker's made-up stories handed down from Mack had been true, in a fashion. Angelle and Aaron and Pierre had all lived in the house during a time of great stress for each of them. The knife I had discovered beneath the floorboards of the pantry could have been the same one given to Aaron, the one that had caused Aaron's brutal beating, but why had it been buried blade first in the ground? And why had a vision of God—or a messenger of God—or my crazy, mixed-up Inner Demon summoned me to find it? For a moment, I wondered if the diary had been hidden somewhere in the house as the knife had been, if Mack or maybe Toby before him had uncovered it from a loosened brick or behind a wall, then wondered what could have caused Hank to reach for the journal out of all the books Mack kept in his place. What did this mean or did it mean nothing at all, merely the intersection of a sequence of random circumstances? Was this an accidental discovery or part of a larger plan? I sat in the chair beside Hank's bed, shifting my eyes every few moments to gage his sleeping and the activity in the nearby hall. Soon, I had found my place again in the journal and was reading without interruption, conscious, however, of Hank's breathing beside me.

June 22, 1822

It is a hateful time now in the household, what with the tragic events of this week. Aaron's health grew stronger, but so did his anger and resolve to be free. On Tuesday he worked a few hours in the storeroom and this seemed to please everyone— Papa, Evangeline, myself. Manny and Grady's tempers were lessened and Angelle's wailing was subdued as she was put to work doing chores in the kitchen. That evening I went to the courtyard, wanting to tell Aaron to slip away later to my room, but he was asleep and Evangeline pressed me not to rouse him. She whispered to me that her prayers had worked, that the gods were busy restoring what had been disturbed and she asked me if I thought that Papa would change his mind about things, if Aaron would be allowed to stay and if Angelle's future would not be condemned to the same fate as her older brother. I told her if things stayed calm, if our tension fell below the detectable surface of our lives, then Papa would surely soften and change his mind—hadn't we seen that behavior before from him? I wanted to tell her that with time all would be as she wanted—that when Papa retired the household would be set free, but I could not make such a promise to her without fear that she would repeat it to mon Père and he would set events into motion to prevent the whole thing from occurring.

The following day Aaron worked as usual in the storeroom, and things did seem to be restored to better times. At dinner, I even heard laughter rising again from the back rooms. I was able to speak privately to Aaron for only a few minutes that day—Papa was active throughout the house and the store, not lingering in his usual way over the journals in his office—but I made it known that Aaron would be welcome in my quarters again at night, if he could find his way there without any problems, and indeed that evening he climbed the columns and lifted himself over my balcony as he had done for many nights in our young lives. I felt such joy again myself to have him in my arms and I kissed and blessed his new scars lightly with my lips. We were intimate and I was gentle with him, not wanting to open any of his wounds, though he wrestled me to the mattress and pinned me with his arms and taunted me with withholding his affection, which he powerfully delivered when I begged him to bestow it. Before I fell asleep he asked me about his Freedom. I confided my plans to him as I always had, explaining that I had not and would not change my mind in this regard, certain that our confidences with each other would remain private. He stayed with me till it was almost dawn, leaving my bed just as the dark sky of the window began to lighten into tones of royal blue.

But the day would not turn out to be of good or promising character. No, it was a hateful day, spiteful and agonizing and unforgettable, and it is why I write now, here, on this page, so that I will never forgive what slavery has brought to these lands and my home and our minds. In the morning when I awoke I noticed that the knife was missing from the top drawer of my bureau where I had kept it hidden from Papa's sight when he had returned it to me. I was certain that Aaron had taken it in the morning hours when he had left my room, but with the hope that he was only reclaiming it as the gift I had presented to him. I didn't confront him on this when I opened the store—he was busy in the back room and there was a rush of early and impatient customers wanting to fill their purchases quickly. Right away, I noticed when the two heavy men entered the store and approached the doorway to Papa's office. I knew at once that they were here to take Aaron away to be sold and I could not believe that Papa had not informed me of this fact. I went to the storeroom to warn Aaron, to tell him if he wanted to flee I would try to detain the men in the store for as long as I could. But before we had finished talking, before the seriousness of moment had a chance to register with Aaron, the two men were at the door of the storeroom. Aaron fled through the back door to the courtyard and rushed up the stairs to the top floor of the slave quarters. He was climbing his way to the roof and certain Freedom when he lost his balance and slipped to the balcony below. I thought the fall would have only just stunned him, and I watched as his determination lifted him up to continue and try again. As he stood I could tell he was disoriented and that the two men were too close for him to safely escape. They were within reach of him when Aaron's posture shifted and he tumbled against the railing. The weight of his body broke the wood banisters free and he fell into the courtyard below. I stood there and watched my own heart burst with pain, confused as to whether it was accidental or planned. He was dead before he could draw another breath, his head twisted unnaturally in the fall.

But oh, if that were only the worst of the day. The store was closed, the haughty Creole customers pushed out into the streets, and the doors locked up. All of the slaves were shackled and restrained until Aaron's body had been carted away. Where his body fell I found the knife, picked it up and kept it in my pocket, rubbing the handle minute after minute, praying through some kind of mad black haze that this could bring him back to life.

Throughout the day there were sobs and moans from the back of the house, many of which pierced me in ways that caused me more distress than recounting the tragic fall I had witnessed earlier. Papa forbid the slaves any further news of Aaron, though I had heard he was carted and buried in a ditch not far out of town without even a marker for a proper Christian. I could not relay this sad news to Evangeline and that evening I stood on the balcony of my room and watched the fires burning through the windows of the slave quarters below me, certain that more trouble was forthcoming. And it was.

The journal ended there: beyond the last line were about twenty blank pages. I was shaken by the thought that Hank's fall might be connected to Aaron's death—that the figure I had hallucinated lying on the bricks of the courtyard might have been the ghost of a slave—and that Hank might still be in danger because he had survived. As I was thumbing through the back pages, looking for any remaining writing or markings or clues to the fate of Pierre and Angelle, a middle-aged doctor entered the room and I put the book aside. He was tall and thin, gray hair combed back from his face but wiry and oily and thick about his neck. He seemed not at all concerned about Hank's results from the various tests, saying his vital signs were stable—blood pressure, hearing, cholesterol were all in acceptable ranges. It seemed maddening to me that they would test his cholesterol, of all things, or his body fat ratio, when what he needed was X rays and CAT scans and MRIs and I know I confronted the doctor too angrily on this. I was only reacting in my old, trained-to-cripple-the-establishment activist ways, a product of years and years of dealing with Mack's ineffectual doctors and my worry that the truth of what was happening would never surface. I hated this doctor, in fact, because he *was* a doctor, full of a knowledge I did not own and could not tap into, a wisdom that he could use to purposely exclude me from knowing the real facts of what was happening to Hank—or could still happen to him. As I continued to question the doctor he drew his head back into the collar of his jacket, like a turtle, and kept his eyes pinned to the chart he carried, clearly uneasy, wanting to flee the raging Medea I had become, as quickly as professionally acceptable.

"How much longer will he sleep?" I asked.

"A while," the doctor said, not wanting to commit to anything definite.

"And the drip?" I asked him with superhuman eyes, hoping to see through his frivolous mask. Hank had been hooked up to an IV when he had been returned to the room.

"Just fluids," the doctor answered.

"Nothing else?"

He didn't answer me and placed the chart on the holder of the door and I followed him out into the hall; he clearly no longer wanted to deal with me, and just as I asked him for a list of what medications Hank had already been given while at the hospital I noticed someone passing by me and behind the doctor. It was a dark-haired young black man—in T-shirt and jeans and wearing a puka shell necklace—and I knew right away that I needed to leave the doctor and follow him. It was the ghost of Toby again, ready to lead me to another place—I was certain of it. I ran down the hall to catch up with him. He passed through the door that led to the stairwell, moving right through it. *Yes, okay,* I thought, catching my breath, *he is a ghost—he just proved that to me.* I was now casting my faith and fate to metaphysics and medicine. I opened the door with a brisk twist of the knob, noisily followed him down two flights of stairs and into another hallway of the hospital, into a patient room where he moved towards the window and disappeared into the daylight.

"What?" I asked out loud to no one. The room was empty. Nothing but two vacant hospital beds, the sheets firm and unruffled, tucked tightly beneath the mattress. "What do you want me to know? Why are you doing this?"

For a moment I lost belief in myself—I was drunk, tired, beaten down into a throbbing pulp of pain—how could the same ghost appear in two different places—how could Toby haunt both the guesthouse and

a corridor of a hospital? Everything seemed highly illogical, even my
new-found though still skeptical acceptance of a possible spirit world, and
I felt a depression overwhelming me—a belief that I was now a seriously ill
schizophrenic-psychotic and that my future path was destined for hospital
wards and medication and abandonment and poverty and a closet full
of bleached white straitjackets. A wail moved through my body, like the
shriek the shriveled Bette Davis gives to the hoary Joan Crawford in the
climax of their best scenes together, and I stood at the doorway ready to go
postal or at least consider Hari-Kari.

Outside the room, nurses and interns and orderlies passed by the
doorway without any recognition of me and I concentrated on calming my
breathing, feeling the air pass in and out of my lungs, into my bloodstream,
into my legs and thighs and stomach and chest, up to my shoulders and
my arms and my neck and eyes. In the daylight of the room I waited for the
image of Toby to reappear, for the dust motes to swirl and twirl around in
the air and bring me some sort of sign or moment of recognition. I stood
deepening my breathing, clearing my mind as if I were in a yoga class and
ready to meditate and contort my body into unnatural positions. I did
this for a few seconds—a few seconds that felt like hours because I was
so impatient. "Energy is only taking the form that you allow it to take,"
Griffin had told me—or my internal manifestation of Griffin had told me.
"You are shaping it. It's not shaping itself. You'll understand this when the
time comes to know it."

Slowly the haze of a memory returned to me, the rays of lights and
patches of shadows shifted and flickered to form recognizable bodies and
figures. And then I sensed what it was that I felt I must know—or remember.
What Toby was trying to show me. Toby had died at this hospital. That was
why I could see him both here and at the house. That made sense. It was
logical. And this could be the room where I had first met Parker all those

years ago—this was where Mack had been brought when he was struggling to survive pneumonia. The room ticked and buzzed with the rising energy of amanuensis and the walls faded away, revealing bundles of wires strung inside, cables and pipes and wooden beams held together by the dusty, dirty joints of metal and nails and I felt such an energy around me that I imagined that I could pass through the walls myself if I gave it a try. But this force was not enlightenment or joy. Instead, I felt a new outbreak of sweat dampen my armpits and drip along the sides of my ears and a flash of fear caught me like a tidal wave. Now I felt that Parker was somehow in trouble too, not just Hank. This was a sign. Nothing was an accident. Something else was going to go wrong and it was going to happen to Parker next. Toby was trying to warn me that Parker was in trouble. That was it. Hank was safe. He had *survived* an accident. Parker was in trouble. Something was going to happen to Parker.

I tried to calm myself, tried to bring a rational thought into all this paranormal disbelief. Was I going crazy? Was I oversaddled and megadepressed and ultra-addicted and having a nervous breakdown? Was I upset about Mack? About Hank's accident? Was I trying to read too much into things going wrong? I was letting a hallucination warn me that my world was falling apart, when every day I confronted one big mess after another. What kind of drama queen had I become? Where was God *now?* Where was logic? And order? And reason? And why did the next drink seem so far away?

Again, I went to the pay phone in the hallway and dialed the guesthouse, trying to pretend that I was merely a stout, breathless man making a phone call and not a lunatic looking for confirmation that the sky was falling down on top of him and his dead body would be discovered with dirty underwear. No one picked up in the office and when there was no answer in the café, I called the operator and asked to be connected with the funeral home where Mack's body had been taken. The receptionist informed me that the hearse had left for the cemetery about ten minutes prior to my call. I tried to ask the receptionist about Parker, describing him as politely and complimentarily as I could and asking if a portly, wheezing gentleman had been noticed in the group present at the service, but she said she had not been able to meet anyone in the room, and that she was, in fact, located in an office downstairs and not near the reception areas at all. *Shit,* I mumbled to myself. *God was not going to help me out at all today.*

I left the hospital as quickly as I could, running through the streets till I reached the streetcar stop. Riding towards the cemetery I caught sight of my reflection in the windows and made a futile attempt to pat a cowlick down at the back of my scalp, more concerned, however, at the haggard look the three-day gray beard had given my face because I now appeared to be a mental patient on the lam after escaping his maximum security cell. I wanted another drink badly. Anything—uniced, lukewarm, stinking, with or without soda—and I even prayed to God that he would send me a bottle to ease my fears or at least one minute sip of a golden syrup to help me make it through this ride. Of course, that went unanswered, and I felt my anxiety welling up in my chest and about to burst into another scream, but I practiced breathing, thinking of things I could say to friends at the graveside when I reached the service, till the streetcar stopped and I began running towards the entrance of the cemetery.

I'd always imagined that my constant and unending work at the guesthouse kept me in good physical condition, but I was out of breath after the first block and had to stop and slow my pace, my heart pounding at my ribs as my hands swished at my side like those of a prissy character actor. Above me the clouds were darkening and gathering and there was certain to be another heavy summer rainstorm soon, but the heat was unbearable and I was drenched with sweat, rivering to my love handles, puddling at the backs of my knees, clustering in the well of my collarbone. I fell into a sort of chanting prayer as I ran and walked and ran and walked, *Please God, if you can hear me, let there be no more trouble. Keep him safe. Keep him safe. Keep all of them safe and out of trouble.*

At the cemetery gates I could see the hearse parked at the curb and I tried to remember the way to the crypt where Mack was to be buried, but I had to adjust my pace because of the way my shoes shifted uneasily against the bleached white shell-and-pebble pathway and I lost my senses of balance and direction in a matter of seconds. Mack had invested in a wall crypt when Toby had died, the plaque had carried his name for years alongside the dates of Toby's birth and death, only waiting for the date of Mack's death to be added. I had given the funeral director all of this information only a day before, had even explained to him where in the cemetery the crypt was located—for years, Mack had left flowers and tokens and notes to Toby, some of them as odd and twisted as Buddy's Voodoo art installations.

I entered an aisle of pediments and statues and tombstones and crypts that quickly became a maze; I was so airless and weak-kneed that I could barely see a few inches in front of my feet. I stumbled through a tour group and a guide remarking over the triple Xs someone had written in chalk on the stucco siding of a tomb—this cemetery had been open for hundreds of years and clandestine Voodoo ceremonies were planned to intrigue and lure visitors, shrines created daily to honor former Voodoo houn'gans and mam'bos and invoke their powers. I ran around another group where the guide was describing a "duel defending the honor of his brother-in-law," only to find myself on a route through a labyrinth of high stone walls and completely disoriented. I retraced my steps, the guides and the groups now suspiciously gone, and I started in another direction along a row of two-level wall crypts. That was when I saw the wolf-like dog, clear as day, running in front of me on the shell path. *My God,* I thought, *this is no accident. There must be a reason for this.* I was certain it was the same one I had seen in the pantry—white fur, long thin snout. It stopped and turned its head towards me and I caught sight of its ice blue eyes. Yes. It was the same one. I could read that in its eyes. And it wanted me to follow it. But what was it doing here? A wolf in a cemetery? It cantered a few steps, turned to make sure I was following, and when it was certain I was, continued to run ahead of me.

Now, instead of trying to find my way to Mack's crypt, I followed the wolf, hopeful it was leading me in the direction I needed to go, recognizing that I had to relinquish control of my own direction and follow the path of God or gods or whatever Higher Psycho was now taking control of me. Ahead on the path, the wolf stopped in front of the ruins of a tomb, climbed up on the crumbling pile of bricks, and disappeared as a patch of strong sunlight moved over the area.

I stopped beside the old tomb, my chest heaving up and down as I tried to catch my breath, my throat dry and clamping tight, my tongue the size of a football and just as unwieldy. On the shell pathway in front of me was a string of dark liquid, black and oil-like, oozing from the stone wall and puddling into reddish tinted pools between the bright white shells. *Blood? Was the tombstone dripping blood? What sort of gothic nightmare had my life become?* Where was Steven Spielberg when he was needed to inspire a better plot? As my eyes followed the dark liquid from the ground to its source on the wall, the names floated into view: *Pierre Dubuisson,* his loving wife *Sarah Wheaton Dubuisson,* and their *Unnamed Child* (all dying in 1836). Above them *Antoine Dubuisson* and the names of his two wives: *Melissa Lefeuvre Dubuisson 1780-1811* and *Elizabeth Sutton Dubuisson 1784-1813,* and above them the three wives of Christian Dubuisson: *Deborah Granville Dubuisson 1773-1813, Cynthia Baptiste Dubuisson 1760-1794,* and *Annette*

Baptiste Dubuisson 1756-1779. The top name on the tomb was *Christian Dubuisson. Born: September 4, 1754. Died: July 19, 1818.*

The wolf had led me to the Dubuisson family crypt. I ran my hand along the names, feeling the letters chiseled into the bricks. What was *this* all about? What was I supposed to find *now?* The oily, bloodlike substance seemed to be seeping through the dates below *Antoine Dubuisson* and as I leaned into read them they seemed to brighten as if ignited into flames:

Born: April 7, 1780 — Died: June 23, 1822.

The last entry in Pierre Dubuisson's journal had been June 22, 1822. If this was what I was supposed to discover, then I had just learned that Antoine Dubuisson had died the day following his slave Aaron's death.

What was I supposed to do with this information? I had no idea what it meant, other than I was tired and hallucinating and crazy because I was now parched and sober and seeing things and believing in some kind of internal hoodoo of my own. *Lord, I could really use a drink right now. Send me a sign that the next drink is not that far away. Anything. Just a little hint or clue.*

I left the spot as quickly as I could, trying to find my way back to the main gates of the cemetery because the sky had grown as black as night. Before I reached the gates, however, I spotted the gathering beside Mack's crypt along the pathway. Stuart, Celia, their two boys, an activist Mack had known for years, and maybe six other friends were standing and listening to the priest, including Lynette and her girlfriend Talla. As I stumbled towards the group I realized that Parker was not among them and concern rose into a burning sensation at the back of my throat. *Parker was missing. Where was Parker?* I was just about to turn away when a cloud of tiny lights rose up from the ground like a startled swarm of fireflies. The fireballs swirled around me as if I were the eye of a hurricane, rising and circling my legs and hips and stomach and chest. For a second I wondered if I were to die, if the lights of souls had come to take me elsewhere, if *I* was to be the next accident, not Parker. My body began to tremble and I heard, or thought I heard, anguished screams, like those of prisoners being tortured. I tried to keep my vision focused, to look through the lights, but the fireballs had become a bright wall preventing me from going any further. I tried to yell at the group ahead of me for help, but I was suddenly as bright and as transparent as a ghost. Just as they were growing brighter, fifolet circling my shoulders and rising up towards my neck, I took a step back and broke through their path.

As I ran away, out of the cemetery, I fell again into another prayer as my feet hit the sidewalk outside the cemetery. *Let him be safe. Let him be okay. Let him be cooking. Please God, let things be back to normal. Let me find Parker in the kitchen where he belongs.*

Four

It's a well-regarded fact that everyone in the Big Easy has a touch of madness about him, tourist, native, and the dearly departed alike. The City That Care Forgot, after all, has a love affair with death, a whiff of the grave hangs about the whole town—sooty cemeteries with their elaborate tombstones, decaying houses that look like crypts, impromptu jazz funerals championing skulls and bones. Necrology has become part of the charm of the town, a lure and an industry as important as the cash-boom days surrounding Mardi Gras. There are Voodoo Gift Shops and Vampire Walking Tours and local goths who whiten their skin and blacken their eyes and lips and lurk in front of neon-lit store windows in hoods and robes, hoping to agitate a few tourists along their paths, many of whom are already stoned or drunk before they reach Bourbon Street. The City of Sin is also a city of few constraints; many visitors have decided the best way to display their newfound lack of inhibitions is to disrobe to as little clothing as is legally possible, which usually translates into a plastic beverage cup never quite placed at the right angle against their publicly-exposed bare body. I've always felt that I was able to maintain a little pocket of cynical sanity among all this foolishness, but now that seemed not to be the case anymore. Here I was myself witnessing ghosts, shape-shifting animals, messengers from my subconscious, and the inexplicable phenomenon of the fluttering lights before my eyes—everything that seemed one day precariously but nonetheless balanced to me was now topsy-turvy. At any moment I expected Parker to awaken from his perpetual slumber and announce that he was now living an undead life as a vampire.

"I'm going crazy," I said to Dwayne. "You have to take this seriously. This is too real to me." We were inside Mack's apartment, searching through a dizzying pile of books and papers and knickknacks he had collected over the years. I had laid out both my dilemma and frustration to Dwayne when I returned to the guesthouse and found things not quite as horrific as I had imagined, though unattended to and therefore somewhat annoying. Everyone grieves differently, I know, and while my reaction to Mack's death was clearly a mental and spiritual crisis, Parker's response was to not work at all and stay in bed. Parker was still asleep in the back room of the downstairs office, though I had been told he had opened his eyelids long enough to permit José to unlock the café's doors so he could manage it for the night. José had recruited his boyfriend Kaku to aide him in the kitchen and Buddy had prepped the tables as usual. Dwayne was on hand because he had heard of Hank's fall—the gay phone tree continuing to do its usual work of sending out a regular flow of gossip to anyone who wanted to know it. And as for the state of the guesthouse and the few paying customers still around—well, luckily the blithely oblivious to the rest of the world honeymoon couple was still behind a Do Not Disturb sign, the crotchety old gentlemen in the Royal Suite had mellowed and left me a nice note saying that they had to catch a flight and would settle their bill by phone, and Stuart, Celia, and the boys had decided to go sightseeing on a riverboat cruise after the funeral instead of packing up all the things in Mack's apartment that Celia had tagged with tiny red circular stickers to indicate what she wanted—but the courtyard had not been swept, the stairwell was full of rancid-smelling trash from last night's food, and everywhere the linen and towels remained unchanged and propagating at a rate unhealthy even by natural standards. (Ah, dear me, if only I had been able to hallucinate *elves* to help me out!)

"You seem a bit high strung to me, but I would think that's the liquor's doing," Dwayne said with a cautious deflection of his eyes.

I had at least taken another slug of high-end whiskey when I had tried to rouse Parker on my own and had received only his grumbled request to leave him be. Now, I was upstairs in Mack's apartment and removing Celia's red stickers from as many things as I could find. She, too, had left behind a note for me to read, though it hadn't been quite as nice as that of the paying guests. "Avery, I've tagged everything we want in Mack's place with little red stickers. When do you think you can have them packed and sent to us?"

But my biggest leap of faith of the day had been my confession to Dwayne about the ghosts I was seeing. He'd already heard secondhand gossip from José and Buddy, but now, in a bit too animated way, I had described seeing Toby, Angelle, Aaron, Pierre, a hungry-looking white wolf, and about a thousand flying souls of light. I'd even confessed to the blood-dripping tombstone and my narrow escape from the cemetery.

"If I'm having a breakdown, I want to be committed to a nicely decorated padded room," I said to Dwayne. "Something with French Provincial furnishings and Laura Ashley linens. But if someone's haunting me, I'd at least like to know what they want from me. Is that too much to ask of a ghost?"

"Well, it's not as easy as all that," Dwayne said, his eyes curiously darting around the room, hoping to see anything paranormal or supernaturally-related. "They just don't blurt it out."

"Scrooge didn't have any problems," I answered. "He knew exactly what he was supposed to do."

"That's fiction," Dwayne said with a timid laugh. "This is real."

"A *real* ghost?" I said. "Don't you find that sort of an absurd comment? Isn't that, what—an *oxymoron*?"

He laughed again and pushed a stray dreadlock over his shoulder with a twist of his neck. "Not really," he said. "More a fascinating insight, I think."

"Have you ever seen a *real* ghost?"

I noticed a shift of pain, or embarrassment, move across his face at my question. "Not yet," he answered. "But I'm still looking."

"But you believe in them?"

"Of course," he answered. "Why shouldn't I? If people can believe that a virgin can give birth without having sex and an old man can part the Red Sea by pounding a cane into the ground, why can't I believe in ghosts?"

"That sort of response would have gotten you burned at the stake in other times and kicked out of a lot of churches around here."

"I'm not sure that everyone can see the same ghost, however," he said. "I certainly couldn't see your ghosts the same way you see them. I think we all have different levels of psychic tuning. You may be more in tune to one particular phenomenon than say Parker or Buddy or myself are in tune with it. Or you may be in tune with one particular ghost over another one. Someone else, even with a heightened sense of ghosts, may see nothing at all. Ghosts are as complex as, well, the *living* are."

"You seem to have a lot of theories for never having seen a ghost," I said, now a bit uncertain that Dwayne could help me banish my specters, let alone witness them along with me.

"Seen one, no, but felt one—no, *many,* actually...*yes,*" he said. "Even though I can't see them, I know they are there. I can sense them. In the air."

"Like an allergy attack, I presume?"

"Yes, well, sort of."

Of course I hadn't confessed *everything* to Dwayne. The hallucinations of the Higher-Power-Inside-Myself-Masquerading-In-The-Physical-Form-of-Griffin and my time-stopped conversation with this Internal Being I had kept, well, private, so as not to convince him that I was a totally overboard lunatic. But I had shared with Dwayne the details of Pierre's diary, and of his affair with Aaron and the death of both Aaron and Antoine. He had found the history credible, but no logic behind the sudden ghostly appearance of both Aaron and Pierre and the other phenomenon. I felt certain that there had to be more clues to all this amongst Mack's belongings. If Toby had uncovered the history of the property, Mack would certainly have kept his papers. Mack never threw anything away. For a practical and uncomplicated man, he had been very sentimental.

"This looks promising," Dwayne said, his fingers slipping between a stack of pages to read the text. He handed me a folder containing papers of various owners of our property, from a photocopy of a lease when it was run as a boarding house in the 1920s to a faded blueprint of the floor plan of the renovations.

"This is too recent," I said, after I had flipped through it quickly. At best, I had hoped that Mack might have included a copy of the transfer of the property to myself and Parker to stifle the threat of eviction by Celia and Stuart, but that was missing, and at the very least, I had hoped I might have uncovered a report of a ghost sighting by a previous resident. But there was nothing. Nothing that might have clued me in to why Antoine died. Or what happened to Pierre. And what became of Angelle. So I went back to removing the red stickers from Mack's belongings to ease my frustration, planning, in my mind, my eventual confrontation with Celia over the fact that if she wanted something of Mack's, she would have to pack it up and ship it out herself. I was not her maid or servant or even her *legal relative* and didn't deserve to be treated as such. Somewhere in this mess of an apartment, Mack had left a written will with instructions that all of his possessions were to be dispersed according to my and Parker's discretion, though I hadn't wanted to resort to that tactic yet, either, preferring, instead, that Celia sentimentally decide on what she wanted to keep herself.

I had made my way to Mack's bookcase, only glancing through his titles—mostly science fiction and fantasy—an extensive collection of Ray Bradbury and Isaac Asimov and the usual boyhood fascination of *Robinson Crusoe, Tom Swift,* and *Lord of the Rings*—all of which Celia had ignored tagging, even as something for her own boys. At the end of the shelf was a tall bright blue book, the gold-print title on the spine unreadable with age, and I pulled it down to get a better look at it, at the same time realizing that I might not be doing so accidentally. The pages of the book were old and yellowing, a few of the corners split off and falling to the floor like dandruff. I opened the book to the title page and read:

OUT OF THE DARKNESS COMETH THE BRIGHTEST LIGHT
The Narrative of the Life
of
Evangeline Dubuisson: A Slave Woman Now Free
With Introduction by Reverend Bishop Claiborne,
and
Commendatory Notices from Reverend Gordon Spaulding,
Superintendent of The Home for Little
Wanderers, Providence, R.I.,
and
Reverend Jules Wainwright, Sudbury, Mass.

BOSTON:
JAMES ARLINGTON, PUBLISHER,
229 SUMMER STREET

1878

I flipped the page to the table of contents and scanned the chapter listings and subheadings: **Early Life in Hayti, Home in New Orleans, A Family Changes, The Move North, The Underground Railroad, The War Years,** and the last chapter, **Liberty Gained.**

On the following page was a tintype of an elderly black woman in a high-collared dress with a cameo brooch at her neck, her wiry black-and gray hair pinned behind the back of her head; in her lap was a thick, worn edition of the Bible with a satin ribbon page marker. She looked weathered and wrinkled, the folds in her dress complementing the creases from her smile, an intelligence of survival behind her unfocused eyes. The caption beneath the photograph read: **Evangeline Dubuisson at age Ninety-Three.** The following page held the introductory letter from Bishop Claiborne:

None but those who resided in the South during the time of slavery can realize the terrible punishments that were visited upon the slaves. Virtue and self-respect were denied them. There have been many histories written, but they do not tell a thousandth part of what has been done in the ages past. Consider that here in this Bible land, where we have the light, where the Gospel was preached Sunday after Sunday in all portions of the South, and where ministers read from the pulpit that God has made of one blood all nations of men, that nevertheless, with the knowledge and teachers of the word of God, the slaves were reduced to a level with the brute. The half was never told concerning this race that was in bondage nearly two hundred and fifty years.

It was in the fall of 1875 that I met Evangeline Dubuisson in her 93rd year, taking the surname of her first master, a prominent merchant of Hayti and New Orleans, La. She was sold in the State of Louisiana many years before the war, and lived in the State of Virginia until her Liberation brought her to Providence, R.I. I have spent hours with her listening to her telling of her mother's capture in Africa and her own birthing in Hayti and years of bondage in New Orleans and the death of her children from the hands of Fate. If we could only know the conflicts, the defeats, the victories of the soul—we should see that the humblest and most uneventful life is more thrillingly wonderful than any romance that was ever written. All this is emphatically true of thousands upon thousands born and reared in slavery.

It was the lot of the subject of this brief biography to have been born in Hayti and to have fled the colony during a time of great unrest. Yet Evangeline Dubuisson has not been entirely so lucky in all her long life. She was born a slave, born in an island that was nominally Christian, and yet she was born a slave. She was born in a land of Bibles and sanctuaries and Sabbaths, and yet she was born a slave. Let all the people everywhere in all our borders thank God that the shame and sin and curse of slavery has been done away with. Evangeline Dubuisson may have been born a slave, but the pure soul that looked out of her flashing eyes was never in bondage to any miserable being calling himself her master. Redeemed from the galling yoke her body was compelled for years to wear, she has lived a pure and spotless life. Though poor and unknown among men, the angels of God have camped around her for, lo!, these many years; and she has been able, by the abounding grace of God, to walk the rough and dusty paths of a toilsome life with garments spotless and whole. The biographies of saintly, enduring spirits like that of Evangeline Dubuisson will be read, and will serve to inspire the discouraged and down-trodden to put their trust in the almighty arm of Jehovah, who alone works deliverance and salvation to all those who put that trust in him.

E. H. CLAIBORNE

There followed similar introductory notes by two other ministers, revealing the information that Evangeline was freed in Virginia, and detailing her "salvation" in 1838 by renouncing her Catholic and "Voudou" pasts and becoming a Baptist in Providence, and then a publisher's introductory letter, begging the reader's pardon for the book's defects in style and composition, "inasmuch it is written by an operative tradesman." I scanned the first chapter, which detailed Evangeline's mother's capture in Western Africa and her arrival in "Hayti" to work on the Dubuisson plantation, Evangeline's father's short life and death as a slave on another plantation of the colony, Evie's birth on July 4, 1792 in Haiti, Christian Dubuisson's bedding of his slave Jeanine (Evangeline's aunt) after the passing of his first wife, the birth of Christian's son Antoine and Christian's vow to raise his first son as a free man, and the Dubuisson family's escape with their slaves from Haiti in 1791 to avoid the slave riots. The Dubuissons first settled in a house on Rampart Street, near the waterfront, and Christian's second wife, Cynthia, died at age thirty-four during a miscarriage. Evie's mother, the family slave, Marietta, was also not fortunate in America, dying in 1796 at the age of thirty-eight when Evie was fourteen, and I pictured a young slave girl suddenly in tears, distraught and feeling abandoned and forced into a new role in the household.

Evie's first sexual encounter was at age seventeen, when her Master, Christian Dubuisson, raped her in his office. ("I had come in to the room to deliver a parcel when he complimented me on my disposition—I had been humming a tune Mama had taught me. He inquired about my health and asked that he might inspect my well-being. There were questions about relations with other men, particularly other slaves, and my 'no sirs,' were followed by his fondling of me.")

In 1800, Antoine married Melissa Lefeuvre, the same year Evie gave birth to her first child, a son, Aaron, fathered by Christian but raised in the household as a slave. Evangeline (or the book's author) went to great length to disparage the different treatments of the two half-brothers Aaron and Antoine, both born of slaves but with one being raised as a free man and the other "reduced to the toil of a beast of burden," and an image of Aaron I had retained from Pierre's diary, of a man strong and hardened and scarred, swept across my mind; I could picture his dark muscular arms pulling with all his strength against chains and iron shackles, the raw, shoeless feet running through the muddy streets of the Quarter. What an unfortunate scenario, I thought, pinned down by society and your family.

"You can never understand the slave mother's emotions as she clasps her new-born child," Evangeline wrote, "and knows that a Master's word can at any moment take it from her embrace."

Little attention was paid to the birth of Pierre the following year, but with my imagination I saw the two young boys, Aaron and Pierre, growing up together, finding time to play in the courtyard, one better dressed than the other, one growing stronger and angrier, but both passing along the gossip of the household through whispers and nods and suspicious glances, an intimate bond between them no one else detected—Pierre, compassionate and curious, Aaron, determined and aroused. The impending tragedy of their story made me sigh and look away, remembering all my undone tasks of the day, then I returned my attention to the book, flipping eagerly through the pages in search of photographs or drawings or something to help deflect my emotional involvement in the story. I was as sentimental and romantic as Mack had been, or at least I was until the nonstop no-break life of this place had reared up its foul head and swallowed me whole.

A few pages later I read that four years after Pierre's birth Christian had married his third wife, Deborah Granville, a second cousin of his first wife, but continued to sleep with both Evie and her aunt Jeanine, after Deborah's miscarriage and her subsequent inability to have any children.

Evie also wrote strongly of her confrontations with her mistress Deborah. ("Mistress had no more feeling for me than that she had for a cat. She used to beat me and pull my ears till they were sore. She would crack me on the head with a key or any thing she could get her hands on till blood would ooze out of my poor head. I could do nothing to please Mistress. Sometimes she tied me up by my thumbs. One time I completely blacked out and was punished further with a whipping for not accomplishing my daily chores.") Deborah also warned Evie not to bear Christian any further children and in 1806, when Evie was twenty-four (and her son Aaron was six), she aborted a child and her grief seemed to rise up off the pages, pushed into the currents of air in Mack's apartment by the old, weeping spin of the air conditioner. ("We never had any more dancing on Sunday nor Monday after Master married that woman," she wrote. "Life was dark for us all the time.")

Fascinated and unsettled, I read that Antoine's wife, Melissa, died in 1811 at the age of thirty-one, and the following year he was married to a British woman, Elizabeth Sutton. But the next year the family home was filled with more grief, when Elizabeth, Deborah, and Jeanine all died during a yellow fever epidemic. Out of grief, Christian turned to Evie for comfort, and the following year she gave birth to Angelle. Four years later Christian died of a heart attack at age sixty-four and Antoine began to sleep with his father's mistress and the family slave, and Evie wrote of the experience as "a kindness and comfort when there was often none in the household."

Of course, nothing was mentioned in Evie's book about Aaron and Pierre's sexual explorations with each other, though she did write that they were "great boyhood friends and good companions" and "the intolerance of the fathers was not present in their sons." I imagined their trysts happening throughout the store and the house at rushed and unexpected times — in the dim light of sunrise while others were in their last minutes of sleep, Aaron would hover over Pierre's body; in the black corners of closed-up shop, Pierre would kiss Aaron's neck and stroke his crotch. I allowed myself to speculate about their encounters: the size of Aaron's thigh, the slenderness of Pierre's fingers, the dark bushy growth of wiry hair at their groins; their orgasms would arrive swiftly, fearfully, but their embraces would linger, till one pushed the other abruptly away to keep them from being exposed to the rest of the household.

The new store and home on Dumaine Street was opened in 1820 and Evie wrote that the new location seemed to be cursed from the outset, when the first house on the property was consumed by fire. "Even though our quarters were newly built at the rear of the house, it was forever in need of repair — daily, mortar seemed to fall out of the walls and the wind and rain and heat work to create ever-present tunnels of unhappiness."

So this place has been an unsteady ruin since Day One, I thought. Perhaps the Dubuisson family was not at fault for creating our miserable and shabby home but the architect who had designed the building. Maybe he had purposely neglected the place, too busy spending his commission dancing with quadroons or smoking opium or drinking absinthe. (Ah, *absinthe,* now there was something to put on my To Do list. *Buy a bottle of absinthe, at any cost, and really knock myself out.*)

Finally towards the end of the third chapter I reached Evangeline's account of the death of the two half-brothers, her son Aaron and her Master Antoine.

> Master had no feeling for his half-brother Aaron and one
> day he overhead Aaron talking about Freedom; and I tell you,
> he half killed him that day. He beat Aaron a while and then
> would make old Manny beat him a while. They gave Aaron nine
> hundred lashes and then made him wash all over in salt water.

Poor Aaron, I don't know where he is today. He was raised a
Catholic and I know he prayed that if he could not have Liberty
he would be taken away from the bonds of the flesh. He is in
Purgatory, I reckon; for the Catholics say the priest can hold
mass and get any body out for so much money. Nobody held
mass for Aaron, and he will have to stay in Purgatory. Master
accused Aaron of trying to buy his Freedom by stealing his
property, and Aaron leapt to his death from the roof of the
new store to escape more punishment. Master had his body
dragged away to be buried in a ditch but old Manny told me
many years later, when we had both been sold and were living in
Virginia, that he had helped young Master Pierre bury the body
in a side corner of the courtyard with what little possessions
he had. Manny said young Master Pierre loved my boy Aaron
like a brother and wept when he placed a knife in the ground
as a tombstone before covering it over with dirt to hide it from
sight.

God took vengeance on Master Antoine. He took sick with
fever a day later and we all did not think he was bad off. We had
been used to his being sickly now and then, and thought that he
would soon be up. But he never left his bed alive. They sent for
the priest just before he died. He greased him with something,
I believe, and they say he took the sacrament from the priest
that day. He died just like he lived. Master did not live right,
and he did not die right, just like the old saying, "Just as the
tree falls, just so it lies." So many times I used to want to talk to
him about the blessing of his own Freedom, what he was given
when others were not, but it was not my place, even when we
were intimate. There was several masses for Master Antoine, and
he was buried at the family plot, though we were not present
because many of us had fallen ill too or we were not allowed to
grieve ourselves in that fashion.

I had many a hard spell of sickness since the death of Master Antoine and the doctors said I could not live beyond a certain time, but every time they said so Doctor Jesus said she shall live, for because I live she shall live also; and He came to me and laid His strong arm around me and raised me up by the power of His might, to see the salvation of our God in the land of the living. And today I can praise His name for His wonderful love to the children of man.

I was also given a great comfort with my daughter Angelle. Angelle, like many of us, was familiar with the healing virtues of plants and herbs. We were trained and taught in such things by generations of women-folk and in New Orleans we were part of the Voudou société, though we had both been Christened in the Catholic faith at our births. The Voudou was a popular activity for our kind—both free and in bondage—and I will not criticize or belittle it now, because it lifted our spirits, set us dancing and brought us faith and the belief of a better life during hard moments when we most needed it. It also kept the Masters fearful and suspicious of us at times when we needed more than faith and strength on our side, though its unusual ways could also bring us more harm than we deserved. Angelle had a special talent with herbs and potions and healings, particularly as she grew older, and many women-folk visited her room at the back of the slave quarters at night to receive a special potion she would make to help them relieve their aches and cramping.

There was a great change in the household after Master Antoine's death, young Master Pierre had growing up to do real fast. He was given a heavy burden at a young age, and he had promised many of us in the household that he would one day give us our Liberty when he became the Master of the house, but he did not keep his promise to any one of us. Still, he was the kindest Master of us all in those wretched days of slavery and burden. We were no longer beaten and my work was no longer extended to the store or the storerooms, but confined to the living rooms of the house and the kitchen. Manny and Grady's burdens were also lifted somewhat when Master Pierre hired an Irishman to help out in the store, instead of buying another slave to replace our poor lost soul of Aaron. He gave wages to the Irishman and said to old Manny and Grady when the business became profitable again, they would have their Freedom, too, but of course that did not happen.

Angelle was the most disappointed of all of us when we were not granted our Liberty—she had inherited the same need and desire and determination as her older brother Aaron had, particularly since she sensed so strongly its possibility and could remember the miserable fate of her older brother. As she became more skilled in potions and treatments she tried many times to use these to influence Master Pierre's disposition, always without his knowledge, of course, and also without any success. As he became older and more worried about the success of his store, Master Pierre became an aloof and distant Master to us, and this also summoned up the greatest fear possible in young Angelle. She had always believed her beauty and her charm would bring her her Freedom if her talents and her daily prayers and offerings to the Loa gods of the Voudou could not. Daily, she sought out the young Master in the store, inquiring if she could bring him tea or mend the collar of his shirt or jacket or some such ruse that she could use to cast a bewitchment over the young Master. Master Pierre was a handsome fellow and he was always capable of rejecting Angelle's flirtation by agreeing to some minor whim of hers and sending her away. He was always kind to her, even in the last tragic moments of his life. Angelle began visiting Master Pierre at night, in his room, bringing him a sleeping potion one time when the day's events at the store had agitated him. Next, she began visiting him every evening, and he came to want her in the ways that men want women, and she felt that this hold over him was now her easiest path to Liberty.

Angelle had been brought up by her father, Christian Dubuisson, to believe that she would one day be free and not a placée but the Mistress of the house, and the unfortunate turn of events in the business and the household had always distressed her. Now she was convinced that she was in love with young Master Pierre, and he with her, so she received a brutal and shocking blow when he announced one evening that he was to be married to a woman from Mississippi, someone whose father's plantation and farming enterprise would be an important market and outlet for Master Pierre's expanding business and trade.

My lovely, beloved Angelle did not take this news well at all and she retreated from the Master's bedroom and began to talk of him in the most offensive ways, and she began to create potions and charms to prevent the arrival of Mistress Sarah, and then when the fine lady finally arrived, Angelle went about creating ones to bring their marriage union harm and displeasure.

Angelle had gained a great reputation in the Voudou société in those days and her ill-will of her Master and Mistress soon became common knowledge to everyone within the marketplace of New Orleans. She softened, however, when Mistress Sarah became pregnant with her first child and Angelle gave her an Erzulie bath for good fortune and brought her herbs and perfumes to ease the growing aches and pains of her changing body. Angelle even went so far as predicting what happiness Mistress Sarah and her child would have in their future. When both the baby and Mistress Sarah died during childbirth, many in the société believed Angelle had been only pretending to aide instead of helping her Mistress and had instead cursed the family. It was a great blow to her character, and even the women-folk who had once championed Angelle now found her insolent and sinister because she had harmed a newly-born child.

News of this made its way to Master Pierre, of course, but even in his grief he did not believe that Angelle was capable of such ill will and destruction. Then Master Pierre himself fell ill, terribly ill, in the days after the death of Mistress Sarah and her young unnamed daughter and all of us in the household were worried that his imminent death would be the ruination of us all. For if he died while we were all still slaves in his household and business, then we would surely be sold again as slaves to another master, someone who could be far, far worse than the kind young Master Pierre.

Angelle tried her best to aide him, bringing him broths and lotions and special treatments. The day of his death, Angelle tried to save us all by convincing the police that she was now the Mistress of the household by revealing a letter that Master Christian had written proclaiming the intended Liberty for his daughter, but when she was brought before a Judge the letter was deemed a forgery and a fake and Angelle was yoked and flogged in Place d'Armes in a most hideous and pitiable display. She died only hours later, weak and dispirited, when Manny and I returned her to her bed while awaiting the arrival of our new Master, Edward Wheaton, Mistress Sarah's father.

The subsequent pages held the news that Sarah's father had sold the Dubuisson house and business to a merchant from Baton Rouge; Grady became the property of Master Wheaton, but Manny and Evangeline were sold to a plantation owner in Virginia. As I flipped through the remaining pages of the book, I tried to convince myself that yes, of course, this was what I had been looking for—that Aaron's knife was what I had discovered beneath the floor of the pantry, that the tombstone marker confirmed all this, and it was the ghosts of Aaron, Pierre, and Angelle that I had witnessed in the courtyard, if witnessing ghosts were even possible, and that I had not only been caught up in conundrums of their daily lives, but also trapped in the mysterious details surrounding their deaths. Yes, it was a localized supernatural problem, not a personalized spiritual one, as I had worried about ever since hallucinating my Inner Confusion as a potential Sex Idol. I lifted my eyes away from the pages of the book and my throat instantly tightened as if it were awaiting another drink, like a detective from a B-movie in search of a good bolt of black market rye to figure out an ensuing game plan. As I got up off the chair where I had been reading, I noticed that Dwayne was reading the handwritten pages of a composition book.

I asked him if he wanted anything to drink, and when he looked up at me he seemed to be annoyed that I had interrupted him. He shook his head and said, "No, not yet, I'm almost done with this," which discouraged me from refilling my own glass and a wave of guilt washed over me for abandoning the day's work necessary to keep the guesthouse running.

I walked out of the apartment and stood beside the broken balcony railing, overwhelmed by the work that lay ahead for me. I felt guilty for everything: for the dirty laundry piling up, decaying and stinking; for the sure-to-be-rotting unsold food at the café, for avoiding Celia and Stuart, and for wanting desperately to be with Hank at the hospital but unable to summon up the courage that I might be facing more bad news. My back tensed and my vision blackened and I saw myself standing at a distance from where my body actually was, noticing how tired and frustrated and overweight I looked. *What a sorry mess I've become,* I thought and wondered if this twin of mine could get to work while I relaxed. It was then that I heard a baby crying. Turning towards the sound, which seemed to be coming from the main building, I saw myself regarding my own image as I turned away. My double had turned to investigate the sound of the crying, too, and I could see him walking away from me as well as the path he was exploring with his own eyes. I stopped walking to make sure this was not some sort of trick or hocus pocus or stirring madness of my own mind, but when I turned around and looked behind me I saw myself still standing by the broken railing looking aghast at my own image. *How did I get like this?* one—or both of us—thought. *I've got to pull myself together. Never go this long without shaving. Diet some. Work out at a gym. Stop drinking so much—it's going entirely to our waist. And it's making me—us—look like we're tottering maniacal clowns in ill-fitting, threadbare costumes!*

The crying was louder and it seemed not to be a baby at all but a strange mix of high-pitched female voices. The one of me who was the mobile one tried the door to the Royal Suite first where the sound seemed to be the loudest and, stepping inside, it took me a moment before my eyes adjusted to the dimmer light, as if a fog had settled in, not the sort of suffocating fog that swallows up everything in a milky blur but a mist that was even and almost transparent.

Why had everything become so strange and problematic? Out of order or helter-skelter? Why did I have to work at this—this—this figuring out of the unnatural order of things? I stared into the empty room for what seemed to be a long time. At first I thought the room had been trashed and burned by guests because the layout was different—the small couch was missing and the bed, which was usually at the center of the room, was now at the far end. But then I smelled a strange odor, dank and musty, and the flames of candles placed around the room came into focus. I felt a chill at my back as the mist seemed to lift and I saw a woman approach me. She was dressed in a white blouse with a brooch at the center of it and she wore a dark scarf over her hair and a long dark-colored skirt which looked like the bottom half of a period costume of the nineteenth century. When she spoke to me and reached her hand out to guide me farther into the room, I could neither hear her nor feel her touch, though the wailing sound which I had heard on the balcony continued to flutter through the room like a breeze rustling the dry leaves of autumn trees.

I moved deeper into the room and saw that a man—or the faint appearance of a black man—was lying in the bed beneath the covers—and that there was another woman—young and black-skinned and dressed in dark, shabby period clothes standing beside the bed, pressing a rag against the sleeping man's forehead. Another dark-skinned woman—shorter and older with wisps of gray hair visible at the hairline of her scarf—made the sign of the cross with her right hand as I approached the bed and I looked down at my hands and saw that I was carrying a Bible and a crucifix, though I had not entered the room with either one.

It seemed to me then that they must have been waiting for a priest and arriving as he was expected, I had been mistaken for such a man. I tried to hand the Bible and the crucifix to one of the women, but they were still only ghostly images and not of strong enough physical substance to take the items from me.

Standing beside the bed and regarding the dying man I knew that I had somehow conjured up Pierre's death scene, that the elderly woman was Evangeline and the sobbing girl was Angelle. I tried to catch their eyes, but they would not meet my gaze. *Why was I here? What was I supposed to do? Why was this lingering in my mind?* My mood changed and I was annoyed that I had reached such a level of exhaustion that I was now hallucinating death scenes out of another century (and not a good old-fashioned romp in the hay). Then it occurred to me that perhaps I wasn't manifesting my restlessness over death but subconsciously confronting my disbelief that an afterlife even existed. Might that account for what I was witnessing? I had long ago abandoned any pretense of practicing any religion regularly and with it any belief that those who had died were sent to heaven, hell or the limbo in between. "Earth to earth, ashes to ashes" was not just a religious sentiment but a scientific fact of mortality for me. Where did we go after that? Nowhere, in my opinion. I'd carefully removed the belief of God from my daily life because His religions had failed to incorporate the physical meaning of mine.

Beside the bed was a dresser with a pitcher and bowl on top for washing in front of a mirror. As I placed the Bible and the crucifix on the top of the dresser I caught my image in the mirror—or tried to see my image in the mirror. What I saw was not myself but a man who had my portly physique and who was dressed as a priest. But my face was not visible. In its place was a bright white light, and as I tried to look closer and deeper into the mirror for the details of my own face, it occurred to me that perhaps this was not at all about the unsettling spirits of this tiny plot on Dumaine Street, but related to my lack of faith and my disbelief that a God or a greater Higher Power to whom we are all accountable in the end even existed. Hadn't I summoned up a vision of a Troubled Psyche as an internal manifestation, rather than as an external force to be reckoned with? Was there really something greater at work? Something or someone beyond my recognition?

I felt the presence of the light in a deep and profound manner, sensed that answers were to be forthcoming in my continued search for understanding. In the mirror I examined and squinted until I finally found the details of my own green eyes and in doing so I saw my grandfather standing before his pious congregation. It was an image of the backside of him I remembered from the age of seven or eight, the year it dawned on me how badly he was subjecting our family to danger, freshly shaved and dressed in his best white shirt and saggy black pants, his hand pressed against the scalp of a sickly man with skin the consistency of paste, shouting, "Rise up, child of God, you are healed! God be saved!"

I don't believe that my grandfather ever healed anyone by faith, but it had been good enough theatrics for quite a number of years to bring around a crowd to his church three or four times a week or whenever he took the lot of us on the road to his tent-revivals across the South. St. Mark's Church of God with Signs Following always guaranteed a rowdy service, the praising and testifying and hymn-singing incorporating smelly fiery rags; mason jars full of milky, poisoned water; and an irritable rattlesnake my grandfather would pull out of a blond wooden box and lift above his head and pass along to anyone possessed by the Holy Spirit. Every time I entered that church I was seized with fear and, in the memory of the mirror, I realized that the weeping sound I had heard when I approached the room was not that of a sickly infant but of the wailing worshippers anointed by the presence of the Holy Spirit and accompanied by the tiny tambourine I had banged against the side of my pants as my grandfather had instructed me to do. My father had continued the faith my grandfather began; the handling of serpents and speaking in tongues were a mandate from God for both of them. I suppose this should have made me iron-spirited myself, the son of evangelists, but instead I was aware of how freakishly my family was regarded by my classmates and how badly I wished to distance myself once I had found fault with them and their so-called powers from God. I was ostracized for both our poverty and our Bible-thumping. At school I was ridiculed and teased and I tried to let my faith keep me as strong as it could make me, but I was something of a sissy boy and too smart for my own good and I isolated myself instead of reaching out and finding friends.

In our church it was thought that it tested one's faith to drink poisoned water or pick up a poisonous snake—God wouldn't allow the poison to kill you as long as you had faith in Him. It was as simple and as easy as that. *Believe.* And in my early childhood I wanted desperately to belong to this reverent tribe of chanting men and women, to not feel like I was different, to be a part of the show for God, and I was lucky that we were never allowed to handle snakes in our services until we reached the age of eighteen, though my grandfather found no reason for me not to pass my hands over the body of a serpent or follow him into the woods to find a new rattler when he felt his current one was becoming old or docile or bored.

And every week there was someone to be saved or healed or both. The congregation sat on wobbly wooden benches that had been around for decades, their eyes examining the family of us for signs of promise and hope and messages from God. They watched my father open-mouthed and astonished as if he were suspended in air, walking a tightrope without a balancing beam; my grandfather they regarded as steadfast and certain as the weathered, old family Bible he carried in his grasp.

"Is there someone here who needs the grace of God?" my father would begin the services. "Someone whom God has delivered to us?" My father spoke in a raspy tenor's voice, his articulation as practiced as an opera singer's. Sitting up front with my mother and my two brothers and sisters, I looked out at the rows of hopeful men and women and their families, waiting to be moved by the spirit of God. One Sunday I sat before the congregation and saw not their expectations but the lights of their souls. Where each nose and mouth and eyes should have been was instead an orb of glowing light. *Yes, I was loony even as a boy.* I sat there thrilled and mesmerized by a hall of lights, convinced that God had given me a special gift. I was close to fourteen then, felt my body changing on a daily basis from a child into a young man and all of its accompanying hormonal urges and desires worried me, and I rose up and spoke in tongues, which was really just a young boy's acting gibberish because he was starved for attention, feeling exiled by his classmates and alienated from his family.

When I told my father and grandfather later about what I felt was my special gift, they drew their eyes wide in disbelief and angrily told me that it was a sin to lie and that God would punish me for deceiving my elders if what I said proved to be a sham. No one in our church had ever seen the Holy Spirit as a burning light inside each one of us. No one had dared to step over from reality into that fine realm of fantasy. *Yes,* I laughed at my memory, *I was a high-maintenance would-be drama queen even as a boy. Only then I thought I might find an audience.*

But I *had* seen the orbs. And I continued to believe they existed, even though the next time I was in church they were not there, gone, as if I had woken up from a dream or they had been banished as the devils my father had judged them. *Begone you spooks of my imagination or I will drop a house on you!* But the lights continued in my imagination or I continued to conjure them up. Sitting there, I softened them, lengthened them, widened them until they took the phantom details and shapes of their owners. Had what I recognized then as a young man been the same sort of phenomenon I was witnessing years later in the pantry and at the cemetery? The energy of the human soul, the energy left behind that can give the spirit a ghostly shape? Was this, in fact, a gift from God? Or was the gift something else? Something more? The next step? Was the gift or power not the ability of sight—of witnessing the lights—but the power to understand them—or understand their power? Was this to be part of my task, what the celestial Griffin had alluded to?

Ah, if the lights had only made me smarter. Or had they? As a young man God tempted me and I failed Him, or so I rationalized for years until I broke away from my family and our church. The first time I masturbated I was filled with shame, as if I had caught a sickness that God could not heal. Sex was shameful and painful if not done for begetting children, according to my family's religion, but there was a pleasure burning at my groin, a need to touch myself again, make the orgasm repeat again and again. If God was everywhere, saw every sin of the sinner, then He must also know exactly what I was working with down there and understand the pleasure I had felt when I held it and stroked it; this was how I stumbled into the conception that perhaps the God mankind had created was somehow wrong, or false, or unjust. *Missing in action from the misery of my life.*

I wanted desperately to be a part of something else—the world of my classmates, the world outside of my family's church. I wanted to be as easy going and athletic as the other boys at school were, palling around with each other, smoking cigarettes in the parking lot and drinking so much beer on the weekends that I would puke and pass out. The first time I lit up a cigarette with my friend Craig I was thrilled and shamed because it was forbidden by my religion. The first time I arrived home drunk I was giddy with happiness even though I tiptoed to my bed consumed by fear that my father would wake and beat the happiness out of me because alcohol was forbidden in our household and denomination. The first time I let Craig's mouth reach my cock, I was filled with more thrill and shame. *What would my father make of this transgression?* I wondered. *What does God think of this pleasure? Was this a sin that could be forgiven? Was this a disease that could be cured?* But at the depth of this desire—my passion to feel this burning and rising and releasing again and again with another man—I knew that it was not sinful but natural and instinctual. Who else did I want to do this to me? Not a girl. Or a woman. Or a prostitute. No, I wanted the captain of the football team to go down on me, or maybe let me go down on him. And God was simply watching me as he always was. I was only acting as I felt I should act. Where was the sin in that? What cure did I need to seek?

One Sunday in church my grandfather was bitten between his fingers by a water moccasin a worshipper had brought to the service. It was his twenty-second bite but he died within twenty minutes, his arm swelling and turning black while my father pressed his hand against my grandfather's heart attempting to heal him with the power of the Holy Spirit. My grandfather died because he was not anointed by the Trinity, or so our religion theorized, and I considered this to be my fault because my rising sins had infected my family, and I reached for the serpent as my grandfather's step faltered. The snake bit me just above my thumb, but because my grandfather had already received most of the venom I only felt a prick and a slight dizziness. As I held the snake and passed him along to the man who had brought him, I felt a sickness mounting my body, and there seemed to be some weight or burden inside me that was growing stronger. I bent over, pierced by an intense hopelessness in my stomach, and vomited my breakfast at my mother's feet. Then at once the experience was gone and I succumbed to blackness.

I came to in my bed sometime later, my father pressing his hand against my forehead and saying, "the beginning of wisdom is to fear the Lord." I remained ill for almost a week, missing my grandfather's funeral, and I know my thrashing about and slow recovery involved more than my receiving a snakebite. When I felt better, was able to stand and keep food in my stomach, I confessed my sin to my father: the joy of wanting another man. My father reacted like he had been bitten by a serpent himself. "How can this be?" he asked me, his face mottled with anger. "When you know you will spend eternity in the fires of hell?" But at the depth of my soul I knew my newfound pleasures were not a sin, yet because of this I also knew that I was not the devout religious warrior of my father's faith. This was no backsliding; in the eyes of my father and his religion I was a transgressor, and I had no option but to leave the church and the faith and my family or be tossed out by all of them.

And so I became a big-time sinner headed for New Orleans, and sin I did, with as many men as I could meet. I sinned with a deacon from

Nebraska who had an enormous corn-fed cock, sinned with a grown-up altar boy from Boston who wanted to be handcuffed, sinned and sinned some more with a choir director from Atlanta into water sports. I sinned with Mack, sinned a lot more with Parker. Five years after I had landed in New Orleans I heard that my mother had been bitten by a snake and died, and the following year my older brother left behind two young children when a rattler sank its fangs into his forearm, and after that I lost contact with my family until close to a decade later when I read an article on the Internet about my father being arrested for trying to murder his second wife by convincing her to stick her hand into a cage of angry snakes.

So sinning was in the blood, I thought when I read that article, though by then the definition of sinning had changed for me. Sinning was pleasure—a drink when I wanted one and sex when I found it. In the mirror of the room I saw the shape and form of the man on the bed behind me rise up from the sheets, swing his bare legs across the side of the bed, stand up in all of his powerful nude glory and approach me from behind. A part of the man had the features I had designed for Pierre, but a part of him also possessed Hank's lithe physique, and when he reached out for my reflection, the arm and forearm that embraced me sported the dark wiry hair and flamboyant tattoos of Griffin. My own clothes had fallen away from my body and I did my best to let the sight in the mirror of my sagging and aging physique not repel my desire as the arm and hand and fingers traveled down and grasped my rising cock. I stood there, feet firmly planted against the floor, willing myself first to resist becoming aroused, and then when I was unsuccessful at that, an orgasm. *What was this all about now? Was this a test or was I going mad? Was God showing me I was a man driven by desire? Or was He simply showing me that he was here, with me now, that He had, in fact, been with me throughout my entire life?*

The wailing sound in the room increased in pitch, the sound brightened and tumbled and changed direction and I checked my body to make sure I hadn't been committed to the asylum and jacketed in white. Soon the wailing sounded like it was laughter and when the hand stroking my cock became the mouth and stubbly scalp of Griffin that I had encountered in the pantry, my focus shifted so that I could enjoy the sensation. The dimensions of the mirror shifted too, the carved wooden features of the frame, the blurry black patches where aging had worn down the reflection to the tin surface, and it was then that I saw the figure again of the shabbily-dressed young black woman standing behind me, her face lifted up and laughing. *Or was this a trick?*

I turned, expecting to confront Angelle, but instead I was met with darkness, a black cloud that seemed to surround my body first, then penetrate my skin like a downpour of rain, dampening the flesh and blackening my consciousness. I felt myself rising up, as if I had been lifted into the sky, and I had a momentary recollection of a drug-induced hallucination I had one night when I went clubbing during my first months in New Orleans and someone gave me a hit of MDA. *MDA?* I thought, *that was decades ago, not even close to being a fashionable club drug today. Why was I recalling this now? This ethereal lightness of body but with a black consciousness? Why did it feel like I was a part of my body but also apart from it?* Then I felt my body rotating, aware that I was no longer rising up but falling, descending through the blackness at a rapid speed towards a fate I could only fearfully await. It made me remember Hank's fall from the balcony, those agonizing seconds when I recognized what was happening but was unsure of what the result would be. I thought of Toby falling and Aaron jumping and the longer my body dropped through the blackness, the more troubled my breathing became.

The pain arrived first against my back, stinging lashes and welts that burned my skin, my wrists and ankles surrounded by heavy metal rings that held me in place, preventing my writhing or rolling over. My back felt both aggravated and infected, as though pus was swarming around needle pricks, ready to explode like volcanoes. *Was this what it was like to die as a slave? I thought next. Or what it is like to truly suffer? Was this God's punishment? An obstacle? Or part of the passage to insight?* I tried to erase the ache of the stinging at my back by concentrating on my breathing—gulps of air in and out of my mouth, saliva puddling around my tongue, sputtering and drooling as I quietly prayed for help. The pain grew in intensity and I felt the aches of other parts of my body, a string of pain flutter through my stomach and intestines, the open flesh and sores on my heel and at my toes, the salty sweat at the back of my neck dripping down my spine and blistering the scars of the lashes. All I could think of was how I wanted to go back to my own life, my life of dirty laundry and constant chores and endless challenges from hostile guests and mutinous employees and self-absorbed friends and backstabbing ex-lovers that now didn't seem like such a miserable life at all. *Please God,* I prayed. *Please bring me back home. If I click my heels three times, will I be there? And I won't wish for another thing.*

My prayer was met with laughter, the same high-pitched laughter that had drawn me to the Royal Suite. The laughter changed and it was again similar to sobbing, and just when I was trying to isolate one voice from among the many different pitches, one voice that I might be able to recognize at another time, I was aware that I was back standing on the balcony. Dwayne was standing beside me and speaking, oblivious to whatever I had been imagining, and I only caught the last few words of what he was telling me, "It must have been painful for him to talk about."

"Could this be a spiritual problem?" I asked, interrupting him, as if I had run up the stairs and unexpectedly discovered him walking out of the apartment. "Could our ghosts have something to do with religion?"

"Religion?" Dwayne answered, "I'm not sure what you mean."

"Religion teaches us about the afterlife. Eternal happiness. Rest in peace. All that sort of crap. All of our ghosts were living people who met unfortunate deaths. Aaron. Angelle. Even Toby. Of course we don't know much about ghosts because God intended us to know very little."

Dwayne was shifting uneasily back and forth on the heels of his feet, and I knew that what I would say next would meet with skepticism. "Maybe a prayer would settle them," I added. A little, hastily intoned prayer, in fact, had just now lifted me up from my own blackness, though I was hesitant to confess it. Perhaps prayer could restore our household to its blissful chaos.

"A prayer?"

"Yes. Right now. Maybe it would work. Maybe if we prayed."

"Maybe your sightings are a spiritual issue," Dwayne said. "And a prayer might work for you. Or lots of prayers, since there seem to be more than one ghost. But Toby saw the ghosts too. And his was a psychological problem, not a spiritual one."

"What do you mean?"

"This," he said and he handed me the composition book he had been reading in Mack's apartment.

"I think you should read this," he said to me. "It's a bit sad. Mack was writing journal entries in the final days his boyfriend Toby was alive. It started as a record of dreams—Toby's dreams—so Toby could tell them to his psychiatrist. Then it became a sort of chronicle of descent. It seemed to start as some kind of sleeping sickness. I think his ghosts were psychological."

Five

In many spiritual traditions, it is recognized from the outset that what is sought, what is hungered for, cannot be found, and that the spiritual question must be seen as an end in itself. Seek, but do not find. Desire faith, desire not understanding. But like the religion I left behind when I left my family, that road seemed too narrow for me and that sort of logic would also lead me to overlook the meaning of my ghostly visitors—appreciate them, welcome them, but do not try to find out what they want. Who could live with that continual sense of unbalance, learning but never understanding? Or maybe I was just a control freak, wanting everything to be in order—or the order I wanted it to be in.

Reluctantly, I accepted the composition book from Dwayne, knowing it would likely be an unpleasant read and holding it as if it were a too-heavy dumbbell he was passing along to me at the gym, one that, as soon as he turned away from me, I would drop to the floor. I had not known this particular information about Toby—Mack had always kept the specific details of his relationship with Toby private, and the facts surrounding Toby's death were seldom mentioned between us. I had not been the kind of lover or friend to pry into them, fearing, for instance, that what I could discover would cause me jealousy. But now I was fearful of what I might discover regarding my own fate. Could this be proof that I was crazy, too? Would I jump to my death? Would I be pushed into oblivion?

I took the composition book in my hand—it was the kind of notebook that college students carted to and from classrooms, scuffed at the corners and decorated with initials and slogans and phone numbers of potential dates—and I handed Dwayne Evangeline's memoir, trying to find the words to tell him that this held the clues to the history of my ghosts, but finding, instead, only the phrase, "Would you like a drink before you start this?"

He declined my offer and I went into Mack's kitchen and found a small tumbler and the bottle of bourbon I had brought upstairs a few days before, and poured myself a shot. I took a seat at the small table in the kitchen and opened the composition book, my index finger nervously running along the first few sentences. The first entry was 5/1/77 and Mack had started the first page in pencil, as if he thought he might change his mind or embellish and rewrite his first thoughts, but by the end of the second page he was writing in ink in a clear, practiced script, revealing some of the disturbing thoughts that were swirling through his own mind as he tried to record what was inside Toby's.

> Last week Dr. Stephenson suggested that Toby keep a daily diary or a list of his significant thoughts and moments that might help him address his rising depression and the nightmares he is experiencing when he sleeps. At night, Toby complains of long periods of insomnia, followed by moments when he falls into a sleep and experiences a nightmare that only wakes him and prevents him from wanting to return to sleep. He says this is the cause of his mind shutting down during the day when he needs to read and study, why he zones out into a state of semiconsciousness that is as unnerving as his dreams, and this, in turn, is causing him to be depressed (or more depressed than he usually is). I've always thought that Toby expects too much from the world and works way too hard—not manual labor or physical stuff, but mental work—that he reads far too much and for too long a period. In fact, he does not get enough physical

exercise to make him sleep better. I've told him more than once that if he took breaks, walked around the Quarter, got out of the apartment, he would not be so despondent all the time and might be tired enough to fall asleep and sleep soundly through the night. But he only tries to force me into an argument when I suggest this. His temper is at his sleeve these days. He's ready to fight back with, "What do you know? You're not a doctor." So I told him to do what the doctor asked, keep a journal, but his response was to claim that he does not have enough time to write it all down, which is why, in a last ditch effort to keep things working for us, I told him I would do this for him.

Toby is always complaining of a lack of time—meaning he is not working fast enough on his book, though when I ask him about what deadlines he must make, he says that he should work faster because there is so much to understand. Then, when he admits that he cannot keep up with his reading, when something interrupts him, something like the basic need for a drink of water or a trip to the bathroom, he grows defeated and agitated. He snaps at me whenever I ask if I can help him, and he grows angry—not at me, but inside, angry at himself. His irritability has vanquished his appetite and his lack of sleep has made his eyes grow large and moist and full of the need for something he cannot quite articulate. We barely touch each other anymore—in bed, he will no longer allow me to hold him and he is too restless for me to try to pin down. Nightly, he tosses from one side to the other, raising his head to reshape his pillow or draw his body into another position.

Last night Toby had falling dreams, strange dreams in which he seemed to be moving through a tunnel or a dark, empty space. I tried to ask Toby what might have triggered these, something during the day that could have made him feel this way, but he said he always feels like something is tugging at him, a nagging list of things he has not completed. When

I asked him what it was that he had not completed, he would not answer me, then snapped, "You wouldn't understand." I told him I am trying to help and trying to understand, but this seemed to agitate him only more and he grew silent and was unable to read, rocking back and forth in his chair with his arms hugging his knees, like a mental patient. Things are not good for him and are becoming worse for us. I can't see us going on like this for much longer.

5/2/77

More falling dreams last night. I asked Toby to give me some more specific details about the dream but all he said was that it started right away, as soon as he closed his eyes, and he only woke up when he felt his hand burn and twitch. He said later in the night, when his eyes were so heavy he couldn't keep them open anymore, he dreamed again about the young woman, a young black woman that he has seen in his dreams several times in the last few days. I asked him if she were a relative—his older sister, his mother when she was younger—but she was not familiar to him, except in the dream. She seemed to be rising out of sleep herself.

When I asked him who she might be, who he might have created in his dream, he said she might have been from the book he had been reading since last week, a book about a slave who had lived in the house where our apartment is located. Toby had been told some of the history of the house by Mrs. Mallalieu, the woman who rented him the apartment, and last week she gave him a copy of a book that had been published about one of the slave women who had worked in the house when it was first built in the early 1800s. Toby said he began seeing the young slave girl almost the first night he started to read the book. First, she was only a shape—a bodiless dark shape as if she were a stain on the floor, then he found her eyes and next the rest of her face took on details.

He says that one night—a few nights ago—he dreamed he could see the texture of her dress in his dream—the wide weave of the fabric, the stains and tears in the cloth. Last night this texture—this stained and torn fabric—constituted the walls of his second—or third—falling dream. Last night he said he saw her while he was awake—or dreamed he was awake—he was so uncertain what state of consciousness or unconsciousness he was in. He was dreaming that he was rising out of a dream to find her beside him and rising out of sleep herself.

5/3/77

Last night he dreamed he was falling into the bricks of the courtyard, never reaching them but falling above them, turning and twisting around in the air as he fell through the blackness, his skin feeling prickly and painful as if it were covered with sores. He awoke sweating and went to the bathroom and rinsed off. I told him that the heat might be causing some of his misery this time. The humidity of yesterday was miserable and thick and hung in our bedroom all through the evening. But he was so tired and listless he did not even have the energy to fight with me and this has made me somewhat worried. This morning I walked down to Canal and bought a window fan and assembled it and put it in the bedroom window. I hope that will help out tonight. I had suggested that we get an air conditioner, but Toby was against the expense—he's not even working at the grill anymore so there has been no income other than what I can cobble together for the two of us. Toby could not even read today—he stayed in bed all day, comatose with his eyes opened, the fan blowing hot air across his body. I brought him ice and soda before I went out to work, but he only looked at me as if I were some stranger.

5/4/77

This morning Dr. Stephenson said falling dreams were quite common and contrary to popular myth, you would not die should you fail to wake up before you hit the ground. He indicated that the cause of these dreams might be that Toby felt insecure or anxious—either in his work or his relationship—a rather useless and expensive insight, I told Toby after we had left the appointment, since that was why Toby went to him in the first place. Toby was insecure because he could not complete his work, and as for us—our relationship—we have always had difficulty publicly defining it because we are so condemned—by the Bible, by the government, by our neighbors, even by psychiatrists who treat this as a disease instead of as a conscious way of living. Toby makes it clear that he wants everyone to know that we are boyfriends and lovers (though not much lately if you ask me because he has become so distant and aloof), but he cannot handle the taunts and jeers when he walks down the street. Since he was a boy, Toby has had "sissy" issues as Dr. Stephenson describes it, and he refuses to act any differently than what feels natural to him. Toby said that he just wants respect—not just for us but for his work, too—and because he doesn't receive it for either, he is depressed. At least now he has admitted his depression exists, as well as a cause for it, so I have told him that we are taking steps in the right direction.

Dr. Stephenson addressed some of the reasons why Toby felt respect from the outside world was necessary to him and then said that this sense of inferiority could be a triggering factor for the falling dreams: a fear of failure at achieving what he wants and who he wants to be. Toby did not tell Dr. Stephenson about the young slave girl in his dreams during his session today because he felt the doctor would not understand, since he was not a black man himself. Toby also felt that it wasn't necessary to mention her—the doctor had already agreed to give him a prescription for sleeping pills, which was what Toby had gone to him for in the first place and he had never wanted to participate in all this dream analogy. I am not at all optimistic that the sleeping pills will help because Toby has still not found a way through his depression, even though he has admitted to it. Today he read for a few hours, grew agitated, paced around the apartment waiting to take the sleeping pill, and finally took a sleeping pill before he went to bed.

So Toby had been a high-maintenance boyfriend, too, and Mack had his hands full and plenty to worry about. The following pages detailed Toby's inability to cope with the sleeping pills: a restless night of sweating and vomiting, a restless day without work, followed by another restless night of sweating and vomiting. I could see Mack as the carepartner and not the patient I had known him as for years, devotedly bringing wet washrags to wipe along Toby's brow and lips, helping him change into a clean T-shirt, checking on him as he slept through the night. In the diary Mack elaborated on Toby's agitation one minute and his lethargy the next and I knew that even though Mack was describing some of his own agitation and nervousness, in reality I'm sure he was handling it differently, more patiently, like the compassionate man I had always known him to be. As the next three days progressed Toby's inability to hold any food down continued and Mack missed work to try and get him to drink broth or milkshakes or eat any kind of bread or crackers. The dreams—or nightmares—had momentarily stopped, but Toby now complained of blinding headaches, and of seeing lights materializing around objects, "tiny fireballs that seemed to possess a mind of their own," reminding him that death was imminent. Though Mack never wrote that these lights might be fifolet, Toby believed that they were angels, awakened to guide him into an afterlife, and it made me remember that I had begun reading the journal hoping to find an insight to my own predicament. Toby seemed to be preparing himself for death, or perhaps I was reading that meaning into the diary because I knew of his eventual fate. But if the fifolet were angels, as Toby felt they were, was my heart-stopping pause during last night's wake and my most recent painful thrashing predictions of my own destructive path? Was I to die next? Was it my time to go? *Not now,* I thought, *give me some more time. My house is not in order. Please God, give me a few extra years, at least, if that is what lies ahead for me. Let me experience the joys of central air-conditioning, if only for a day.*

Suspiciously, I began to read more entries. Mack recorded next that Toby began to talk more about death—his death—what kind of funeral he wanted, what kind of mass he wanted, what kind of music was to be played and performed, where he wanted to be buried in the cemetery—he told Mack that ever since he was a boy he had wandered through St. Louis and Lafayette cemeteries—that the cemeteries throughout the city were what had inspired him to work his way through college. For one college course, he had charted the vaults and pathways of St. Louis Cemetery III, which had been set aside by the city for African American Catholics. Death had kept Toby going, or so Mack related it—the whole city was some kind of graveyard, people buried in plots, ditches, scattered cemeteries; as land values grew greater and the city expanded, bodies had been exhumed and reburied, and Toby had spent years studying one site after another. Toby was convinced that his tombstone should carry an elaborately carved angel, with large outspread wings as if it were lifting the tomb off the ground, and in my imagination I conjured up a wide spread of feathered wings but instead of lifting Toby they were engulfing me and pitching me back into darkness. I knew I was succumbing to my own fear of death, imagining what would happen if I were to die—not how painful an experience it might be for myself, but how it would affect others—who would help out Parker, check on Hank, clean the toilets and change the towels, tell customers not to be frightened by Buddy's Voodoo art? This fear quickly evaporated into guilt because I was avoiding all these things at this very moment, trying to find a reason why I had seen the ghosts; why I had discovered the knife, Evangeline's memoir, and now this, Mack's diary of Toby's last days and a warning of my own.

Mack wrote of his ensuing argument with Toby over the unnecessary expense of such a funeral—Mack would have preferred to have invested in an air conditioner for the apartment than put a down payment on a tombstone, and the following session with Dr. Stephenson revealed that the doctor believed that this was Toby trying to change or transform himself or his relationship with Mack, and that perhaps Toby felt strangled or stifled by Mack and this was a manifestation of his desire for freedom from the situation.

This was not at all what Toby wanted to hear. Toby soon became so despondent at the idea of a breakup with Mack that during the session he yelled back at the doctor for being insensitive to the special kind of relationship he and Mack shared. Before returning home, Mack had promised that he would not leave Toby and they visited with a priest in the hopes of beginning the formal paperwork for their interment together in one of the local cemeteries. The priest had balked at the idea, they were young men and had years ahead of them and he said that he could not honestly present them as a couple before the eyes of God, but Toby had said God would not overlook their friendship with each other and that they would find a way to the cemetery plots with or without the priest's help. The priest, of course, had known both young men, had, in fact, even had a secretive sexual history with both of them, and it occurred to me while reading Mack's description of him that I might have slept with this man, too, my first year in the Big Easy. Only after a private barter arrangement with the priest, whereby Mack agreed to do some repair work in the church offices, did the possibility of a burial together begin to take shape.

That night Mack, depressed himself now, wrote about death—his own death—how far off and remote it seemed to him but how far off and remote his relationship with Toby had also become. "If I were to die now I know that Toby would not survive himself for more than a few days," he wrote, but mentioned that things had "already changed and transformed" between himself and Toby—all of the passion and affection between them had been "bled dry" and he had been left with his own emptiness. He didn't want to die. But he wanted to change. Or go back to the way things were. He missed the adventurous young Toby who used to kiss him impulsively on the street, pull him out of the kitchen before dinner and into the bedroom, who used to wake at night—not from dreams or nightmares—but from the desire for sex again and again and again. "In our early months we were always grappling with each other, pulling off our T-shirts and reaching our hands beneath each other's shorts, stroking and sucking each other off with a passionate fury and bliss. That's what I miss. Not the sex. The passion of being with someone who wants to passionately be with me."

"Yes, that's what I miss," he added. "But then I've changed myself, ever since my parents' death."

Mack wrote that all of Toby's infatuation with and talk of death had happened at a time when he was feeling vulnerable himself—his parents had been recently killed in a car accident and he had been both drawn to and repulsed by his need to keep in contact with his sister because of an insurance settlement, "even though she understands nothing about the kind of life I am trying to carve out for myself."

At least she's consistent, I thought. *Celia was a bitch even back then.* I flipped through the diary, scanned a few paragraphs, and then came to a section where Mack noted that Toby slept peacefully through the night, "not so much as a twitch," Mack wrote, "which made me wonder if he was even alive." This was followed by a day of productivity for Toby, at work on a book he had begun while in graduate school, pounding away at the keys of his old manual typewriter, suddenly suspicious of the new "electric" one Mack had recently bought him. There followed a few more days like this—stretching almost to two weeks—and then there was the entry on May 14, 1977.

Last night Toby dreamed of suicide. I thought we had reached a better place. He had been happy. Intimate. As if he had never become depressed. Things were loving between us again. But the heat was trapped in the room last night, stifling hot and the fan was not able to move any bit of air around. He began with the falling dream, only this time, he said, he had jumped—not been pushed or pulled into a void. I tried to get him to say why he had jumped, but at my questioning he tensed up and would not speak to me. I tried to let it go but his behavior had finally made me angry and upset and I could feel a depression overwhelming me, too. I asked him again why he had jumped and he said because he heard a crying sound. Someone was crying.

I tried to get him to describe the crying more, but he wouldn't and he tried to avoid me. I followed him around the apartment, made him irritated until he told me what he had heard. He said it was a baby. A ghost of a baby who had died in the house about a year before I moved in with him. A downstairs neighbor had brought a sickly baby home from the hospital and it had died in the house. The police had interrogated everyone in the building about any suspicious behavior. Toby denied any involvement in the baby's death, but he said he had been ridiculed when he told a reporter that the house was a notorious haven for ghosts—that no one had taken him seriously—or his work seriously—and now because no one respected him he was hearing her crying—she was trying to taunt him because he could not convince anyone that the ghosts were real.

I asked him if he had seen the baby, or the ghost of the baby, but he said it wasn't a visual experience but a "chilling out-of-body sensation." I told him we needed to make another appointment with Dr. Stephenson; if the nightmares had turned into ghosts then he needed help. More help.

He said that he didn't want the ghosts to go away. That what he was doing was trying to prove that they were real. But he hadn't realized how much pain there was involved. He said he felt like a psychic lightening rod, burning itself up with energy.

I made an appointment for Toby to see Dr. Stephenson again tomorrow. I won't let him go crazy. I won't let him self-destruct. Toby, Toby, we have to get you better.

After this, there was an account of the session the next day with Dr. Stephenson, wherein Toby described his interest in the occult; since his boyhood, Toby had spent afternoons with his aunt, his mother's older sister, who had taught him Voodoo potions and rituals. Toby said he had been raised a Baptist, but that there had always been a Catholic and Voodoo background to his family, with the women in the house talking about love potions to find or bring back a man or how to cure a broken heart. His first supernatural encounter was at the age of eight when he was at the Lafayette Cemetery one afternoon and something—or someone—made an urn topple off a pediment and crash on the pathway in front of him and he narrowly escaped his own death. "The ghost had warned him to stay away," Mack wrote of Toby's adventure. "But it only made him want to remain and find more. That's just the way Toby always was." *Spooked*, I thought. *Like we all were.*

Over the years, Toby had heard stories about ghosts and vampires from other boys, and he knew which houses in town were haunted because he had heard about them for so long. He said he knew firsthand that there were a lot of facts behind all this silliness; an uneasy death always left some kind of stain. By studying these ghosts, these paranormal activities, Toby had learned to address them both realistically and psychically — he had learned how to sense the presence of a ghost whether or not he could actually see it.

I tried to give credence to this sort of incredible power — Dwayne had also hinted that he could sense the presence of a ghost, the same way Parker could tell how much garlic or salt had been put into an entrée. For myself, I could sense the layers of history of a place, particularly of streets and buildings, recognizing the cracks in walls and giant water stains were the results of time and weather and decay, but the supernatural presences seemed elusive to me, unobserved and undetected by any of my senses unless they appeared visually to me, ready to hit me on the head (or whip me on the back). They had a power over me. I didn't possess the gift to find them. They found me. (Lucky *me*.)

Dr. Stephenson addressed Toby's interest in the supernatural as being a way to consciously conquer issues of being different, being scared, being pegged as a sissy boy throughout his childhood. This only irritated Toby further — being called a sissy boy again. He felt he was not a sissy, but smart and studious, as intelligent as any white man who had gotten a scholarship to study archeology to see if the things in the Bible were true. How different was that from what he wanted to do — prove or dispel what haunts and influences us?

The next few entries detailed Toby's increasing visions of ghosts and haunting sounds at the building where they were living—the "balls of light" and the "crying baby" gave way to "slaves running across the courtyard" and screams of "bodies being tortured." Mack never saw or heard any of these things himself, nor did any of his neighbors when he stopped and asked them if they had noticed any unusual occurrences around the property. "I'm beginning to wonder if his nightmares have had some kind of psychiatric impact," he wrote in one entry. "If Toby is not emotionally disturbed but mentally ill."

This chillingly made me wonder if all the booze I had consumed since arriving at the Mouth of the Mississippi had waterlogged my brain and I was a mental case, too, waiting to be institutionalized. Toby persisted in his belief that these hauntings were real, not imaginary or psychotic, particularly as one ghost seemed to haunt him more and more, "the slave girl Angelle," Mack wrote, "who died in this house without attaining her freedom."

5/24/77

Tonight, another dream of Angelle. Toby said that she comes to him full of pain. He dreamed of being whipped, scars crisscrossing his back, his hands and feet shackled by iron chains, a metal yoke around his neck. It was only when he stumbled upright and slowly followed her to a bridge, a strange but beautiful black wrought-iron bridge surrounded by mist, that he was able to shake the pain and find sleep. This morning he confessed that he has also seen the slave girl in the courtyard during his waking hours—a ghostly presence seeking him out, following him up the stairs, watching his movements. At first, he thought she meant him no harm, but yesterday when he went to get a drink, he gagged trying to swallow and when he spit out the water the sink was full of blood, and he was sure it was the slave girl trying to punish him for something that might have happened to her. Now he says that whenever he thinks of me, she is there, in front of him, trying to show him her scars, her hands outstretched, ready to guide him across some elaborately designed bridge to another land.

There followed more sleepless nights. Toby began to see Angelle during the day, not during his dreams, especially "right before a thunderstorm, when the atmosphere is full of humidity and electricity." Another ghost had also taken shape. Another slave. A man who is shoeless and running across the courtyard that Toby had come to believe was Angelle's older brother, Aaron. The similarities with my own paranormal encounters were also a surreal reminder of my recent theological leap of insight. Why hadn't Toby recognized that his passion in ghosts, in all things supernatural, might have been a path to God, not towards danger or death? *Or was I wrong? Was I headed towards falling or leaping or jumping myself?*

Mack wrote of trying to find ways to believe in the ghosts, reading the book Mrs. Mallalieu had given to Toby, Evangeline Dubuisson's slave narrative. He related a conversation he had with Mrs. Mallalieu and her theories on Toby's ghostly sightings (of which she had experienced none herself), though she had confessed to some strange happenings around the property. "Ever since that poor baby died here last year or so, it's been a real sad place. Things just never work right here anymore. The electricity in 2D keeps shorting out, the hot water heater shuts itself off for no reason." She complained of trash everywhere, growing at impossible rates as if it were being blown in from other houses. "She probably wants us all out of the place so she can have it all to herself," Mrs. Mallalieu said. "She can have it if you ask me. I can't even get the tenant's names to stay on the mailboxes."

Mack looked for help from many places—from his professors at Tulane, bringing back books and photocopies of old newspaper articles for Toby to read. Mack also detailed his frustrations with reaching out in his quest to decide if ghosts were real or imaginary, seeking advice again from the priest.

6/2/77

I should have known better than to go back to Father Gerald for advice—he only had one thing on his mind and it was something a little more than just offering comfort. There is no such thing as a ghost in the Bible, he said. The dead go either to Heaven or Hell to await Judgment Day. When I asked Father Gerald if he believed that ghosts exist, if he had ever seen one, he said, "Of course not, no, how could I be a man of God and believe such a thing?" That did not prevent him from hugging me, pressing his cheek against mine, and clutching me a little too long for a man of God to get away with and keep his respect or the respect of a parishioner. I know he wanted me to make the next move, but I felt as if Toby were watching me, waiting for me to fall and give him a reason to end things between us.

How can I believe that he is seeing ghosts when I have never seen one myself, and can't even imagine what it would be like? There are no falling pictures in the apartment, no cracked mirrors, no plates tumbling to the floor. Nothing that leads me to believe that there are ghosts present in our home. I cannot see what he sees and hears. No one can see what he sees and hears.

This evening I tried another approach. Maybe they are not trying to frighten him, but trying to communicate with him. He responded that they are torturing him, trying to make him pay for their sins. They are not talking to him. They are punishing him. His reaction makes me believe the issue is within himself, not with the appearance of ghosts. I think he has decided to drive himself mad. His behavior is spiraling out of control.

Finally, another session with Dr. Stephenson and Toby was put on different medication, this time to treat depression and not insomnia. In the following pages Mack wrote of Toby's continued loss of energy and as I saw him detailing Toby's spiral downward, I understood the guilt Mack must have felt over the part he had played during Toby's final days.

6/9/77

Toby sleeps for hours now, as if he cannot get enough sleep. When he wakes to turn over, to take a drink of water, I ask him if there was anything, anything or anyone in his dreams. He says they are empty now; it's like he's in a deep blackness but he doesn't feel rested, wanting only for me to leave him alone so that he can go back to sleep because he is tired, too tired to stay awake.

As the entries progressed, becoming shorter and shorter now, Mack kept lists of what Toby had eaten during the day, whether or not he was running a fever or felt faint or light-headed before going to sleep, whether or not there had been any strenuous activity (lifting, washing, exercising, and such) throughout the day. And at the bottom of the next page was another chilling moment.

6/14/77

Toby complained of a new dream today and a part of me seemed relieved that he was dreaming again, that his energy might be returning, until he recounted the nightmare. This dream was different from the others. He said this time he was no longer falling, it was as if he were being sucked into a black void

or the deep unhappiness of something. He wanted to cry out
from the pain but he could not speak; something (or someone)
had taken his voice away, as if it had been stolen.

Stolen? That was exactly the kind of dream Parker had complained
about yesterday. The passage made me stand up from the table and close
the composition book. Parker was still sleeping downstairs. I had thought
that Parker was out of harm's way when I returned from the cemetery and
found him still sluggish and sleeping in the back room of the office—what
harm could come to him while I went upstairs with Dwayne and went
through Mack's belongings? Now I believed that I might have left him in
more danger by allowing him to sleep—that the site of the bed in the back
room of our office was most likely the site where Angelle had slept when
she had worked in the household and that whatever sleeping misfortunes
Toby might have experienced could also be happening to Parker.

Dwayne was still reading Evangeline's memoir when I walked through
the front room and opened the apartment door and stepped back out onto
the balcony. This time I did not find my hideously harried doppelganger
waiting for me, but as the sight of the broken railing reminded me first of
Hank's accident and his absence and then Mack's death, I stopped and felt
a strong, swirling motion behind me, as if something were pushing against
my back, a finger prod sending me to the edge. I resisted the urge to step
outside myself, to split my psyche from my body and try to regard my
predicaments in a more detached manner, as I had done before—as if it
were a superhuman technique I had now accepted and mastered and could
do at any moment. The longer I stood and looked down at the courtyard,
I came to believe that I was not so much being pushed as pulled by a cold
force beneath me, as if someone had pointed a monstrous vacuum cleaner
at my feet and I was a stubborn piece of dirt refusing to budge. It felt as

if I were being sucked down, yanked by the shoulders and calves of my legs into a black, miserable unhappiness. Could this be what had caused Hank's accident? Could this be what had caused Toby's death? Could this be what had sent Aaron tumbling over the railing? But what if this was all a part of God's plan? That none of this was accidental? Where was the meaning to all that was happening here?

As I made my way down the exterior staircase I tried to convince myself that Parker was not really in danger, that I had already worked through this issue once and didn't need to revisit it, that this was all just silly coincidence and I was only a highly-strung miserable, old drunk. Surely Parker was just sleeping off the exhaustion of cooking for years and years for ungrateful customers and whatever had really plagued and troubled Toby was not the same as what was tiring Parker. And if it were some part of a divine plan, how could I stop it? With prayer? *What could a prayer do to help us out now?*

When I reached the bottom stairs and stepped onto the courtyard, however, I broke into a light run, or, rather, at my excessive weight and heft I moved with a sort of farcical skip across the bricks.

Inside the front room of the office, I took in the blinking light of the answering machine, the newly arrived fax that waited in a tray of the printer to be read, and the dark, blank, turned-off computer screen. The door to the back room was closed and I grabbed the doorknob, expecting to be jolted with a highly-charged electrical current or met with the force of hurricane-like winds when I turned it and opened the door. I was ready to battle whatever ghostly or divine messenger materialized if it meant saving Parker. Instead, I was greeted by an empty bed. Parker was not in the room, the bed had been tidied and made up, the bedspread tight and flat against the mattress, the pillows plumped and tilted as if they had not been used for days.

I tried to think of the best possible scenario, that Parker was safe and about somewhere, possibly at work again in the café, but my imagination found a worse and more unfortunate fate for him. What had happened to Parker in the hour or so Dwayne and I had been upstairs in Mack's apartment? Was he, too, now at the hospital? Had I missed hearing another ambulance arrive and cart him away? Had I been too absorbed in finding out the reasons for my ghosts to worry about Parker?

I looked around the room for a message from Parker, but there was nothing on the bed or the small dresser in the room, and then I went into the office and looked for some kind of note. When I found nothing there, either, I stopped and listened to the messages on the answering machine, but there were only two of them, both from nervous-sounding customers requesting future reservations.

Outside, the light purple colors of twilight were now settling against the bricks and furniture and fountain of the courtyard and, as I was headed towards the back door of the café's kitchen, I noticed a lamp shining in the second floor apartment window, the window behind which Parker and I had once lived together during our blissful, early years together as a couple of fools in love, which I had relinquished to Parker and his newer boyfriends. As I made my way back to the enclosed stairwell to see if Parker had gone upstairs to the apartment, I heard a high-pitched laugh hitting and spilling around the enclosed space of the courtyard. It was a woman's laugh and it seemed to be taunting me as I walked across the bricks—at one point far away and then the next right against my earlobe. *Yes, I was going crazy. No, there was no God. But if I believed there was, could I pray and all would be forgiven? Could we simply get on with our lives?*

The woman's laughter grew louder as I made my way up the creaking wooden stairs—and I would have been certain that it was Angelle's laugh were it not for another voice—a second, darker, more alto-pitched tone,

but also certainly a woman's laugh—followed by a third, fainter laugh—
the low, heavy, heave of a man's guttural laugh. By the time I reached the
French doors of the second-floor apartment it sounded like the laughter
was coming from inside the building and only lightly passing through the
panes of glass. As I pressed my ear to the door, I detected a faint smell of
something burning and all at once assumed that Charlie Ray must have
returned, cigarette in hand, and that he had roused Parker and they had
come upstairs to their apartment for a quick sexual reunion. I twisted the
doorknob of the French doors, again expecting some kind of electrical
jolt or hurricane wind to greet me, or at least the bitter smell of Charlie
Ray's unfiltered cigarette smoke. Instead, as the door pushed open, I found
Parker seated at his small dining table with a lit cigar in his left hand.
Lynette and Talla were seated on either side of him and the room was full
of a bitter, hazy stench.

"There you are, hon," Talla said, her bright red-painted lips forming a
wide circle of surprise. "We're just doing a little cleansing ritual here."

"Smells like you're stinking up the place," I answered her, feeling
cynical and adolescent. My eyes met Parker's and I sensed that he was not
in whatever danger zone I had imagined him to be in, but I was also not
the kind of guy to let him off the hook so easily. "At least you woke the
resident zombie up," I said looking directly at him. Parker had even shaved
and was wearing a clean T-shirt and shorts, his scraggly rim of hair damp,
perhaps the result of a recent shower.

Talla rose from her chair, swept across the room, and embraced me,
engulfing me in a cloud of honeysuckle-scented perfume, her jewelry
accessories jangling as she tried to hug me with a strength I wouldn't forget.
"We're sure sorry about Mack," she said and squeezed me again. "You've
got some mighty strong spirits around here, that's for sure. Now, you need
to take a puff of this, too, darlin'. You probably need this more than Parker

does. I should've come around here earlier and I bet that I could have saved poor ole Hank some of that hurtin' he must feel right now." She released me from her bear hold and took the cigar out of Parker's hand and stretched it out towards me. "Now go ahead, only you have to do it backwards. The lit end goes in your mouth."

"Whatever are you talking about?" I answered her, a rush of nausea at the back of my throat as the sweetness of her perfume met the stench of the cigar. I knew Talla detected the annoyance in my voice because I saw Lynette's reaction as she arched one of her eyebrows to display her own disapproval of my response to her lover.

"Just try it," Lynette said, her eyes bulging wide to let me know I should just play the game and see it through to the end and not be a difficult contestant. "What harm can it do to you? If it helps things out, well, all the better."

"What harm can it do me?" I asked, my annoyance rising. Talla always seemed to be treading a fine line between the metaphysical and outrageous kink. "You want me to put the lit end of a cigar in my mouth to help me out?"

"It's to help purify you," Talla said. "It'll make it a little easier for us talk to the spirits."

"Are you crazy?"

"Sit down," Parker said in a small but stern voice and I shot him a quizzical look that silently questioned who had suddenly voted him to be the alpha male. "We're going to have a séance."

"A séance?" I said back to him. "Are you out of your mind?"

"No," he answered. "And we're only trying to keep you from losing yours."

"We're concerned about you," Lynette said. "And don't worry, this is not an intervention, but when we saw you at the cemetery you looked like a tulip being pissed on by a great dane. You didn't even come over to us so, of course, we're going to find out what's going on. We're here to help you. Lorda mercy, Avery, you've been our *ahijado* for like forever."

"Sweetie, a proper cleansing takes a good week—fasting and covering the body with salt and herbs and such," Talla said. "But I fear we're short of time here. And we don't want to make ourselves too vulnerable to the spirits. Too much spiritual preparation and we could all end up inebriated, you know, talking like we're a bunch of silly ole gals at a Tupperware party. Or worse—possessed like that poor young thing in that scary, scary movie that I certainly walked out of when I was a little girl because I just couldn't believe such a thing could happen to anyone and watching that stream of pea green vomit was just too much even for me. It's a rather delicate balance, you know, communing with the spirits. And there's a great deal of unrest about this place. Parker's already told us all about your seeing ghosts and the unfortunate incident in the pantry."

I blushed deeply, out of embarrassment and confusion. By "pantry" I felt certain Talla was referring to my rather swift and indiscreet encounter with Griffin, which had played itself over and over in my consciousness like a videotape. "How did you know about the pantry?" I asked Parker.

"You told me last night," Parker said. "You know, while we were... in bed." He slid something across the table for me to see and I realized it was the knife, the knife I had discovered beneath the planks of the pantry floor and had hidden in the refrigerator. They were not referring to my encounter with Griffin at all but my discovery of the knife.

"I don't remember what I told you."

"See," Lynette said, a bit too quickly. "You need us more than you think."

"We're convinced that you're living in a thin place," Talla added. "A special place where the visible and invisible worlds are at their closest proximity to each other. It's an old Celtic belief that even the early Christians recognized. It's why many monasteries were built in such lofty, holy places—at the border between two worlds."

"We were just explaining it to Parker," Lynette said.

"In certain places, at certain hours, with certain people, certain things can be seen," Talla added.

"And what do you expect a séance to accomplish?" I asked.

Talla drew her chin towards her neck then tilted it upwards, as if to indicate I had asked another foolish question of her. "Well, I think we need to talk to the spirits to see what they want from you."

"I'm afraid I already know that," I answered. "They want to be free—free of this house, of history, of having to commune with idiots like us."

"You need to have a little more positive energy if we are to be successful with the spirits," Talla said. "They are only waiting for us to contact them. They long for forgiveness and peace and need a living person to ask what the trouble is and offer help. It's as simple as that."

She gathered up a deck of cards from in front of her and I noticed that they had indeed set the room up for a séance. The lights had been dimmed—the lamp I had noticed on near the window was barely glowing. Three white candles on the table had been lit, alongside three large coins; Talla wore several beaded necklaces and had on a yellow turban with a sparkling brooch at the center, as if it might help her sensitive brainwaves communicate better with the more gentle spirits she was hoping to invoke. How she was going to handle a household of angry slaves, I had no idea. She flipped over several cards and laid them in front of her, using the *rap-rap-rap* of her long, painted fingernails to show that she might be thinking—*deeply*—about something.

"Is this a reading or a séance?" I asked.

"Hush," she said. "It helps the reception."

She placed her fingertips against one of the cards. "The Page of Wands," she said. "You're in some kind of danger."

"Of being considered a fool, that's for sure," I said.

"You must be positive if this is to work," she said, shooting me an annoyed glance.

"Is it because of the knife?" Lynette asked "Should we return the knife to the place it belongs?"

"You're not serious, are you?" I asked Lynette. I couldn't believe that she had become a willing participant in this nonsense her girlfriend was unleashing on us—no, *me*. Yes, I was certain I had ghosts, but no, I didn't believe they wanted to talk to any of us, particularly Talla. But then again, I did think that I was going crazy. Or at least on my way to becoming a mad, screw-lose old man who at any moment would start mumbling to himself.

Talla fluttered her eyelids, tilted her head back and let out a deep, mournful and showy, "Yesssss." She popped her eyes open and leaned forward as if to press her breasts against the tabletop. "We must all join hands in a circle to contain our energy."

Parker stared at me until I acquiesced and sat down at the end of the table beside Talla. I let out a deep and dramatic sigh and placed my palms on the table so that my fingertips touched Lynette's on my left and Talla's on my right, feeling as uncomfortable as if I had been unexpectedly drawn into a conservative prayer group hell-bent on ridding the world of people exactly like us.

"Clear your mind and level your breathing," Talla said in a calm voice, as if we were now part of a meditation class. "Feel the energy and the emptiness about us until it begins to take shape. Imagine the shape before you and not at your back. Keep the energy within your sight until it manifests itself out of the darkness."

Lynette and Parker had been sitting with their eyes closed and Lynette fluttered her eyelids open and whispered to me to close my eyes. I did so reluctantly and we sat in silence for an awkward moment, then, for more dramatic effect, Talla shifted the tone of her voice to the highest possible moan she could make and still be heard by human ears. As her voice fell octave after octave after octave and then returned to its normal register, she began to describe "the energy before her."

"A girl," Talla said. "Dark. Big eyes. Very unhappy. And a red glow around her. She is very dangerous. No...she's misunderstood. She's dangerous because she's misunderstood. She knows nothing of the knife. The knife means nothing to her."

"Who does the knife belong to?" Lynette asked.

"Someone full of guilt," Talla answered. "Guilt surrounds the knife. And its owner. But he is protecting us. He is the protector. And surrounded by shadows. There is a stronger shadow at his back. Another man. Another shadow protecting him. The young girl swirls around them as if she knows them or is trying to confuse us."

There was another moment of silence and then Talla said, "No. The knife is his but not his. It was a gift. The knife was never intended to bring harm but to please. It was a gift."

I felt a tingle at my arms, aware that Talla had uncovered within a few minutes a simplistic version of the background that had taken me two days to unravel. The coincidence caused me to be aware of the feverish heat of my skin and the coldness of the air about me, as if I had been sitting in the draft of the air conditioner (which I wasn't). I felt the shifting shapes of gray and purple beneath my eyelids slide into a deeper blackness, as if I had fallen asleep. My heart was beating stronger than normal and I tried not to be alarmed by the pounding of it inside my rib cage, but after a minute or two I felt the same clutch inside my chest that I had felt the night before on the courtyard and I fluttered my eyelids and let out a gasp. Before my closed eyes the colors changed, purples into blues that lightened into paler and paler versions until it was white and then yellowish and next became the reddish eyes that I had seen in the pantry. I felt another clutch at my chest, as if a human hand were squeezing the muscle of my heart, and the pain of it forced my eyes open and I stood up from my chair, breaking the circle of hands of the séance. Lynette and Talla and Parker were still seated, their eyes closed, unaware that I had broken free; once again, time seemed stopped, frozen—their chests were not even rising with breaths. Now, out of the dim light of the room, the energy swirled and swirled into bright sequins of light which gradually took the form of Griffin, the darkly dressed Griffin, his skin pale and luminescent and now emitting all of the light in the room. He moved across the room towards me, floating as he had done before, and this time I spoke to him without moving my lips, since I had recognized that he was the embodiment of my conscience and he no longer needed to "hear" my voice.

"That was a rather showy entrance, if you ask me," I said.

"You were expecting?"

"Well, a ghost, not an internal manifestation of my psyche."

"Rather spooky, nonetheless, if you ask me," he said. "You have to admit, she has some talent."

"And you interrupted her right at the good point," I said. "I wanted to hear what they have to say to her. Or through her. Or *whatever.*"

"Have you learned nothing?" he said. "Ghosts don't speak. They do not say things through people—or mediums or at séances—that they did not say during their lifetimes. They are here to remind us of our pasts—the things we've learned or the things we've forgotten. They are only repeating their history to us. They are not talking to us. Their *actions* are speaking to us."

"Then how can I help them?"

"Help them? Or help yourself?"

"Well, get things back to normal," I said. "Or just back to where we were before they began to disrupt things. How do I make them go away?"

"You can never make them go away," Griffin said. "History does not leave us. But when you understand history, when you understand their actions, the balance of the present will naturally return."

"So what do I do?" I asked.

"Use your whole body as a tool to do what is right...."

"For the glory of God," I finished for him. "I know the passage. Romans 6:13. Then you're a messenger from God. Or are you *God?*"

"If that is who you wish me to be. I have been called many things."

I didn't know if I should kneel or bow, if what he said was true, but since he was a part of me, from the deepest core of myself, I did neither and asked instead, "So, what do I do? Do I just have to wait and see, is that it? Any more clues? I could use some help here, you know. If I'm to serve some kind of purpose. This body I've got isn't in the greatest sort of shape if it's got to be a *tool.*"

"It is all before you now," he said. "You only need to remember."

I felt another clutch at my chest and I doubled myself to hold the pain inside. When I righted my body and lifted my eyes up again, Griffin was gone, the room was dark and I was seated at the table, my spread fingertips still touching those of Talla and Lynette, as if I had never moved away. "There is great love here," Talla said. "This is a house full of love but it is clouded with sadness and pain. We must accept the sadness and return to the love. The energy of the love of this house. Love must rule this house again."

Now, with my eyes still open, the darkness of the room began to shift and change into shapes again. Soon, it did not seem as if I were in one room of the house but in all rooms of both buildings of the main house and the old slave quarters, the soft glowing lamp of the apartment was present, but so was the glow of the computer screen of the office and the dark purple bedspread of the Burgundy Suite and the mirror over the dresser of the Royal Suite. Slowly, into all these places came the shapes of beings — first, a leg or a neck or a foot or a forearm; then another leg and a chest and a thigh and a shoulder. Not all of the limbs and body parts belonged to men, but the men were in the foreground, as if the curves of breasts and hips and collarbones of women had been reduced and blurred and placed just out of my vision. The room widened and the shapes began to assemble into arrangements of bodies — nude bodies, bodies of men moving against each other, groping and clutching and brushing and holding hands and thighs and shoulders and groins, as if I were standing on a balcony overlooking the unfolding of an orgy. Slowly more and more specific details fell into place — triceps and thighs and cocks and buttocks, freckles and roots and scars and birthmarks and pigments of skin — and then body parts began to distinguish themselves not as a group, but as individuals. As each man's shape came into view it was clear that he was not alone but a part of a pair, couples of men were kissing or hugging or sucking or dancing or fucking. Into all this action floated the memory of history and the couples became people or situations I knew. Over there, by the rug and the fire were Mack and Toby during the first year of their relationship — and over there, in the old bed with the gold fabric headboard were Mack and Parker the night they met. And there I was with Parker too, the night he moved in with me in this apartment, and there we were again, older, heavier, as we were the night before, struggling to arouse each other but surrounded by a golden aura that seemed present everywhere now in this large room. Into all of this flowed the couplings of Dwayne and Buddy, José and Kaku, even the two crotchety gentlemen who had recently rented the Royal Suite. I was filled with a great sense of power, as if I were seeing Time as God saw it. But I did not understand why it was in front of me. Soon, I realized I was no longer standing on the balcony but moving through the space like a goldfish in water, swimming from the foreground into the background, finding men and bodies and shapes that I had no memory of until I came to a pair of young men, one light skinned, the other dark, and stood over them and watched them sleep in each other's arms. Just as I was trying to make out the details of their faces, just as I had recognized that this was a vision of Aaron and Pierre, I felt a presence watching me now—at first, it seemed to dart out of my view, as if a bird, startled, were flying higher to another branch. Then I felt a shadow move over me, circling me, and the shapes in front of me were beginning to change. No longer were they of men having sex, arms and legs and thighs being caressed by hands and kissed by lips, but they were bodies full of scars, puffy and tender, full of scabs and puss and pain. I tried to avert my eyes, tried to follow the shadow that was now circling around me and give it detail. Just as the old, threadbare fabric of a dress fell into view and I recognized the face of the woman I had seen in the reflection of the water of the courtyard fountain, I heard a hard rapping sound inside my skull—a sort of rattling noise as if windowpane were being tapped against. The rapping continued and the images swiftly broke apart and I was again seated at the table. As the room of the apartment and the table and the candles came back into recognition, I saw that Parker had broken the circle, stood up from his chair and was walking towards the French doors of the balcony where the rapping sound was coming from.

He opened the door and there stood Celia, so clearly in the structure of her face and posture Mack's sister, but more deliberately in her annoyed expression her own different, greedy and unhappy version of the same genetic background.

"I hope I'm not intruding," she said, as she glanced into the room. "But I wanted to resolve the issue of whether I should arrange for the sale of this building before I leave tomorrow morning and what sort of timing would work for everyone if a new owner wanted you to vacate."

Six

The hardest thing about believing in the existence of a spirit world of troubled souls and wandering phantoms is not so much convincing yourself of the presence of ghosts sharing your living space, but convincing those around you that you have not lost your sanity (or, in my particular instance, sobriety). If I had my choice of spirits I'd chose the bottled kind any day over a spooky one, though the former can be just as deadly as the latter; I never once believed that any of my heavy-duty on-the-job drinking was the catalyst for all this paranormal activity. But I was the only one witnessing the resident poltergeists at our particular address on Dumaine Street and the precious fate of my mental health lay not entirely in my own mind or even in the hands of my otherworldly companions, but depended on the gracious acceptance and generosity of the real folks who had to convince themselves that I was truthfully being haunted. Luckily, I live in what is considered today one of the most haunted cities of the planet, if there *are* such things as people seeing ghosts. And even as things began to fall further apart and I began to question my own sanity and future, I never lost faith that somehow the natural order of things could be restored. But it was a surprise to me, nonetheless, that it was Parker—sleepy, cranky, I'm-just-tired-of-it-all-right-now Parker—who shifted the downward flow of the random order of our little universe into the opposite direction when he broke the circle of the séance, stood up from the table, and met Celia at the French doors of the balcony. "Sell this place?" Parker said to her, after she had asked whether or not she should try to sell our home. "Honey, the market here is just never as strong as it is elsewhere in the country. This kind of space and old world charm would get us a couple of million for sure if we were in New York or Los Angeles. But this is N'awlins, darlin'. We're nothing but a charming dump."

I was appalled that Parker could hear Celia lay claim to both our home and businesses and not immediately refute her bid for it, but I was also aware that Parker T. Steinberg was not a confrontational man and if he were going to set her straight he would do so gradually and politely as any converted Southern gentleman would. "Avery and I could never get back what we've invested in this place," he added. "We've *depreciated*. No one repays you for the sweat and tears and lousy backs and dishwater hands from all the hard work."

Lynette and Talla had begun to talk softly at their end of the table, Talla laying out her tarot cards in a row in front of her and tapping her fingernail vigorously against one in particular. I just knew she was trying to predict the outcome of this conversation and wanting nothing to do with such nonsense, I ignored her. I stood up from my chair and joined Parker and Celia near the doors, ready to fight but not willing to argue myself. "I wouldn't think you would even be interested in a run-down place like this," I said, hoping to discourage her. "We're having a bit of a paranormal problem at the moment. Ghosts and all."

Celia arched her left eyebrow at my news and said, "I would think that would make it more valuable. Particularly in a city known for its ghosts."

"I would think there would be advantages," Parker said. "And disadvantages. Right now, I think our ghosts might have the upper hand on us."

"Then you've seen them?" I asked, suddenly more concerned about what Parker had witnessed than the possibility that Celia would pull the rug out from under us.

"I didn't say that," he said. "You said that."

"We're in a bit in a pickle, Miss Celia," I said, trying to be charming and not to let my annoyance with Parker show. "One rather nasty spirit wants to take the house away from us. Can I get you a drink?"

Celia shook her head no, her eyes wide and delighted at our predicament, the dollar signs literally floating to the surface of her irises. She stood by the doorway with her feet slightly apart, her hands folded across her breasts, as if she were tempting us to try and knock her down. Or out.

"But it's not hers to give away," Parker said. "So, of course, we're going to have to fight and find a way around her. We're very proud of this place, in spite of it falling down on top of us." He gave me a sort of "A-ha! There-you-go!" look and used his right hand to push the French doors open and lead Celia outside onto the balcony with a slight brush of his big palm against her tiny shoulder. "Did you try any of the specials that José made tonight?"

Again, she shook her head no and I stood behind them, all of our gazes directed at the splashing water of the fountain and the beautifully illuminated plants and bricks of the courtyard below us. At that moment I actually prayed for a ghost to appear, to scare the hell out of all of us and send Celia packing and out of our lives. Of course, there was not a specter to be found when you really wanted one, when it would really have been useful to have an unearthly visitor, and the night was lovely and dark and enchanting, with just a bit of a breeze going. Racing through my mind were all of the unaccomplished tasks for the day, from the unconfirmed reservations to the unstocked toiletries. And then there was Hank. I needed to find out how he was doing. I felt my patience with it all disappearing again, evaporating into the darkness.

"We barely had dinner," Celia said to Parker. "The boys wanted beignets. They stuffed themselves full and then turned cranky from all the sugar. Stuart's downstairs, trying to get them to sleep."

"Come taste the sausage and grits," Parker said to her. "José's got a magic touch with it. It's as hot and spicy as anything you'll find in the Quarter."

I'd always considered myself lucky that Parker was more even-tempered than myself. Had it been me alone, I might have pushed Celia over the balcony and just told the police, "Whoops, I guess it was just another spooky accident in a chain of spooky accidents." Celia followed Parker down the staircase and he withdrew a chair for her at the courtyard table and motioned for her to sit, while I went through the back door of the café and asked José to make us some small tasting plates of his entrées for the night. I tried to make a light joke to Kaku, who was up to his forearms in dishwater, for agreeing to help José out in the kitchen, remarking that even vegetarians had to wash out messy meaty pots every now and then, but he gave me a scowl, or a look that I took to be a faux-scowl, when he lifted the corners of his lips into a smile. (*Ah, at least someone still has a sense of humor around this place,* I thought. *Maybe we should work out a way for Kaku to stick around more often.*) Next Buddy came in through the swinging dining room door and placed an order on the counter for José and nodded hello to me. "Full house tonight, Mister D," he said. "You don't mind if Dwayne eats something at the bar, do you?"

"Of course not," I answered him, glad to see that Dwayne had found his way out of Mack's apartment for a break. While José was preparing the plates, I followed Buddy back into the dining room and opened a bottle of wine. Dwayne was seated on a bar stool, a tumbler of something in front of him and his head bowed towards a file folder of newspaper clippings he was reading, most likely something else uncovered from Mack's apartment.

He had a calm, satisfied look about him, as if he'd just had an incredible sexual experience, and I immediately wondered if he had abandoned Mack's buried treasures to fool around a few minutes with Buddy. Dwayne lifted his eyes up to me as I reached for some clean wineglasses and we nodded to each other, colleagues in arms; we'd both learned a lot about the history and mishaps of the property that day and we were now soldiers in a new war.

"I'd completely forgotten about this," he said, indicating the paper he was reading. "It was the stuff Parker showed me when I first asked him about the history of the place a few months ago when I was putting together the walking tour. He'd put it behind the mirror after I was done with it."

"You don't happen to see the deed to the property in there, do you?" I asked Dwayne, realizing the moment the question escaped my mouth that Parker must have filed the deed away the same way he had filed away the old file of newspaper clippings—behind something else, tucked away for a moment until he thought of another, better place for it—and then just forgotten about it.

"I always liked this one," Dwayne said, "about the baby and the wolf."

"*What?*" I asked him a bit too suspiciously. "*What do you mean?*"

He lifted up a yellowed newspaper clipping and handed it over the counter to me. The story was dated June 26, 1975, and it read:

Police Drop Investigation
Father Blames Wolf for Infant's Death

Homicide detectives have dropped their investigation into the June death of a fourteen-day-old infant, the New Orleans Police Department reported Friday.

"We don't suspect any foul play," police spokesman Detective Mitchell Rebeiro said.

The baby had been born with severe medical problems and died June 23 of natural causes at the home of its parents, Rebeiro said. A source close to the investigation said that the baby was breathing on his own and wasn't ill and that the father said he saw a strange animal present in the room moments before the baby's death. The animal was described as dog- or wolf-like, with white hair or fur and a large snout and bright red eyes.

A source identified the infant as Sante Vassallo, the son of Anthony and Meredith Vassallo. Rebeiro and Catherine Martinez, public information officer for the medical center where the infant was pronounced dead, would not confirm the details of the father's account or the names of the infant or his parents.

The Vassallos did not return telephone calls seeking information.

Martinez issued a brief statement Thursday about the death:

"Because we do not have the parents' permission to discuss the details of this case, we have no further information to provide at this time." A source close to the investigation reported that there were no unnatural marks, bruises, cuts, or swellings present on the infant's body which might have caused the death.

Residents at the building where the Vassallos live speculated on the details surrounding the infant's death. "No one in the building owns a dog or a wolf that could have crept into the room," Marian Mallalieu, the building's owner, said. "I don't allow pets in the building."

Toby Ridenour, another resident of the building, said that the baby's crying could be heard in the building's rear courtyard and "might have woken up some of our resident spirits."

Ridenour, a graduate psychology student at Tulane, said he had spent the last two years studying the history of paranormal activity in the French Quarter. "Accounts of strange wolf-like animals in and around New Orleans have been noted since the colonists arrived," Ridenour said. "And there are the legends that they brought with them, like the loup garou."

The French colonists arrived with the myth of the loup garou or werewolf-beings of half-man and half-wolf, called rougarou by the Cajuns, Ridenour explained.

"The Irish had the Banshees and the Phooka. Voodoo cults had the Loa gods and shape-shifters. And after many years they all began to blend together," Ridenour said.

Ridenour has researched the paranormal activity of several locations in the French Quarter and hopes to compile his findings into a book. "In the mid-eighteenth century this particular property was often seen by residents as one of the gateways to the otherworld of the dead," Ridenour noted about the building where he lives. "This house has a long history of deaths from yellow fever or untimely illnesses and had been the site of one of the original cemeteries used by the first settlers, before the bodies had been relocated to the St. Louis Cemetery."

Ridenour, who occupies the apartment above the Vassallos, explained that the infant's father had been interested in the history of the building but had scoffed at the notion of there being resident ghosts.

"Some days you can feel the energy of one world pulling you through to the next," Ridenour said. "Many mourners believed that departing souls would be met by a wolf and escorted away to make the journey easier, much like the legend of Cerberus at the gates of Hades."

Detective Rebeiro would not speculate on the activity of poltergeists at the site of the infant's death or of the father's

mental state at the time of the infant's death. Martinez said
hospital officials would also not comment on the report of the
father's sighting of a "wolf-like creature." The hospital declined
to release medical records of the infant.

I placed the article on the counter and thought, *Just as things were
getting better, now I find this out—we're living on top of what was once hallowed
ground. A cemetery. Of course we're being haunted. Of course I'm seeing ghosts.
It all makes sense to me now. We're living at the gateway to the world of the dead.
And the wolf was the escort of souls, to keep away the fear of moving from one
world to the next. I saw the wolf only minutes before I learned of Mack's death.
Now it's all starting to make sense. Sort of.*

I tried not to act too disturbed as I gathered up the glasses and the
bottle of wine. I was sharing my home with the undead. Ghosts. Phantoms.
Poltergeists. Dead babies. *Wolves.* "Do you talk about this on your tour?"
I asked Dwayne.

"About the baby?" he answered. "No, not anymore. I did a few times
and it got the women very upset, so I stopped."

"The cemetery?" I asked. "Do you mention that this was the site of one
of the original cemeteries?"

"Of course," he said. "I remember Mack told me about it first, before
I ever saw the clipping. He said he knew it when he bought the building.
Said it was part of the quirkiness of the place."

Why didn't I know this? I thought, making my way through the dining
room. *How could this have escaped me?* The Gateway of the Dead. The
Doorway to Another World. A cemetery. It was too impossible to believe,
and yet I needed something just like this at this very moment to back up
my recent experiences.

Outside, at the courtyard table, I put the wineglasses down and poured Parker and Celia drinks. Celia was talking about ghosts now. Mack's ghosts. It was too surreal to believe and too genuine to disbelieve.

"I was here one weekend when he was in school," Celia said. "No. It was after his graduation and he had moved in here with Tommy— no, Toby—that was the guy's name. Of course, I thought they were just roommates, but Mack wouldn't let me stay here and I always thought it was because he didn't want me to find out about him and Toby. He said there were all sorts of problems going on here—no hot water for a spell, the electricity was out. And that there was a baby that cried all the time and I would never get any sleep. I told him that it probably wouldn't bother me, but he said it would because the baby wasn't alive. He said it was a ghost of a dead baby. I thought it was the silliest thing I ever heard of until I heard it for myself one afternoon when I came over to find him. I was staying at a rooming house on Esplanade he had found for me. Of course I learned everything about Mack that day. That he was living with Toby and they were more than just roommates. We had started in on a fight—I asked him how could he do this, told him that Mom and Dad would never have allowed it to happen if he were living closer to home. He said that things were different, especially since Mom and Dad were dead, so what did it matter? And then the baby started up crying. Screaming something just awful. It was about two in the afternoon when it began, then it stopped about forty minutes later. It was very upsetting. It wasn't the crying of a healthy baby. It was a baby screaming for comfort. That whole day was so unpleasant. I know I must have been too sensitive to everything around me because we had just lost our parents and Mack's boyfriend just seemed so weirded out—like he was on drugs or something. It was just awful. An awful time."

"Mack knew a lot about our ghosts," I said to Celia. "Apparently we're on the site of the cemetery of the original settlement."

I glanced at Parker but he did not flinch at my revelation, which meant he had been aware of it all the time, probably for years and years and years and years. I tried to hold my irritation inside, but he glanced at me and arched an eyebrow, as if to say, *So? So what? I've known that for years and years and years, you silly old fool!*

"I think I remember his friend telling me about that," Celia said. "It was very long ago. It was all a part of a book he was writing. I was always uneasy when I was around him. He was a very pretty boy, the kind of guy who never grows up, which is why I never liked him too much, but he was always acting so strange. I know that is a silly reason to dislike someone, isn't it? I remember the night Mack called to tell me he had died. I said, 'Well, at least you can get out of that dump and come back home.' That's when he told me he was buying the building. I still find it shocking he actually paid money for this place. And now it's mine. I'm not sure what to do with it because I knew it meant so much to him."

"I'm afraid it's not yours to decide," Parker said. "Mack sold us the building more than a decade ago. It's why we started up the café and the guesthouse."

"But he never mentioned this to me," Celia said. "Why didn't he tell me?"

"Perhaps he was too proud of the place to admit that he had sold it," Parker said. "Or too proud to admit that he had to sell it to survive. Avery and I framed the bill of sale and hung it over the kitchen grills. It's right there, if you want to inspect it, right next to all our licenses and inspection certificates."

Of course, that's where it was. Why hadn't I remembered this? I excused myself to check on the plates of food. In the kitchen, José was now demonstrating to Kaku how to carve a radish into a flower, his crotch pressed against Kaku's ass as he reached around his boyfriend to work on the counter. They regarded me as if I had intruded on an intimate moment (which I obviously had) and I glanced to the wall above the grills and there it was, the deed, the glass frame splattered with grease and sauces and who knows what else—the living toil of our day-to-day lives, no doubt. I felt suddenly pleased but tired, exhausted, as if every problem had suddenly been solved, when only one was out of the way. I felt a heaviness move through my body, my arms stayed at my side, my shoulders rounded, my knees locked and my feet froze in place. It seemed, now, as if time had stopped my body and I was conscious of not being able to move any part of it—or to find the energy or the desire to want to move any part of it—yet the movement continued in the room around me, without me—Kaku laughing, José grinding and carving, the gas flame of the stove flickering, the meat and oil simmering and cackling, the second hand of the wall clock circling with a *tick-tick-tick*.

That was when she appeared before me. Angelle. One minute she had not been there and the next moment she was, as visible and solid a form as José and Kaku. There was a look of despair to her, her clothes seemed ragged, threadbare, torn as if they had once been ripped off of her and hastily put back on to defend her modesty. Her hairline was visible beneath a dimly striped scarf, her eyes large and moist, and around her neck she wore several beads and amulets threaded through dark string, including the crucifix similar to one I had seen earlier in the upstairs room. In her hands she held an envelope that she was trying to hand to me. *Of course,* I thought, *she must have worked in the kitchen.* The café's kitchen had also been the kitchen of the original Dubuisson house. And the letter inside the envelope must have been how Angelle had hoped to receive her freedom.

At my feet the floor tiles of the kitchen began to brighten, a mass of tiny, flickering lights rising to my ankles. Next, I was no longer in the kitchen, but in a bright, empty, cloudy place. The cloudy mass of glittering light at my feet moved as if blown by wind, a bright current of cottony substance headed towards a white stucco wall and a black gate which remained closed, causing the mass to circle back and swirl again at my feet. Beyond the wall and the gate was a bridge, tall, dark, looming, reminding me of what Mack and Toby had described seeing.

But the gate that led to the bridge was locked; nothing—or no one—was capable of reaching it. I tried to move my feet and realized that I was no longer pinned in place and could walk about freely, so I walked to the large, black iron doors and shook them, but they would not open; the lock on the gates was surrounded by a chain held by another lock. Kaku and José and the kitchen equipment had disappeared with the rising lights, but Angelle was standing beside the locked gate, pleading, exactly as she had appeared to me in the kitchen. She dropped to her knees, her elbows barely visible in the cloudy light, her head bent towards the ground as if to ask for forgiveness.

If she wasn't responsible for Pierre's death, I thought next, *then she must fear that she might be, that even if she did not kill him, her actions might have contributed to his death. Maybe this is why she is not at peace.*

I knelt, sinking into the cloudy mass of white light, and was once again in front of Angelle. I reached out to where her hands were, clasped them within my own, and bowed my head and said a prayer. *Please Lord, forgive her. She asks for forgiveness for her part in Pierre's death.*

When I lifted my head I noticed that her shape was changing. She was no longer cold and solid and fleshy, but brighter, transparent, and her form continued to thin and disappear. Her expression changed into one of relief, then astonishment, then gratitude. When she had disappeared completely into a small cloud of light, I realized I was no longer on my knees but standing, and no longer in this cloud-like limbo outside the locked black gate but back in the crazy activity of the kitchen with José and Kaku, who showed no indication that they had witnessed the ghost of Angelle or her transformation. *So a prayer worked,* I thought. *A simple prayer is all that it takes. Have faith. Keep God a part of your life and He will keep you a part of His.*

The spell broke as if I had emerged from underwater, prompting a coughing jag that stopped José's seduction of his boyfriend long enough for him to pat me on the back and ask if I were all right. I nodded and said that I needed Kaku to help me carry out the trays of food to the courtyard table, but I was not in the least bit hungry and didn't wish to join Celia, so I took two plates up the staircase and brought them to Lynette and Talla, who were still sitting at the dining room table in Parker's apartment.

"Everything, okay, hon?" Talla asked, when I opened the door. "We wanted to stay outta the way for a bit, you know."

"We're not gonna be evicted," I said. "At least not by Celia. I think she understands that the place is ours. But I could use your help with something else that is troubling me."

"What is it, sweetie?" Talla asked, pleased that I had, possibly for the first time, turned to her for assistance. Lynette took a fork and sampled the sausage, flapped her hand in front of her mouth when she found it spicier than she expected, and I went to the kitchen to fetch her a glass of water. "What can we do?" Talla yelled through the rooms.

"I'm confused," I began, returning with the glasses and setting them on the table. "Are you religious or superstitious?"

"What do you mean, hon?" Talla asked, only long enough to meet my gaze and then swallow a gulp of water.

"What God do you believe in? Which is the right one?"

"There is no right one or wrong one," Lynette answered for her girlfriend, while Talla furrowed her brow and caught her breath—she had just sampled a bit of José's spicy sausage dish.

She tapped the corner of her mouth with her napkin and then said, "Well, I've sort of cobbled something together that works for me. *Us*."

"A cafeteria spiritualist?"

"You can call it that, hon."

"How do you know one god is better than the other?"

"Better?" Talla asked.

"You mean are we monotheistic?" Lynette asked.

"I look at it like this." Talla laid her fork down against the rim of the plate. "Why do I like pink better than green? I just do. I think I look better in pink than I do in green. I think there are some parts of religion that fit me better than others—makes me feel more worthy and worthwhile—but in the end? Who knows in the end? The end is a mystery. And that's what we're only trying to understand. All of us."

"But what if I told you it's not," I said, watching her expression change to one of suspicion, as if I had just told her the earth was square and orbits the sun in a rectangular path. "That there is an afterlife and sometimes it's a difficult journey to get there. Which is what is happening in this house at this moment."

"I'd say you made a remarkable about-face, since you were so skeptical only a few moments ago about our séance."

"Let's just say I've been enlightened," I answered her. "And you helped convince me that there is a problem. Though I wasn't sure what it was exactly before you started."

"And now you are?" Lynette asked.

"What if I said that what we have going on here is a portal problem," I began to explain, trying to hold back an urge to laugh at the situation

I had found myself in. It was so absurd, *truly* absurd. I was becoming a messenger for the dead. "I need your help in moving it somewhere else."

She took my news that we were living at the gateway of the deceased without a bit of surprise or a condescending attitude towards me that I might really, truly, be bonkers. I tried to be as serious as I could as I laid out my course of action—for which I needed and wanted Talla's help. Of course, I had no idea if my suggestion would work—whether she could perform some sort of nonsensical chant or tribal ritual that would let the lost souls of the departed follow her through the streets of the French Quarter so that they could find eternal peace and rest and closure at the St. Louis Cemetery a few blocks away, where I suggested she lead them in a Pied Piper sort of way. A Ceremony for Relocating Ghosts was probably not going to be something that she would find written instructions for in her *Voodoo Handbook of Practical Knowledge* or *Advanced Witches Guide to Magick and Spells*, but Talla said she was up for the challenge; in fact, she seemed to become possessed and enlarged by the idea of it, pumping up her lungs and breasts with deep gulps of air and saying she knew she had the self-confidence to accomplish such a thing because I was expressing my confidence in her abilities. I, of course, felt as if I had become a lunatic, as idiotic and foolish as any drunken tourist wandering down Bourbon Street and flabbergasted to find a tour guide dressed in a cape and wearing a skeleton mask ready to offer me a free drink coupon.

"I would need a few weeks to do the proper cleansing," Talla said.

"We don't have that kind of time," I answered, running the tip of my finger across the sauce that was at the side of the plate. The flavoring was fiery hot when I brought it to my lips and it reminded me that I wanted another drink because I was beginning to feel a bit *too* sober to believe any of this was possible. "I think we're at a bit of a crisis point right now. How about a bit sooner? *A lot sooner.*"

"Well, I have to do a little prep work first, hon," she said. "Find the right words. Mood. Clothes, too. I need to feel relaxed doing this. Nothing restricting or binding. I'll meet you back here at three. How about that?"

"Tomorrow afternoon?" I answered. "Fine. I'll have to get Parker to cover for me with the check-ins."

"No, sweetie. Tonight. Later tonight. I think it's best we do such a thing at a time the spirits are comfortable and there's not too many people around to ogle at them and make them nervous and mad and upset. When the night is at its darkest and things are quieter around here."

"Of course," I said, wondering how I would make it up till that hour of the night and still be able to function the next day. "And do me a favor," I added. "Let's not tell the others about it right away. Let me ease up to it if we need them to help out. I may want them to sleep through it all—so they're not ogling or worried that we're hanging out with, you know, a bunch of ghosts and lost souls. Especially Parker. No need to mention it to him at all. He'd only be worried."

No sense in everyone knowing what kind of fool I've become, I thought, though I laughed at my own idiotic behavior, and Lynette smiled at me, pleased to see that I had confided in her girlfriend.

"I hear ya, hon," Talla answered and winked, as if she were in on the ruse. "Outta sight, outta mind."

After I saw them out and watched as they said their good-byes to the others in the courtyard, I entered my working mode, bagging up the growing garbage from the café and then returning to Parker's apartment, taking the dishes into the kitchen and wiping down the table. I used Parker's phone to call the hospital and speak to Hank, but when there was no answer in his room, I asked to speak to the nurses' station and was told that he had been given a sedative and was sleeping. I hung up without leaving a message and washed the dishes and placed them in the dish tray, finding the warm soapy water mildly tranquilizing, when another plan came into my mind because of a lack of faith in the one I had just devised with Talla. Back in the dining room, I reached for the antique knife where it had been left on the table, folded the blade into the handle casing and shoved it into my pants pocket. Then, in the bedroom, I found my boyhood Bible in the bookshelf, where I had kept it for years without ever opening it. The rim of it was covered with dust and I blew it off, watching the thick cluster of motes travel into the air and fall into a heap on the floor where I would sooner or later need to vacuum it up, knowing well that Parker wouldn't do it himself, probably would not even notice it.

Was this desperation or true faith? I thought, sitting on the edge of the bed, going over in my mind my newest theory, my newest insight into the problems at hand. What if the ghosts and God were related somehow? What if it all had to do with the psychic consciousness and something beyond it, what the mind of the living believed before the soul died, whether the religion was Catholic, Baptist, or Buddhist? What if God created ghosts in the same way that he created men and women and animals and plants— but for ghosts, he had created windows or passages from one world to the next to allow them to pass along meanings or messages from the world of the divine and the afterlife to the world of the living? Of course this theory meant that I must accept the fact of the existence of a Higher Power and that life was not just a random clashing of misadventures and unlikely coincidences as I had always felt my life had warranted and exhibited. This wasn't accidental. God had planned it. And the ghosts, in a sense, proved to me His existence.

What would my father think about all this? My theory of divine correlation between God and ghosts and man? If I were to tell my father and grandfather that I had seen a ghost, they would have called me idiotic and foolish—certainly no different than how I already felt. My grandfather would have said such things are only superstitions and superstitions belong to the realm of the uneducated and uncivilized, though my father might have considered that they were the visions of a sinner unable to accept the power of the Holy Spirit. But if I had said to my father that I had been given a message from God, that an Angel had materialized and presented me with a challenge, they would have given weight and credence to this possibility of a miracle and a meaning. My grandfather would have said that I must be a man and find a way to understand God's message to me. *God's message? Was that what this was all about?* Was God talking to me in a way that he felt I would accept hearing from him, me, the sarcastic heretic and cynical heathen that I had become in society's eyes, if not my own? In these moments between me and my discovery of the gates of heaven and hell I saw it all as it should be—what had truly happened and what I had to do about it. (Or so I convinced myself. At least I was ready to believe my own interpretation of it.) *The plans I have for you are plans to prosper you and not to harm you, plans to give you hope and a future.*

Traveling back down the staircase with my Bible in hand and my divine plan in mind, I made a short mental list as I approached the courtyard. (God had certainly not expanded the number of my brain cells, so I knew to keep it short.) Parker was standing near the doorway of the Dauphine Suite talking to Celia when I grabbed the key inside the doorway of the kitchen and unlocked the pantry. I set the Bible on a shelf and set about pulling up the cypress planks of the floor that I had removed and replaced two nights before, and then used the large serving spoon to dig at the dirt, a bubble of light rising out of the ground as I cleared out a hole. I pushed the spoon into the earth with an energy I had not possessed in many years, an enlightened power of understanding, a way through the storminess of my daily life (but not without a skeptical, girlish giggle). The dirt seemed to understand this, or seemed to explain it to the rising lights; they broke through the soil, hovered and orbited around my task, illuminating my sense of purpose and awe.

I took a break from my digging to sip from a fancy bottle of appropriately long-aged, expensive whiskey that I felt was needed to mark the occasion of my newfound spiritual wisdom. I took more than a few sips, really, wanting to feel a bit intoxicated, more receptive to seeing and greeting my otherworldly residents and the would-be messenger from God. Suddenly there was a twinge of my eyelids, followed by a harsher thump at my chest and a darkness enveloping my brow, and I reached for the Bible where I had left it on the shelf, lifted it up and pressed it against my body and prayed deeper than I had ever prayed in my life. *"Please God, please let this be the right path for all of us. Please give us strength and wisdom and guide us safely through all of this."*

When my vision slowly returned through the glowing, glittering orbs of light, Griffin was standing at the doorway of the pantry. This time, he was dressed in his white leather outfit, but he did not step inside the small room. He remained at the doorway, behind him two huge wings of white feathers that grew from his shoulder blades and spread out behind him in the night, preventing him from stepping inside the pantry.

"It's a bit dangerous to your health doing it that way," Griffin said, his voice now sounding divine and omniscient, splitting into tones of higher and lower octaves. "We don't usually appear when we're summoned."

"I thought I might merit a special case," I said.

"I know what you're thinking," Griffin said. "I did not lie to you. I only made you see me as I knew you would accept me. It was always a part of the plan."

"Why didn't you ask me? I'm sure I could have found time in my busy schedule to relocate a few lost souls for you."

"They're only stragglers, really," he said. "But they got too excited that this particular way was open again because of your friend's recent death—much like a fire escape door being opened, you know, when it is needed."

"Is this world so bad for them?" I asked. "Is that the problem?"

"The problem is that they are neither part of this world, nor part of the other. That is why they are so uneasy."

"And Mack? Will he be at peace?"

"His destiny has always been set."

"And Angelle? Will she be forgiven, if she was guilty of murder? Will she be able to leave and find peace?"

"There is a place for everyone."

"I'll only do this for you if I can have something in return," I said.

"I'm not in the habit of making bargains or granting wishes," he said. "Or answering prayers. That would make it, what?—a miracle. I can only listen to your thoughts and help you find direction."

"I'm not a selfish man," I continued. "I'll move these souls for you to another place. All lock, stock, and barrel of them. Including the baby. We'll give them all the respect and attention they deserve, but I want something in return."

"I cannot restore life that has been taken away," he said. "That is not a part of the natural order of things. Be certain your friend Mack is now fine, his spirit at ease. He is already quite beloved where he is now. His friend prepared the way for him."

"I didn't get a chance to say good-bye," I said. "All those years went by while I was so busy working. It feels like he left too quickly."

"He already knows of your love," Griffin said. "But I can bring him reassurance of that. Gladly, I will do so."

"But that's not it," I said. "That's not what I want."

"You want more?" Griffin asked. "You're sure you're not a selfish man?"

"No more than any other living soul on the planet," I answered. "I want Hank to be okay and healthy and happy. You shouldn't have caught him up in all of this. That wasn't fair."

"Life is never fair," Griffin said. "And I cannot change the course of fate. That is not within my powers. But your friend was never in any real harm or danger. He was always intended to mend and grow into a stronger man. That is part of the lessons of life, as you yourself know. I cannot change that direction, though I can speed it up a bit. I'm sure in the morning you'll find his doctors baffled by his recovery. As for where he goes next, that is his decision."

"Thank you," I said.

"What lovely words," Griffin said. "We seldom hear those, you know. It's become a too, too greedy planet."

"And what of Angelle?"

"So you are a greedy man," he said. "To ask of so many things."

"How can I help her? What must I do so she won't be left behind?"

"I have said before that you will know what to do when the time comes," he said. "But be certain that she wants only to be included, to be part of your history and part of your family."

"Will I see you again?" I asked him. "Or will you follow the others?"

"I am in all places," he answered me. "As you learned as a boy."

This time Griffin's departure was grandly theatrical. The white of his outfit and his feathers and skin became brighter and broke apart into a thousand orbs of glittering lights. I watched them flicker and dance in front of my eyes, tiny lights pixelating and dancing and spinning and twirling, as if a giant disco ball had been suspended in front of me and I had been drugged into watching it spin. I shook myself back to consciousness, tossed my head back and forth and turned my back on the lights, retrieving the knife from my pocket and flicking open the blade. The blade caught the reflections of the lights and I stood and watched the lights dancing on its edge. In my most dramatic and campy fashion, as if I knew a TV reality show camera crew was standing right behind me and filming my every move, I waved the knife through the air, as a shaman or a baton twirling majorette might do, and then fell to my knees, shoving the blade into the dirt beneath the pantry floor where I had discovered it. The lights behind me moved into the space above me and were drawn towards the earth, as if the air pressure of the room had been changed. The lights spun round and round the blade of the knife, disappearing one by one into the dirt. Slowly, the room returned to normal, lit only by the dim glow of evening and the tiny exposed lightbulb near the ceiling.

I replaced the dirt on top of the knife, replaced the cypress floor planking, and hid the opened bottle of good whiskey on the back shelf of the pantry where I knew I could find it later, if needed. I felt a burning and trembling and I weaved my fingers into each other, astonished at how I had become so suddenly religious and bold. I returned to my knees, bowed my head to the ground, ran through a list of thanks, wondering if I was worthy enough to talk to God, to be chosen for this task, or if it was all simply an accident—that I happened to have been the closest moron to be recruited for the mission. Or perhaps I was now completely crazy—not only seeing ghosts, but *believing* I was talking with messengers from heaven, an angel with wings. Maybe the spiritual problem was not a spiritual one at all but a mental one? Perhaps my drinking and working and exhaustion was making me physically sick? Perhaps this was all an issue of my health. Perhaps I was nothing but a tired old man haunted by his exhaustion.

Buddy was in the café kitchen when I hung the pantry key back on the wall and he asked me to check the credit card modem at the waiter's station inside the dining room; something was wrong with the connection and he had not been able to verify the card numbers all night.

Oh great, I thought, *now I'm doing it all for free. Relocating the dead and feeding the starved living pro bono.* I tried not to let the potential loss of income annoy me—I had entered a stabilized zone at last by just accepting my fate as what fate would have it be—and, at the waiter's station, I placed my Bible beside the register and bent down on my knees to check the modem cables. The floor was both oily and sticky and its uncleanliness made me suddenly worried that we were in some kind of health code violation, then soon enough I forgot about it when I discovered that one of the port connections in the back of the modem was loose. *Nobody else could do this?* I thought, straining the muscles of my neck. I huffed and puffed and stretched and contorted myself to rehook the phone line to the port at the back of the box, then huffed and squirmed and rolled over to stand upright again, running my fingers through what remained of my hair, hoping to pat it back down into place. When I tried processing a credit card number a few minutes later, the modem was working fine and, as Buddy passed behind me carrying plates to a table near the window, I told him all was okay and that he should put through all the card numbers he had been unable to process as soon as possible, to make sure we had not been entertaining criminals along with our ghosts.

At the bar, Dwayne was still reading through the file of clippings and I poured myself another shot of high-end bourbon. While I sipped at my drink, I wrote on a pad of paper a list of names: Aaron, Angelle, Antoine, Pierre, Sarah, Sarah's baby, Mack, Toby. While I was asking Dwayne about the proper spelling of the last name of the fourteen-day-old baby from the newspaper article, Buddy approached the bar and placed my Bible on the counter—I had left it behind at the waiter's station.

"I'm sure you don't want to lose this, Mister D," Buddy said, his eyelids blinking rapidly as if a speck of dirt was preventing him from keeping them open.

Before he walked away, I clutched his wrist and asked him, "How much do you remember from seminary?"

"What do you mean?" he asked, his blinking slowing but occurring with more force. He shot Dwayne a nervous glance, as if they had often discussed my peculiarities at length in private and here I was, once again, acting out true to form.

"I'd like to do a mass tonight," I said. "I don't think there is enough time to locate a priest and convince him to do it right away. And you've had some religious training. You could do it."

"A mass?" Buddy answered. "You want me to lead a mass?"

"Yes, you know, read a few things from the Good Book," I said. "Something worthwhile about life on earth in the physical sense and how God takes care of us later, wherever we end up. Then read these names off and say how dear they were to the living, what good lives they lived, and how much they are missed. That sort of thing." I handed him my list of names and Buddy looked at my handwriting. "And be sure to mention that their souls are now at rest. Particularly this one—Aaron. We'll do it right after we close up here. It'll only take a few minutes."

"But I'm not qualified to officiate at a mass," Buddy said, his eyes now wide and stationary from fear.

"You shouldn't put yourself down like that," I answered him. "Of course, you're qualified. God sees all men as equal."

"Then why can't you do this?" Buddy asked, blinking rapidly again. "If we are all so equal."

"Because I don't know the Bible as well as you do," I lied. "And I would probably not find as many good and comforting words as you could to soothe a graveyard of uneasy souls, because you've had some training in that regard. You proved how worthy and important all this is to you just now. I misplaced the Bible. You brought it to me. That shows how much more important this is to you than to myself."

Buddy gave Dwayne another one of those "Can-you-believe-this-dude?" sort of looks. "I'll ask José to help you out," I added. "I think he was an altar boy in Texas."

"This isn't a way to get rid of some ghosts, is it?" Dwayne asked.

"Well, that could be a motive, yes," I answered, not ready to reveal all aspects of my plan. "There's a great deal of unrest here—as we all know—and it's not like we're trying to exorcise them. Just trying to make them comfortable and happy and part of our family. I would just like all parties who reside here to be in harmony with each other. We're all in this together, you know, as we spin around the big, fat universe. One giant, happy, dysfunctional family. Maybe one or two of our resident phantoms will show themselves to us later, you know, if we're lucky. Before they go…well, to sleep or whatever state it is they finally get to when they are at rest."

I could tell that Dwayne was intrigued with my plan and eager to get the mass going, hoping that this might finally be his chance to spot a real, honest-to-goodness ghost for the first time. Buddy, however, was still skeptical. And spooked. "You're making a great assumption that they are all Catholic," he said, as if he could outsmart my plan. "I'm not sure a mass is the right thing to do."

"Good point," I answered him and Dwayne seemed impressed with Buddy's logic. "But historically, I think the majority of them might have been baptized as Catholics. Please feel free to add any specific ecumenical words or thoughts from other denominations or cults or philosophies you'd like to make it a more inclusive service. I don't think any of them will mind. They might even be flattered. A few invocations of the Loa gods might be worthwhile, now that I think of it. But let's not do anything sacrificial. No blood, please. I just think that might make some of them upset. But a few Latin phrases could be worthwhile, too—for those old souls who expect that sort of thing. And let's get Kaku involved, too. Have a perspective of another culture. He might think of something we're missing. A missing element, that's right. You'll talk to him, won't you? There is only one God looking out for all of us, you know, even if we all have a different name for Him."

I could feel Buddy's disbelief hitting the back of my neck as I walked away. In the kitchen, I explained to José we would be gathering in the courtyard after work to pay our respects to a few departed souls, recent and otherwise.

"A Voodoo thing?" he asked with a little too much enthusiasm.

"Not just Voodoo," I answered. "An inclusive memorial." Then I mentioned that if Kaku wanted to stay for the services, too, he was most welcome. "He's making himself rather indispensable here. I honestly don't think we could do it without him."

It was close to midnight when the last customers had left and we finished cleaning the dining room and kitchen. Parker had come in as Kaku was wiping down the sinks and counters and José was restocking the spices and grabbed a bottle of wine and four glasses. "Come have a nightcap with Celia and Stuart, if you want," Parker said to me. "She's finally mellowing out a bit. I actually think I saw the beginning of a tear."

"You're not still sitting outside in the courtyard, are you?" I asked him. I wasn't too worried about Parker's disapproval of my planned requiem; I had been dodging that mood for years, but even though Parker had mentioned that Celia was mellowing, she was certain to agitate any restless spirit we might be trying to soothe.

"Their suite," Parker said. "The kids are asleep. I just thought I would try and be a gracious host."

"You're always gracious," I said, trying to flatter him into disappearing without me. "Good cop to my bad one. I'm gonna hang out a bit with the boys, if you don't mind. Make sure all is well here. And with them. We don't want the whole household to be grumpy."

"Thank you for doing this," he said, and the tone of his voice made me suspicious that he could read my mind...or my intentions. "I'll be back on course in a day or two. And I want to talk to José about doing more of the cooking."

"Yes, I knew that's what you were thinking," I said, trying to move him along. "I'll tell him how happy you are."

After Parker left I gave José and Kaku the formal long-stemmed gold candles we used for special occasions in the café and we assembled on the courtyard with our reluctant shepherd, Buddy, who stood perturbed, one hand aggressively placed against his hip as though it would convince me to change my mind. I chose a spot to the side of the fountain, our backs to doors and windows of the old slave quarters, but facing Buddy and the Good Word he held up to his chest. Kaku was taking all of this very seriously, as was Dwayne. Buddy and José, however, were clearly spooked and agitated or annoyed—for all of their delight in some of the creepy details of Voodoo and witches' spells and the hope of discovering lost treasures, they were both clearly thin-skinned—eyes darting nervously around the courtyard and giggling like little girls.

"Well, let's go at it," I said to Buddy.

Buddy started solidly with the Beatitudes, "Blessed are the poor in spirit, for theirs is the kingdom of heaven..." Then he began Psalm 39 in a tentative voice, "Show me, O Lord, my life's end and the number of my days," his voice darkening as he reached the passage, "Man is a mere phantom as he goes to and fro," as if he remembered a comment from a professor or mentor on how to better project his voice and make himself seem authoritative. Next he read a passage from the New Testament on the resurrection of the dead: "But if it is preached that Christ has been raised from the dead, how can some of you say there is no resurrection of the dead? If there is no resurrection of the dead, then not even Christ has been raised. And if Christ has not been raised, our preaching is useless and so is your faith."

Graciously, Buddy mellowed as he read while the rest of us cast our eyes suspiciously around us, waiting for a gust of wind to blow, the roof behind us to collapse, the ground to split beneath us, a mist of fog to envelop us, but none of this happened. I could feel Dwayne shifting anxiously beside me, heard José clearing his throat as he stared at the flame of the gold candle he held tightly in his hand. Suddenly, the flame of Kaku's candle was extinguished, and Buddy momentarily stopped his reading to watch José relight it with his own.

Then, Buddy continued. "But someone may ask, 'How are the dead raised? With what kind of body will they come?' How foolish! What you sow does not come to life unless it dies. When you sow, you do not plant the body that will be, but just a seed, perhaps of wheat or of something else. But God gives it a body as he has determined, and to each kind of seed he gives its own body. All flesh is not the same: Men have one kind of flesh, animals have another, birds another and fish another. There are also heavenly bodies and there are earthly bodies; but the splendor of the heavenly bodies is one kind, and the splendor of the earthly bodies is another. The sun has one kind of splendor, the moon another and the stars another; and star differs from star in splendor. So will it be with the resurrection of the dead. The body that is sown is perishable, it is raised imperishable; it is sown in dishonor, it is raised in glory; it is sown in weakness, it is raised in power; it is sown a natural body, it is raised a spiritual body. If there is a natural body, there is also a spiritual body. So it is written: 'The first man Adam became a living being'; the last Adam, a life-giving spirit. The spiritual did not come first, but the natural, and after that the spiritual. The first man was of the dust of the earth, the second man from heaven. As was the earthly man, so are those who are of the earth; and as is the man from heaven, so also are those who are of heaven."

"Is there anything you'd like to say, Mister D?" Buddy asked at the end of his reading.

"Say?"

"Add?"

I smiled because he had slyly caught me off guard. I had orchestrated the service but had not expected to participate in it. "Well, yes," I answered, stalling a moment as I collected my thoughts. I'd missed both Mack's wake and funeral and I suddenly understood that if I used this moment and said something, I could offer closure not only to myself, but maybe to the others as well. "I'd like all of us—the living and the dead—to think of this place here—this little pocket of the world—as a home. Not as a business or a tourist destination or a museum of trapped memories. But as the place where we are all welcome. Where we can come to and go from freely as a family does. In fact, I'd like to think of us all as one big family of the living and the dead. Miss Angelle. Aaron. Pierre Dubuisson. Toby. Mack. Our new friends Dwayne and Kaku. I think that was how Mack saw us and how he kept us together and that's how I'd like to see it kept up. The present and the past together. Harmonious."

Next followed the list of names of remembrance that I had given to Buddy to read. At the conclusion of Buddy's reading of the list, Dwayne added, "May their memory be for a blessing," and added something in French, which made all of us stop and look at him in confusion.

"For those old-timers who might expect that sort of thing," he said.

Then Kaku began speaking in a singing sort of way, "Yajna-vidya maha-vidya," he went, his voice a tone higher than its usual register. "Guhya-vidya cha shobhane, atma-vidya cha devi tvam, vimukti-phala-dayini." This ended with him closing his eyes and falling into the chant, "Om Hreem Sreem Mahalakshmayai namaha," which José joined in on the second syllable and Dwayne and Buddy on the longer word. I had no idea what it all meant, but the tones of the voices were comforting and soothing as they chanted. As they reached the last tone of their chant, we were cast into an awkward silence, standing for a moment looking away from each other like we had all just finished filming a circle jerk, waiting for someone to make the next move and tell us we could all get dressed. And then behind us came the sound of someone walking down the alleyway and into the courtyard, the heels and toes of the footsteps of boots clacking against the bricks. The shadowy figure stopped in the darkness of the alley when it saw the five of us congregated around a Bible and tall candles and, as I tried to look deeper into the dark space, I felt certain there was a fog or mist or cloud of smoke around the figure's face. Then a hand which had been hidden in the dark at the side of the figure lifted up in the air, and a tiny red ember grew suddenly brighter and there was a bit more smoke cast into the night. The figure took a step forward and I felt a wave of disappointment come over me, even though I knew that his arriving at this moment must be part of something larger than myself, perhaps of a divine plan. In my most Good Samaritan demeanor, I took a step forward and said, "Charlie Ray, we've missed you."

He flicked his cigarette down to the ground and stubbed the butt out with the toe of his boot. I could tell by the heaviness of his eyelids that he was either drunk or stoned or both. There was also a defeatedness about him, too, as if he had searched for a place to stay for the night and had come up here—our humble shelter and ghostly wreck—as his last resort.

"Hey," he said. "I heard about Mack."

"We were just thinking about him, ourselves," I said, referring to the crowd of us. "Parker'll be glad to see you. Would you like a drink? Or some coffee?"

He nodded, which I took to mean he wanted coffee, and behind me I felt our small group ready to disperse. I walked over to Buddy and said, "Well, that should settle them down," and shifted my stance so that I could kiss both of Buddy's cheeks in a sort of haute couture way as a means to express my thanks for his out-of-the-ordinary effort and at the same time greedily test the firmness of his bicep.

We all said our good-byes for the night, and made a few small pledges about work the next day. As I kissed José goodnight, I mentioned that Parker was planning to use him for more cooking in the kitchen. "We've all been impressed with what you've been doing," I said to him. "I think you can talk him into letting you plan a new menu."

"We could make the sauces a bit hotter," José said.

"Let's not get too carried away." I warned him. "We don't want to scare the paying customers away."

He nodded and Kaku slipped his arm around José's waist and I turned away from the two of them just as they were about to fall into a kiss. Charlie Ray had taken a seat at the smallest of the courtyard tables and he engaged in small talk with Buddy, Dwayne, Kaku, and José as they passed him on their way out. In the office, I made a quick cup of instant coffee and, when I brought it out to the courtyard and Charlie Ray, Dwayne and Buddy waved good-bye from the alley. Dwayne shoved his hand into the back pocket of Buddy's jeans and Buddy leaned into his boyfriend and kissed his neck. I watched them for a moment, hoping their public display of affection might go a little further, but they were soon out of eyeshot and I gathered up the gold candles and left them by the office door, then took a seat next to Charlie Ray at the table, instead of continuing cleaning. He had lit another cigarette and, as he blew the smoke out of his lungs, he cast his eyes at the makeshift string of the upstairs balcony where the railing had given way in Hank's fall.

"How's your friend?" he asked me.

"He'll be fine," I answered. "Just shaken up."

Charlie Ray and I had never been the best of friends; we were always distant with each other, polite, never inquiring, our only bond being Parker. I didn't expect much of a connection or conversation with him now, or really in the future, so it came as a surprise to me when he said, next, "I lost my job."

I couldn't imagine that Charlie Ray had put much effort into his job as a personal trainer at one of the uptown gyms, but I kept that thought to myself because he seemed depressed, and just as I was about to offer him some sort of sympathy, he added, "I suppose I've just proved my old man right. He always said I'd never amount to anything."

"Well, you're just down on your luck at the moment, I imagine," I answered him. "And you're much too young to draw conclusions about the course of your life right now. You've still got plenty of time to prove him wrong. Or prove it to yourself, if that's what matters."

He dropped the cigarette to the ground next to his chair and stubbed it out with his boot. I wanted to chide him about his continual littering of the courtyard and my having to go around and clean up his butts, but I didn't; I kept my mouth shut and tried to keep the annoyance away from my face. Next, I wondered if he might have taken clairvoyance lessons from Talla and could read my thoughts, for he leaned over his seat and picked up the butt off the bricks and placed it on top of the table, as if to remember to throw it away later. Now I tried to hold in my astonishment as he took a sip of his coffee.

"I should probably stop smoking," he said. "Not very healthy."

"I should cut back on my drinking," I said. "And I will some day. I think. There's still time."

He nodded and next I said, "Well, don't be so blue. If you need work, there's plenty of it here right now. It might be a while before Hank gets going full steam again. It doesn't pay much, you know that, but you're a part of the family here and we'll help you out if you need help."

He did not accept or refute my offer, but gave me another gentle nod. Behind him, I heard a door open in one of the upstairs rooms and there was a rumble of low voices followed by a high-pitched laugh. We both turned towards the sound to see Parker's large, roundish figure emerge on the balcony and close the opened door. Parker took a few steps, saw us sitting in the courtyard, stopped and said, more to Charlie Ray than me, "Hey."

Charlie Ray got up from the table and met Parker at the bottom of the stairs. I remained seated, watching them embrace and kiss, the dim lights of the courtyard catching the teeth of Parker's smile. Watching them reminded me of imagining Buddy and Dwayne's sex life and when I grew too embarrassed to be regarding what Parker and Charlie Ray might be about to begin, I looked down at my watch, estimated the amount of time before Talla's arrival (about ninety minutes), then got up from my seat and reached for the candles by the office door.

Inside the office, I stored the candles on a shelf, booted up the computer, and checked the reservation book for entries for the rest of the week and the next one. Just when I had returned to the PC to launch a software application, there was a light rap at the door and Parker came partially inside the room, one foot outside the stoop, the shadow of Charlie Ray cast behind him on the bricks.

"Thought you might like this," he said, stretching out a large stack of paper bound together by a rubber band. "Celia took it from Mack's place yesterday to look at. She thought it was his."

I took the papers from Parker and looked down at the top page. Printed in large letters was:

The Ghosts of New Orleans
by Toby Ridenour

"Don't read it before you go to sleep," he added with a crisp laugh, and kissed my forehead when I took it from him at the door. "It might spook you."

I mentioned that I was glad to see that Charlie Ray had returned and Parker offered me an embarrassed nod, not wanting to display his pleasure for fear that it would remind me that all was not well with Hank. After our goodnights, I took the manuscript to the small couch by the old fireplace hearth where I sat and flipped through the pages till I found a table of contents and read Toby's chapter headings under **Part I: Hauntings of The Vieux Carré:** The LaLaurie Mansion, The Beauregard-Keyes House, Marie Laveau's Tomb, Pirate's Alley, The Sultan's House, The Crescent City Bookstore, The French Quarter Courthouse, Le Petit Theatre—they were all legends and anecdotes of ghosts and paranormal disturbances that I had heard about over time from living and working in the Quarter. The manuscript had been typed with the use of a typewriter rather than printed from a computer—or, rather, several typewriters, perhaps over a period of many months or years (and one particular machine split the letters m and n and another created shadows to the letters a, s, and w). The entries seemed to be one part travelogue, another part local history and legend, and a final part academic deconstruction of the paranormal activity on the site, as if Toby set about to deconstruct the scientific and psychological reasons behind the ghost sightings of a particular location. ("This is generally in the area where many clairvoyants have sensed high spirit-energy fields and cold spots, particularly at dusk when both light and temperature are going through rapid changes.")

The final heading under the Hauntings section was the one that caught my attention first—**The Cemeteries of New Orleans**—and I thumbed through the pages till I reached the chapter and read:

> The earliest hauntings in New Orleans may have begun with the Indian tribes who originally used the vast swamplands where the city is now located as a sacred burial spot. The swamplands were also not the favored destination for affluent Parisians and merchants, so the King of France, in an effort to build up the settlement and clear his country's overcrowded prisons, sent over shiploads of murderers, thieves, rapists, and other convicts to be the first labor class and whose deaths could possibly account for many of the malevolent spirits in the Quarter today. Living conditions in the colony were difficult, from the unexpected hurricanes that could arrive, to the alligators, snakes, and mosquitoes indigenous to the marshy area.
>
> The original French Quarter boundaries stopped at Dauphine Street. North of this street was an old ditch, and past that St. Peter's Cemetery, where residents were buried according to social status, religion or heritage. Burials were all below ground at this cemetery; the ditch created to contain the high water table and the excess dirt used to raise the level of the ground inside the cemetery. But since the early settlement was plagued with both fires and epidemics, bodies were often buried wherever space was available and often in unmarked burial sites

throughout the Quarter. This could also explain why the spirit-energy levels are more intense at certain locations than at others. In 1784, the Cabildo ordered St. Peter's Cemetery closed and a new cemetery was authorized in 1789. As the city expanded and grew in population, the property of the St. Peter's Cemetery location became quite valuable and families were asked to relocate the remains of those who had been buried here.

The chapter continued with the creation of the St. Louis Cemetery I, which was then outside the city limits, and the establishment of St. Louis Cemetery II in 1823. I scanned through the descriptions of Lafayette, Metairie, and St. Roch Cemeteries and then flipped through the other pages of the manuscript, randomly reading things that caught my eye, such as "years later a caretaker was also murdered on the property" and "was once a ward for critically maimed or ill men during the Civil War."

I had the sensation that someone was watching me, as interested in my reaction to what I was reading as I was in what I was hoping to discover. It wasn't the presence of a ghost. No, it felt different, more omniscient, or that was my perception of it when I took my fear and changed it. It was God. God was watching me and I knew it. I felt His presence just as strongly as I had when I was a boy and opened the Bible for the first time. And just as I had a few years later, when I discovered my attraction to men and discovered that it was not a sinful desire, but a natural one, the right path to proceed—for *me* to proceed upon. *Yes, this was right. What I was doing was the right path to take.*

Towards the back half of the manuscript was a section called **Superstitions, Myths, Legends, and Facts,** and here Toby had set about explaining the origins and details of such things as the Loup Garou and Le Bal Goula, St. John's Eve in Congo Square, Voodoo Customs and the

Loa Gods, Zombies and The Undead, and Vampire Legends and Gothic Culture, and within these was a typed page that was:

The Wolf at the Door

The big bad wolf is very well known from fairy tales like "Little Red Riding Hood," "The Three Little Pigs," and "The Seven Little Goats." According to these tales the wolf is an evil, vicious, cunning, and rapacious being. Modern usage of the idiom "the wolf at the door" derives from the tales such as "The Three Little Pigs," in which the "big bad wolf" stands outside the home where the three pigs reside and threatens to "huff and puff and blow the house down" (and thereby eat the pigs and end their lives). In such, the phrase "the wolf at the door" has come to mean the potential rise of bankruptcy, failure in business, the creditors lining up to take action, or some kind of imminent "end." The use of the word *wolf* to refer to hunger, appetite, or famine dates back to at least the fifteenth century, and the image of the wolf being at the door representing the threat of starvation is just as old. Our modern word "loophole" is derived from the European term "loup hole" or wolf hole, a spy hole in shelters through which travelers could scan the areas for wolves.

Indo-European mythology generally describes the wolf as being of demonic origin. In the Edda, the ancient Icelandic sagas, the wolf is the symbol of mysterious powers. In Egypt, the wolf was seen as the guardian of the underworld and as god of death. In Greek mythology, this vicious being was turned into fearsome three-headed dog Cerberus, keeper of the entrance to the underworld of Hades. Several cultures believed that domesticated animals such as dogs who were once family pets could return from the dead and act as a spirit guide. The dog is the most common of all spirit guides, connecting the sense of loyalty, trust, friendship, playfulness, and unconditional love. On the Fool card of the tarot, the dog is usually the companion of the Fool, giving unconditional support on the road before them.

Native North American Indian legends also mirror this association of canine creatures and the spirit world. The fox, coyote, lynx, and wolf all have association with creation myths and special powers and functions. The Blackfoot Indians of Canada believed that the nether region of their spirit world was inhabited by packs of wolves. Many tribes believed that wolf howls were the cries of lost spirits trying to return to earth. For the Choctow, the Indian tribe that once roamed in the southern and central regions of Louisiana, legend had it that in the last moments of death, a white wolf was summoned to take the soul to where it had originally been born. French settlers from Arcadia to this region adopted this underworld myth as well, but it was the rise of Voodoo culture from the slaves brought to the region from Haiti and East Africa that further embellished this local belief that wolves were summoned to ease the passage of a recently departed soul to land of the dead. Thus, by the early 1800s in New Orleans, the connotation of the Cajun slang "rougaporte," or "the wolf at the door," was not entirely one signifying potential financial ruin or starvation, but the arrival of death and setting out on the road to the afterlife.

Many cultures, however, have identified the wolf as more demonic than beneficial or spiritual; Christianity equates the wolf to the devil. There are various legends from East-European countries, Russia and Scandinavia telling about the devil's creation of the wolf. Thus the word *wolf* in various cultures has taken on a negative connotation: The Swedish and Norwegian term for wolf is varg; in Icelandic it is vargr, which not only means wolf but also is used for a wicked person. The Gothic word *vargs* stands for murderer, strangler, outlaw, and evil spirit. The verdict "thou art a warg" declared the culprit an outlaw. Those people were banished forever from human society and were forced to live in the wild. Some scholars suggest that the werewolf traditions of Germany and Scandinavia arose from this practice, since the convicted person was thought to no longer be a human being. The Navajo word for wolf also means witch and a person could transform if he or she donned a wolf skin. The French believed that the transformation of a man into a werewolf or "Loup Garou" was more than a physical one; the soul was also cursed and could be passed on to another soul through both site and bite. (For more information on werewolves, see the earlier entry on "Loup Garou and Le Bal Goula.")

But there are also positive traits of the wolf found in mythology. In one of the early East-Indian legends for example, the wolf is described as a sympathetic and helpful animal. There are several legends telling about female wolves nursing children, the most famous being the legend of Romulus and Remus, the founders of Rome. The Mongols viewed themselves as "sons of the blue wolf," descended through Genghis Khan from a mythical wolf that came down from heaven.

In Native North American mythology the wolf was often looked favorably upon. Some tribes identified their clans with particular animals and looked to them for guidance or inspiration. Especially on the Northwest coast the wolf was used as a totem. The wolf was revered because it was a fearless and good hunter. It is often associated with the special spirit power that man had to acquire to become a successful hunter. Some tribes also have creation myths where wolves play an important part, for example the Kwakiutl of British Columbia. One of their myths tells how the ancestors of the people took off their wolf masks and became humans. According to the Ute, a tribe from the Rocky Mountain area of Colorado, the wolf played a major role in how humans came to the earth. The wolf had carried a heavy bag on his back and therefore could only move very slowly. After a while the bag became so heavy, he hardly could walk any farther and decided to lie down. While he was doing so, the bag burst and all the people poured out and went to the different places on earth.

Most often overlooked, however, is the myth of the wolf as the protector of community—or the pack—and in Native American Indian culture someone described as having strong wolf-like characteristics was a person who would fiercely protect his or her family and tribe, be it blood family or adopted spiritual community, from outsiders. Because native peoples, like wolves, defended territory and hunted and killed to survive, they admired the wolf's prowess in doing so. Hence for the Pawnee, another Indian tribe that roamed the central regions of the United States and heavily identified with the wolf, the wolf signaled both territory and ancestors and the things that needed most to be protected and championed, the wolf inside the heart, not the one waiting to be confronted outside the door.

A spirit guide? A white wolf as a guide to the afterlife? Could this describe the creature I had seen in the pantry? Had the wolf come not to surprise me, but to summon Mack? To lead Mack to the next world? Had Mr. Vassallo, the baby's father, seen this sort of spectral wolf too? How could such a myth coexist with a belief in angels and ghosts? Were they all connected? Or was I the connection? Could a continued belief in the mystery of God be the *only* answer, because none of this *could* be answered? Nothing could be explained. It was rational only because of its irrationality. Logical because of its illogic.

As I shuffled the pages to make the stack of paper neater, it occurred to me that I might have known of this manuscript years ago, might have noticed it on a bookshelf one night after having sex with Mack and looked through it later, or seen it under the coffee table as my bare feet landed on the floor on my way to the bathroom and thumbed through later during a boring moment. I might always have known about it but never completely recognized and processed it; I might have shifted it from one side to another as I dusted and cleaned, become so familiar with it that I no longer saw the details of it. It was something to be kept for a day when it *might* be useful, like a phone book. I was reading the section on the marsh gas lights phenomenon of the fifolet (with the mythology that Dwayne, Buddy, and José had accurately described) and the references to Jean Lafitte's treasure, when I heard a noise out on the courtyard and I went to the door. Talla had arrived and was assembling her spiritual paraphernalia in her most dramatic but subdued manner. Dressed in a long black robe gathered with a yellow rope sash at her waist, she was pouring sand atop the courtyard bricks in the design of one small circle inside a larger, and saying in a loud stagey whisper, "I cast this circle to protect and to invite in the spirits. This is a temple between the worlds. So make it be."

"Don't worry, we'll clean it up," Lynette said to me, also in a whispery voice, when she noticed me at the office door. She was nearby, arranging three thick black candles on the courtyard table. She was dressed in a long robe similar to Talla's, though hers was white, not black, and she moved about as if she were helping with a prank and not a solemn service.

"I'm not too worried if it does the job," I answered her, though I couldn't help noticing that Talla was not being sparing with the sand lines she was creating around the courtyard—they were much higher than any anthill I had ever encountered, more like the height of a fortress wall of a sand castle a young child might create on the beach to keep away the waves. *My God,* I thought next, *what kind of monster have I created? Look at that mess I am going to have to clean up!*

"We're almost there," Talla said, completing her task with the bucket of sand and standing upright and straightening the tangled jewelry that lay atop her robe. Within the parameters of the smallest circle, Talla had incorporated the smallest of the courtyard café tables as a sort of altar, moving the chairs against the brick wall behind the fountain. In front of the three giant, thick candles, which Lynette had now lit, was a small metallic bowl that held a strand of incense that was already burning, a thin line of smoke rising into the darkness of the night as if it were a white flag offering surrender. As Talla placed the bucket of sand beneath the table, Lynette lifted a glass jar that I had not noticed before and held it out in front of her between her joined and upturned palms. Talla dropped the robe off her shoulders, exposing her pale breasts and stomach and giving me quite a startle. I hadn't expected the nudity and I tried to avert my eyes as Talla reached her fingers into the jar and began rubbing a dark-colored lotion against her left breast. I tried to suppress my laughter because the underside of her rather large and bulb-shaped breast had suddenly gotten trapped in the long chain necklace she was still wearing, but I was less successful at stifling my shock and nervousness and Lynette cast me a scowl and said, "Avery, please show us some respect. Otherwise, this will not work."

I apologized with a bow and my hands pressed together as if I were a Japanese servant who had just arrived on the scene bearing news that barbarians were at the gate. "You don't mind if I get a drink before we start, do you?" I asked her.

"Hurry up," Talla said. "I'm almost ready to begin."

Inside the office, I poured a shot of bourbon in a glass but drank it before I went back outside, trying to compose myself because it all seemed too ridiculous to me—why had I ever thought this up? On a hook beside the computer I kept strands of Mardi Gras beads we had accumulated over the years, left behind by hungover guests in their rooms, and I slipped one over my neck, hoping, in a silly, sacrilegious way, that it would keep any and all sorts of evil spirits away from me, and realizing that I had also created a mumbo-jumbo gumbo of different beliefs and superstitions myself. I was a cafeteria spiritualist, too, believing in what I needed and wanted to believe in, and right now I wanted to believe that the burning fire of intoxication would help me make it through this senseless and misguided debacle of a ritual of relocating lost souls. Instead of pouring myself another glass of bourbon, I found a half-empty bottle of whiskey beneath the kitchen sink and took it with me to the courtyard without the glass.

Outside, Talla had finished rubbing the dark lotion around both her breasts and her stomach, removed the tangled chain, and was now wearing a bright silver pentagram dangling from a yellow string around her neck and some kind of white animal fur collar about her bare shoulders that I took to represent the skin of a wolf. It reminded me of a scene from a movie where you know only bad things are going to happen, or that the protagonist will suddenly develop superhuman powers and everyone will soon be reduced to dust and rubble. I kept my distance from them, remaining outside the areas of both of the circles, trying not to watch the shocking bobbing and bouncing of Talla's breasts, but drawn, nonetheless, to witnessing the novelty of their movement. *It's not like I've spent a lifetime looking at boobs,* I thought, and lifted the bottle of whiskey to my lips and took a deep sip, feeling the liquor rumble the juices of my stomach and create a puddle of gas which I soon burped up. Talla nodded to me that she was about to begin, then cast her head back and let out a howl, which, even if it hadn't been the deepest quiet of the night, was loud and piercing enough to raise the deadest of the dead.

"Hear me Osiris and Hades and Persephone and Hecate," Talla said, now in a quieter tone, though Lynette had lifted some kind of maracas off the table and was shaking them as Talla continued her chant. Lynette had also bared her breasts, but they were smaller and more firm and without all the shimmer and shaking of her girlfriend's, though I was still shocked to see hers exposed, adorned as they were with dark, round, enormous nipples.

"Hear me Ereshkigal and Morgan and Hel and Cernunnos," Talla continued. "Bring with you Papa Legba and Damballah and Kali and Sedna and Tlazotelotl and Qisaruatsiaq. Baron Samedi be our special guest. Guédé Nibho and Guédé Vi you are also welcome to be with us."

I cast my eyes around the courtyard, waiting for something to happen, for some sort of mist to rise from the ground or the ghosts of lost souls to materialize into the dancing lights of the fifolet, but nothing moved. It suddenly seemed to be all a big blunder to me, a mistake in faith—or faiths—mine as much as Talla's. I wanted to stop everything and say "Let's just pack it all up and call it a night"—I was suddenly exhausted and ready to admit that I had hallucinated all the events of the day, including my time-stopped benediction for Angelle and a conversation with a messenger of God. At worst, I expected Parker to appear on the balcony and ask what the hell was going on and then I would be revealed as a bigger fool than Talla and her spiritual hoodoo—because I had believed in her as much as I did in myself—believed in our ability to reach out and help and change something.

Talla's voice dropped to a stagey whisper and she chanted, "La fanmi semblé, en é o, la fanmi semblé, non." While she chanted, I continued to sip from my bottle, rolling my eyes into the back of my head, thinking, *Oh, God, what have I done now? How do I get the hell out of this? How am I going to be punished this time?*

"All things return to where they have come," Talla said. "All cycles end to begin again. This is neither an ending nor a beginning but a time for all lost souls to be reclaimed, to follow us towards sanctuary and shelter and peace. We are all family and friends here tonight. I ask in the name of the Goddess and all powers of the dead that I have gathered amongst us now that you follow us, let us guide and honor you and bring you everlasting comfort."

Talla opened her eyes and cast her glance about the courtyard, as if this were the moment the undead were to rise from the earth and follow her elsewhere. When nothing happened she strode around the perimeter of her small circle of sand and continued her invocation. "With this circle I have made us strong and bold, grant us the stealth and power of the wolf spirit within us. As the body returns to earth, the heart pours back to the waters of life, the mind returns to the clear sky, the soul returns to the light. Blessed be to all who are here and we wish you well on your journey. Rise up and follow us, follow us to peaceful sanctuary. Let us lead you into the light."

Talla stopped again in the middle of her circle, fell down to her knees and kissed the ground three times and said, "Ouvri barrie pou nous passer." Again we waited for something to rise around us and we each cast our eyes towards the other, wondering if all of this were just foolishness. I took the final sips from my bottle of whiskey and instinctively walked towards the table to place it out of my way so that it would not be accidentally kicked or shattered—thinking that the last thing I needed to have to do tonight before I went to bed was sweep up shards of glass so no one would accidentally cut his feet in the morning. Putting the bottle on the table nearest my line of sight, I passed through the sacred space of the circles and placed the bottle on Talla's altar—right next to the enormous black candles and the smoking twig of incense. Talla broke her concentration and gave me a sigh of disgust. She rose up off the ground to say something to me, but in doing so she moved too quickly and blacked out, falling unconscious to the bricks. Lynette moved to catch Talla as she slowly collapsed to the ground. It was then that I saw the lights begin to rise up between the bricks of the courtyard, tiny flashes of light which turned into streaks and rays as if the ground were breaking apart.

"Do you see them?" I asked Lynette.

"No," she answered me, shaking her head, her eyes wide and suspicious. She had lifted Talla's head into her lap and had checked her breathing.

"Is she okay?" I asked.

"Yes," Lynette said. "She's been teaching herself how to faint and fall. It's nothing I haven't seen her do before."

"But do you see *them?*" I asked again, pointing to the rising rays of light.

"No," she said. "Nothing. It has to be you, Avery. You'll have to be their guide. You'll have to get them to follow you."

"But how the hell am I supposed to do that?" I asked her.

I didn't wait to hear an answer, though I swear I heard her say, *"Pray."*

Instinctively, I lifted my hands above my head, as if to catch the attention of the fifolet with a wave of my arms, the gesture reminding me of the nights I had spent at my grandfather's tent revivals when we all rose up with our hands in the air to accept the Lord and bequeath ourselves salvation. The lights had grown much brighter now and were flowing into the curves of the outer circle of sand, moving in a gaseous sort of fashion above them, like the rings around the planet Saturn. They moved like a river, brightening and thickening as they became more concentrated into a single source of light. Then, as if a gust of wind had moved through the courtyard, the river of light grew taller and thinner and the outer surfaces began to resemble the scales of a snake and I found myself chanting "Amen!" and "Hallelujah!" as if I were back in my father's church ready to seize the serpent. I kept my fear in check, however, ready to accept a bite or a sting and prove myself unworthy of being anointed, but just when I thought the brightness of the light would blind me, I saw the serpent move, shift its course, still in a circular fashion, with one piece rising and leading the way, the trail of light heading towards the altar and into the empty glass bottle I had just placed on the table.

"Do you see it now?" I asked Lynette, pointing to the whiskey bottle full of glowing light on the table where the serpent of bright gas had ended up, as if it had been poured inside it. The bottle was fiery and extraordinary and so white I had to shield my eyes to look at it.

"Nothing," Lynette answered. "Not a thing. Are you sure you haven't been drinking too much?"

Next came a howl from the far end of the courtyard, and there, in the darkness of the alleyway, stood the white wolf I had seen before in the pantry. My heart was beating rapidly, and I could feel a dizziness and my speech was slurring and a thought crossed my mind that I had indeed had too much to drink. *My God, what have I wrought?*

"Do you see the wolf?" I asked Lynette. "There," I said, and pointed to the courtyard.

"No," she answered, and then after a moment's thought, added, "Should I be scared?"

"It's all right," I said to her. "Tell Talla it's worked. Tell her she was magnificent."

I approached the glowing bottle, moved my hand towards the glass, expecting to feel the heat of the light but finding it shockingly cool and manageable. I lifted up the bottle of fiery light and walked to the perimeter of the smallest circle of sand, stepped over the line, then proceeded to the wider circle, stepped over it and continued in what I hoped was a calm and contained manner towards where the wolf was waiting. I had to believe in all things now — religion, sexuality, death, afterlife — the larger whole of the universe and the smallest details of human life. As I grew closer to the wolf, it jumped up on its hind legs and turned itself around, running into the darkness of the alley. I followed it out into the street, skipping like a mad man now to keep up with it, the Mardi Gras beads dancing against my chest. I was the Fool of the tarot card following his canine guide.

Outside the guesthouse, beyond the entrance to the café, I had expected to find a few rowdy stragglers on the streets of the French Quarter; many of the bars I felt sure were now approaching last call and final rounds. But as I ran to keep up with the wolf I was surprised to find myself weaving around and through so many strangely dressed people, as if I were making a way through a costume ball. There was a man in hip boots and a T-shirt with a handlebar mustache, standing beside a horse-drawn carriage where two ladies in long skirts and bonnets were seated. Across the street was a row of men dressed as soldiers — half in Confederate gray and the rest in Yankee blue, their buttons catching the glimmer of the lights in the bottle I held with my hand. Were these ghosts, too? Lost souls waiting to be released from the memory of the past?

Their presence gave me a profound sense of mission. This was my task. What I was supposed to do. *This was it.* God had provided me with these images to move me forward. True nature had been revealed to me and it made me feel both conscious of what I was doing and apprehensive of what other obstacles might be awaiting me. *The path is not always easy.* It was still nighttime as I ran through the streets, quiet and dark, but the people moved around me as though it were daytime, carrying packages beneath their arms, bags of newly-bought groceries and supplies; stepping over horse droppings and puddles of brown soupy dirt as they made their way through the street. I knew the route to the cemetery and the wolf was taking it just as I would, if I were leading the way, but now it all seemed a bit too unfamiliar to me, the gift shop on the corner no longer selling T-shirts and souvenirs but with the sign above it reading Apothecary, the restaurant beside it filled with horses and the clanging rhythm of a blacksmith hitting metal. It was too fantastic to believe that I had shifted into another time and too fantastic to dismiss the possibility that I hadn't— everywhere my eye was drawn to the unfamiliar colors and details—a man with a tall, shiny silk hat and blue-and-yellow striped suspenders, the rusty shackle around the wrists of a shirtless black man, the dirt-crusted fingernails of a soldier gripping a rifle, the red-fringed shawl of a woman held together by a gold brooch in the shape of a leaf. I knew that I could not stop to explore and examine these people and places—could not break from my task to inquire of theirs—my mission was the wolf, following the wolf towards the cemetery and Basin Street. Just when I had convinced myself I had jumped through time, I weaved through a group of college boys in jerseys holding plastic cups of beer, raucous and laughing as one of them bent his head to the sidewalk and let out a moaning puke.

The wolf had scampered across Rampart without any worry of traffic, and I kept him in my sight as I crossed slowly, then swiftly as a car swerved into view and I headed towards Basin Street. At the gates of the cemetery, I stood trying to catch my breath, the wolf now only inches in front of me. The wolf looked back at me, caught my gaze as if to explain something to me, then scampered up the side of a high stucco wall which framed the cemetery boundaries and disappeared onto the other side.

How in the hell am I supposed to do that? I asked myself. *I'm just supposed to magically scamper up the side of a stone wall like a figment of my imagination can do?*

I stood in front of the wall and the locked black gates and took a deep breath, looking inside the bottle of light for some kind of inspiration or guidance. The gates were exactly as I had remembered them from my hallucination in the kitchen earlier in evening and I knew I was facing another challenge or test. I tried to will myself scampering up the wall, my legs just running and forming suction cups and me scaling the white stucco wall like a superhero. But to no avail. I could not move an inch—not even in my imagination. I stood there, deep in the weight of my merely mortal feet, sucking in air and trying to calm my aching heart, which was still beating as if it were trying to escape through my throat. I tried the cemetery gate—but it was both locked and chained with a second lock. For a moment I thought about tossing the bottle—which was still glowing in my hand—over the wall, hoping that would do the trick and settle all those lost souls I now had in my immediate possession.

In my gut, however, in the acidy, heartburny gut of me, I knew that that wouldn't work, and that it wasn't the respectful thing to do—just tossing them over and listening to it crash and shatter—I might as well just have drowned them in the Mississippi. I tried shaking the gates open, then tried squeezing inside through the small opening beneath the chain, but could not make it because of my girth. I considered climbing over the gate, but could not get a good enough grip with only one hand and, the truth of the matter was, I felt too old and fat to accomplish the task. The stucco wall was too high for me to reach up and grasp the top of and try to yank myself over while also carrying the bottle. I felt anger rising inside me at having come this far only to be defeated by the height of a wall and the locks of a gate.

Why, why, why? Why me? I sat down on the ground and started to whimper, suddenly overcome with a wave of nausea and frustration. My mind was tired and the world suddenly felt as if it were spinning around me, as if I were the world's axis, and I closed my eyes in an attempt to steady myself. Here, in the darkness of my mind, it felt as if the ground were tipping, shifting beneath me, and I ran through the events of the last few days, trying to find my way through this, hoping to come to a solution for delivering the bottle and find a way to keep things from spinning out of control. "This energy is only taking the form that you allow it to take," Griffin had said to me, or, rather, the Angel of my demented, inebriated, and overtaxed mind had explained to me. "You are shaping it. It's not shaping itself. You'll understand this when the time comes to show it."

When the time comes to show it. What was before my closed eyes was a swirling serpent of darkness, the antithesis of what I had just witnessed in the courtyard. I could see an undulating motion, the blending of black and gray and purple and green and blue, half matte, half sheen, but round and scaly, tilting and shifting and bending. Like the light it seemed to have an intelligence, a path and a direction it wanted to take. It swirled around me, circled my consciousness, and when I could no longer hold the movement in my mind and was afraid it would rise up and strike me, I opened my eyes to quell the urge to vomit and I noticed that I was no longer sitting on the ground, but lying down, and the ground was no longer the ground but the ground was the wall, and instead of lying down, I was really standing up, and all I needed to do, after all, was simply walk over the wall, as, indeed, the wolf had done before me.

And that was exactly what I remember doing. It was a miracle of physics. When I reached the edge of the cemetery wall, I took a final step and fell over into the darkness. The last thing I remember was falling through space. Falling, falling, falling, but never reaching ground, just falling.

Seven

I'd be remiss if I didn't point out that there are concesstions I have had to make because of my overdrinking. The most obvious is the larger clothing size, but the hardest adjustment has been the nightly loss of sleep. On some nights insomnia overwhelms me and I toss and turn, hoping a better position might do the trick and send calming messages to my brain to allow me to relax and fall asleep. And when sleep comes it is pervaded with dreams, not really nightmares but complicated tales that take more thought to work through than a grown man should have to exert while trying to get a good night's rest. On some nights one dream rises into the next and then into the next till I wake more exhausted than when I went to bed.

It was already hot and bright the morning after when I woke up on the crushed-shell and rock pathway inside the cemetery, and I had made it through the night without either insomnia or the feverish sequence of dreams; in fact, I'd had the best night's sleep I could remember in many years. The empty liquor bottle was still at my side when I stood up and shook the sleep off my body, and I took it with me as I walked through the cemetery gates, now oddly unlocked at this early morning hour.

I felt like I had arrived at the end of an adventure, like the end of *It's a Wonderful Life, A Christmas Carol,* or *The Wizard of Oz,* recognizing all that had happened and what I was supposed to learn from it—the gift of life, the desire for home; that misers can live lonely, spooky lives. On my path back to the house I found myself praying, little prayers of thanks for having survived the night, for all having gone well, for no harm having come to me. Life begins when God gets our attention and I felt that I should be making resolutions of some sort, that this might have been…no, *was* a turning point for me, and that perhaps I should give up drinking for a while, or at least not drink in such large quantities and at all hours of the day. Perhaps I should not be so bossy, lower my expectations and not be so critical of others—or of myself. Perhaps I should relax more, not be so possessive and demanding, let things go undone that I could not do myself, perhaps take time off each day to do something, well, for myself. And perhaps I needed to have more faith in divine intervention; perhaps I should pray more, set up a regular communication with God and the spirit world. But of course all this hope and wishful planning fell away the moment I walked down the alleyway and into the courtyard and found the circular paths of sand still there, trampled on and scattered around the entire courtyard, looking as if a tidal wave had washed ashore sometime during the night.

I spent the next hour cleaning, sweeping the sand up, making a mental list of other things I needed to accomplish throughout the day. Lynette had left me a note jimmied into a crack of the office door that said that she and Talla had waited for my return, then given up and gone back to their home in the Faubourg Marigny to get some sleep, and I should call her in the morning with an update of what had happened. When the sand was swept away, tossed into the bucket and the garbage, and I had packed up the incense holder, the jar of lotion, and the very plastic-feeling animal skin into a shopping bag to return to Talla, I went into the office and dialed Lynette's number.

She didn't answer, but as I was leaving a message on her answering machine, she picked up and said in a breathy, groggy early morning voice, "Avery, I'm so glad you're okay. We were worried."

I asked her if Talla was all right, and when she responded with a hoarse yes, I told her we would catch up later and that she should go back to sleep. I checked the wall clock in the office and decided it wasn't too early to check on Hank at the hospital and when I was put through to his room, he was awake and watching television.

"Is everything okay?" he asked.

"With me?" I answered. "Yes, fine. Why do you ask?"

"Just a strange dream I had last night," he said. "I'll tell you about it later. There was an intern in my room earlier. He said they'll discharge me soon."

I told him I was looking forward to him being back and that I would be by to pick him up later in the morning. When I had hung up the phone, there was a light rapping on the glass of the office door. It was Celia, come to say good-bye. Stuart had carried the sleeping boys out to the car and was now packing away their suitcases.

"There's nothing really that I wanted from upstairs," she said. "You can keep all of Mack's stuff. I'm sure that it means more to you than it would to me. I'd probably never unpack it all anyway."

"Well, of course," I answered her. "And if you change your mind, I'll send you whatever we can."

"I'd like to take this, though," she said. In her hand she held the framed photo of Mack and Toby that Mack had kept on the small side table beside his chair, the photo she had taken of them herself, years before.

"And I'm sure he'd have liked you to have it," I answered.

She leaned over the door stoop wanting a hug from me and I obliged her, patting her back to indicate that all was well between us and that any bad blood spilled was now forgiven. I followed her out into the courtyard and, as she turned to leave, she stopped and looked over her shoulder and said, "Avery, I want to thank you for all you've done. Not just for us these last few days. But for Mack. Thank you for watching over him. Being his guardian angel. I'm sure you made him very happy."

I nodded and thought about correcting her—that Mack had been my—*our* guardian angel—but instead, I gave her a wave of good-bye as she made her way down the alleyway, then noticed someone standing above on the second-floor balcony. It was Charlie Ray.

"Hey. I thought you could use some help this morning," he said.

Wait till you see what thankless work you've go to do first, I thought, and waved him downstairs with a change of my posture, and began showing him the mechanics of the place—the laundry hampers, the linen closet, the contents of the pantry, and then the reservation system in the office. I half expected him to take a cigarette break at any moment, that I was crowding his brain with too much worthless information too quickly, but he simply followed me around and nodded, asking a few questions along the way. When I had sent him to the suite Celia's family had just vacated to strip the beds and sack up the dirty towels, I remained behind in the office and placed another call. It was Felipe who answered, and, after a few pleasantries and chitchat, I asked him if he wanted to take a stab at remodeling one of the guest suites.

He was pleased with the idea and we talked a moment about what I had in mind and then about what he could do with the room. Before he hung up I asked if I could speak with Griffin. When Griffin came to the phone, I asked him (and without any sort of hopeful, flirtatious banter) if he could repair the broken spokes of our wooden balcony and if not, could he suggest a contractor or carpenter who might be able to repair and strengthen the balcony railings.

"I could do that for you," he said. "Save you the expense of hiring a contractor who'll never finish the job."

I thanked him and said that his plan might mean another room for Felipe to design and before we hung up he said that Felipe would be by later in the day to check on measurements. Where I was going to find this money I had no idea—but my newly-restored faith in God made me believe that maybe this money *could* be found. Somehow. *Fix it and it will come.*

Inside the office, I fought off the urge to have a drink so early—so far nothing out of the ordinary had occurred and I sat at the computer and confirmed some reservation requests by e-mail. Parker arrived when I was trying to figure out if I should put a honeymooning couple in the Royal or Burgundy Suite for three nights.

"Want some breakfast?" he asked me. "I thought I'd cook an omelet."

I tried not to let the suggestion bother me—that Parker was up early and wanting to cook and wanting to cook *breakfast.* "Okay," I answered a bit suspiciously, nonetheless. And instead of going to the café's kitchen to cook, he went into the small kitchenette of the office.

A few minutes later we had bacon, toast, and an omelet on a plate in front of each of us, and we were eating at the opposite sides of the office desk instead of at the slim counter in the kitchenette.

"You should do breakfast more often," I said. "This is pretty good."

"It's a thought," he answered. "I could do breakfast and lunch. José could overlap lunch and do dinner. We could keep the café open for more hours, make some more money, not work as hard. I'd have the evenings off."

I nodded, my mouth full of food, then answered. "It's a good thought."

"José's been nagging me to start taking reservations," Parker said. "He said if we created enough of a demand we could raise the prices."

"I always thought José was smarter than he let on," I answered.

We sat and ate some more, then Parker said, "You know, I could always buy your portion of the house if you want out."

"With what?" I asked him and laughed. "You found Jean Lafitte's treasure?"

He smiled and nodded and answered, "How did you know?"

"Well, clue me in to the secret map," I said. "Maybe I can find a pot of gold, too."

Next, Parker put his hand in his shirt pocket and withdrew a tiny little book. A bank book. He handed it over to me.

Inside it was one entry. An absurdly large figure of money deposited more than ten years ago.

"Half of it is yours," he said.

"What do you mean?" I asked him, calculating that half of the absurdly large amount of money was also an absurdly large amount of money.

"Mack's life insurance policy," Parker said. "Remember? He cashed it in when we bought the building from him. He gave it to us to use for his living and medical expenses if we needed it. Same time he made out his living will and gave us his power of attorney."

"Did I know this?"

"Yes," he answered matter-of-factly, scooping up a large portion of eggs with his fork. "But you were distraught at the time. Drunk, really, if you want to know the truth. You couldn't even stand up straight, so I don't blame you if you don't remember it. Mack was in the hospital and you were on a real bender the day we went to the bank. You told me to keep it hidden away for a rainy day. I just thought I would remind you of it now that Mack's gone."

"I just don't remember," I said, wondering how many other important brain cells I had lost over the years. "Are you sure?"

"Yes," he answered. "The account's in both of our names. Half of it is yours."

I lifted our plates from the desk when we were finished eating and carried them to the sink in the kitchen. "You could take a vacation, if you want," Parker said, following behind me.

I looked at him and he knew I wouldn't leave, wouldn't step away from this place we had made our home. "I'd rather have central air-conditioning," I answered him. "Modernize this place."

"I'll clean up," he said, and just as I was about to react like an astonished maid transformed into a upper-class diva, just as I was about to yell out, *"You'll clean, too!"* the office phone rang. It was Hank, asking me to come pick him up at the hospital as soon as possible. Suddenly they were ready to release him and wanted him out of his room as soon as he could leave.

On the cab ride to the hospital I wondered if I was dreaming or if I had awakened into an alternate universe where nothing went wrong, where everyone was polite and easy going and people were friendly and helpful and willing to clean up their own mess, a Stepford kind of French Quarter. As the cab made its way through the streets, into the heavier traffic uptown, I looked for something to ground me back to reality, but the heat that morning was manageable, the sky a brilliant blue—no one was homeless on the street, no one had suitcases propped open or outstretched hands asking for money, the window was cracked and I swore I could breathe in a tinge of fresh, salty sea air. Even the cab driver was talking about his luck, telling me of his hefty earnings the night before at a casino. "Must be something in the air," he said and gave me a toothless smile in the rearview mirror. "Or the way the planets are all lined up in a row. I hope everyone's having a lucky time right now."

Luck? I thought. *Was that it?* Or a calm before a storm? Was something else about to happen, something more ferocious, more disturbing than what had already transpired? When would the other shoe drop, the wolf appear at the door? The scary one, the one with fangs and payment-due high-interest bills.

At the hospital, the hefty, big-breasted nurse in charge of dismissing Hank said she was surprised he was leaving so early and not even having to use a cane to walk. "You must have someone powerful looking out over you," she said.

"We've all been saying our prayers," I said.

"You must have a direct pipeline to The Man, himself," she laughed, her chest rising and falling like an inner tube being pumped with more air. "Anyone else take a tumble like that and they could be here for a few months."

Even Hank's sour spirit had made a turn for the better. "I'm so tired of watching television," he said. "Thank God you're finally here."

"Yes, thank God," I answered him and then helped him convince the pneumatic nurse that he did not need to be escorted out of the hospital in a wheelchair.

In the taxi back to the guesthouse, after I had mentioned that Charlie Ray was helping me out and that I was having Griffin repair the upstairs balcony railing and that I had hired Felipe to redesign a few of the guest rooms, Hank shifted his eyes to the left, thought a second and said, "Maybe you could move upstairs, too. See what it feels like for us in a real apartment, not a tiny little office. I've been thinking…maybe if we took it seriously, we could make things work."

Yes, perhaps I had awoken into an alternate universe, or perhaps there was someone powerful above us balancing out all the events of the prior days. I had been transformed by my participation in a mystery that still had not been actually solved. I hadn't really convinced myself that I *wasn't* going crazy, that I *wasn't* an overworked, inebriated sinner struggling with his inner demons. No one had seen my ghosts. No one had witnessed my angels. Instead, I had only recognized myself inscrutably included within the streaming life of the universe. Life—and afterlife—had been revealed to me—and only me—in all its immense and pulsating splendor and confusion. But why had I been chosen for this task? Was it only to restore—and rejuvenate—my faith in God? Return the disorder of my life back to its natural order so I could start over again? What had I learned that could help me—or anyone—do it any better?

Back at the guesthouse, Griffin and Felipe had arrived, and they greeted Hank in the courtyard when we returned with air kisses as if nothing bad had ever transpired, as if the fall from the balcony had never happened. Hank offered to show Felipe the vacant rooms and he checked the reservation log and took the master key up to the Burgundy Suite, and I hoped, with all my hope, that whatever Hank wanted to transpire between the two of them would happen now while things were at their best. *Grant him this moment,* I prayed with a bit of a smirk at the side of my lips. *Please God, let him have a little fun. Keep him occupied and happy and full of pleasure.*

Upstairs, on the second floor balcony, Griffin was at work measuring the spokes of the railing. He waved me a polite acknowledgment and I wondered if the world I was in was not a dream, then had I dreamed what had happened with Griffin in the pantry? Had that happened with this Griffin or my other, *imagined* Griffin, the all-powerful internal Higher-Powered one? My cock thickened at the memory of it, the memory of that first Griffin, the one at work upstairs. I pushed the urge to explore it aside and went into the office and found the sign I had made years ago that said, LE PETITE PARADIS, in fancy gold script, which had kept falling off the front of the building every time I had tried to nail or secure it in place. The name of the guesthouse had been heavily carved into the wood, but above it, I had had the street address painted onto the wood, and I studied it and decided there was enough space there to amend the sign. I placed it on my office desk, rummaging through a storage closet for the touch-up furniture kits I had not thrown out years before when remodeling the guest rooms. An hour or so later, I had removed the street address from the sign and replaced it with the stenciled, painted words, ANGELLE DUBUISSON'S, in homage and memory of our earliest tenant. I used a blow-dryer to speed up the drying process and found a hammer and nail in the tool kit and took the sign outside.

My hammering drew attention to my project, and once Parker and José were convinced that I was not demolishing the door and had returned to their chores inside the café, Griffin, who had been smoking on the balcony, appeared and offered his assistance. As he stood beside me, his hands straightening the sign, I felt my blood pressure rising, my hair thickening, my libido rising, all the things I had experienced before when he was so close. He seemed to notice my increased interest in him, or, rather, my increased interest in watching him work on my project, and just when I hoped he might let a hand fall and grope me, Charlie Ray came running out of the Royal Suite and said, "I think we have a problem."

In a stressed, high-pitched voice he explained that he had noticed a leak under the sink and when he went to tighten the valve it broke and water was now flooding the bathroom. The bucket of sand I had cleared up that morning was soon emptied and full of water, and I was rapidly trying to find an inexpensive plumber to make a quicker-than-later house call, not an easy feat on even a good day.

Charlie Ray and I took turns emptying the bucket of water into the bathtub and an hour or so later I thought all was well when the plumber arrived, fixed the valve, and left behind an absurdly high bill. We cleaned up the bathroom, sacked up the wet towels, and carted them downstairs

for Lynette to pick up later. In a way I was pleased that the disorder had
returned to our lives, or at least my life. Griffin and Felipe had left, but
José and Buddy had arrived and had opened up the café, and Hank was
inside getting the update of the events of the past few days from Dwayne,
who had arrived with Buddy to check things out. Charlie Ray looked
eager to join them and I told him to take a break and relax before trying to
straighten up the Royal Suite again. I also wanted to take a break and give
Dwayne Toby's manuscript to read. I thought he might find it interesting.
Or enlightening. Or both.

As I was crossing the courtyard to the office I sensed something flying
overhead, but when I looked up there was nothing above me. I had an
impression, however, that all was not at rest and at the office door I turned
and glanced around the courtyard for something suspicious to catch my
eye. But there was nothing. The ferns were still, the hanging plants were
not swaying, the water of the fountain was tinkling, not splashing as
if rocked by the tremor of an earthquake, the fish were swimming, the
household was calm. The newly adjusted sign still hung on the outside of
the office, ANGELLE DUBUISSON'S LE PETITE PARADIS—nothing had knocked
it off. and it hadn't been struck down by wind, lightening, rain, or an act
of retribution by a vengeful spirit.

Inside the office, I found Toby's manuscript where I had left it the
night before. I restacked the pages in a more orderly fashion, circled the
bundle with a rubber band, and carried it outside beneath my arm.

I still felt an uneasiness about the place. I looked at the plants again,
but there was nothing unusual, no movement, no animal or snake
scurrying about. Buddy had not even created a new Voodoo shrine for
me to discover. When I looked at the fountain again, however, I noticed
a glittering light that at first I took to be a reflection, but after a few more
seconds of thought, took to be something else. As I approached it I felt my

heart sink, or, rather, felt it flutter with despair. Had one lost soul been left behind? Had I failed to relocate *all* of our ghosts?

At the fountain I looked into the water but saw nothing but the swimming goldfish, then reached my hand inside to pull out a bottle cap that I had noticed stuck in the corner. The metal of the cap must have been catching the reflection of the sunlight.

When I turned around to cross the courtyard again, a breeze caught my shirt and I looked up again at the sky suddenly darkening above me. Another sudden rainstorm was what I thought first; it was hurricane season, after all, and the weather could be swiftly unpredictable. I felt the thunder move through my body before I recognized the sound—a far-off grumble that grew in strength as it rumbled and roared into violence. Above me, the sky darkened and swirled with gray clouds and vibrated with lightening; then a ray of light broke through and it grew brighter where I stood, sunlight hitting the toes of my sneakers. I felt a clutch at my chest and my heart lost a beat as the roaring sound tore through my body. I dropped the manuscript and the bottle cap, unable to hear the sound of them hitting the ground. I fell to the bricks on my knees, everything blackening out before me. I had been wrong about everything. I wasn't hallucinating or going crazy or seeing ghosts and conversing with the messengers of God, I had been suffering little strokes of warning about the fragility of my heart. This time I felt for certain that I was having a heart attack. A major one. I could not breathe, could not ease the painful thunder inside my chest and ears. This time I wasn't summoning a guide. A guide was summoning me. I felt that this was the end of things for me, not the beginning as I had so safely presumed. I had been wrong all along. My crisis hadn't been a spiritual issue. It was all about my health and mortality. It was time for me to die.

And then the pain was gone as quickly as it had disturbed me and a sweet breath of air filled my lungs. When my vision returned the bright ray of light was still in front of me and it brightened more, until it lost all color. Inside the light I could see a movement, something that looked at first to be tiny motes of dust, but when I studied them harder found them taking shape and movement, a flapping of sorts, as if the wings of an animal were beating, pulsing, pumping, fluttering, waving, as if I were looking inside the inner workings of a heart. Slowly the details came forward and I saw it was Griffin, angel white again but this time much larger than he had ever appeared to me before. I was still certain that it was my time to die, that God had not used me for a task, but instead had warned me to change my ways, make myself healthier, and I had ignored this truer task for the benefit of others.

As Griffin moved closer, deeper into the bright ray of light, beneath his wings came the details of two other figures, one slightly stronger in detail than the other, stepping forward and downward, as if at the end of a footbridge. I felt sure that this was the same bridge Toby had seen in his last days. The same bridge Mack had only dreamed of a few days before. The same one Angelle had been trying to make her way towards. Now it was my turn to cross the bridge from one life into the next.

The larger figure came slowly into focus and I could see that it was Mack. Behind him, at his side, more hazy and shimmering was Toby. And for a moment as the details of their bodies became stronger, more visible, I knew that they had come to take me with them, that it was now my time to go, to follow them to heaven or the rest of my afterlife. I wasn't at all scared to go with them, to follow them into what I felt certain was a beautiful land on the other side of the bridge, only regretful that I had not rightfully prepared the other members of my little family—my band of sinners in this crazy world I had constructed for us in New Orleans—that it was my time to leave. Mack approached where I had fallen on my knees and he bent over and lifted my face towards his own with his fingers at my chin.

He made no sound, of course. Ghosts—or spirits of the departed—do not speak, but in my head I heard his voice saying, "Thank you. I made him bring us to say good-bye."

As I whispered good-bye, I felt someone lifting me by my underarms. It was Parker, asking me, "Are you okay?" The bright light had disappeared and I had simply fallen to the ground.

"Yes," I answered him. "I just slipped on the bricks."

I reached down and picked up the bottle cap and the manuscript and brushed the flecks of sand that whitened the knees of my pants, a new prayer moving through my mind: *Thank you for letting me stay a little longer.* Griffin and Mack and Toby and the bridge were gone, as quickly as I had materialized them. The sky was a bright sheet of blue again, as if the dark clouds and ray of light had never been there or anywhere on the horizon.

"Don't be in such a hurry," Parker said. "Things will get done."

I wanted to shoot him a scowl, then wanted to tell him that Mack had just been here to say good-bye, and that an angel of heaven had made me prostrate before him and had spared my life, but I didn't. Instead, out of the corner of my eye, I caught sight of Dwayne standing at the edge of the alleyway. His face was pale and sweaty, his expression in shock, as if, well, as if he had seen everything. As if he had just seen a ghost. Or an angel. Or the miracle of both.

"Don't believe everything you see," I said when I reached him. "Or it will drive you crazy. Unless, of course, you accept that everyone here is slightly crazy in their own good way—and then you can believe whatever you want."

He shook his head no and his face broke into a light, but worried smile. I handed him the manuscript that had been tucked beneath my arm, and said, "I thought you might like this."

Behind me, I heard José explode out of the back kitchen door, expletives—in several languages—rushing out of his mouth, followed by the *clank-clank-clunk* of something hitting the bricks. Parker and Kaku were there at once, trying to stomp out the fire in the frying pan with the soles of their sneakers and shoes. A fiery hot sauce had finally caught fire. Another Act of God or an Act of Irony? Whatever, no one had the good sense to get the fire extinguisher off the wall, which was what I did next, putting out the fire, then sending Kaku to get the office fan to dispel the smoke from the kitchen.

Next, the extension cord began to overheat and the fuse box blew. Before I knew it another fuse blew, and then another, and the electricity in the café was back on the skids and all was restored to wonderful disorder. (*Thank God. Thank you God for our misadventures and our mishaps and our mistakes. And thank you God for giving us the opportunity to share it together.*)

Sometime later I called an electrician to make a house call, and while I was waiting for him to arrive, I poured myself the first drink of the day.

I've never seen another ghost or angel since that summer, though that doesn't mean there aren't any others around the place. Dwayne still talks about how he sees them here all the time—in the corner of the café, in the upstairs guest rooms, in the shadows of the courtyard. Every night when his tour stops in front of the café, he fondly recalls his first supernatural encounter and how this tiny plot of swampland became our treasured corner of paradise.

Acknowledgments

All of the characters in this book are fictitious, and any resemblance to actual persons, living or dead, is purely coincidental. Among the works that offered me valuable insight into the history, ghosts, and legends of the city of New Orleans were *Beautiful Crescent* by Joan B. Garvey and Mary Lou Widmer, *The Ghosts of New Orleans* by Larry Montz and Daena Smoller, *Shadows and Cypress: Southern Ghost Stories* by Alan Brown, *Dixie Spirits* by Christopher K. Coleman, *Journey into Darkness...Ghosts and Vampires of New Orleans* by Kalila Katherina Smith, and *New Orleans Ghosts* and *New Orleans Ghosts II* by Victor Klein. Also informative were on-site walking tours of the French Quarter offered by New Orleans Ghost Tours and Haunted History Tours and the historical overview of the St. Louis Cemetery prepared by the Historic Preservation Program of the Graduate School of Fine Arts of the University of Pennsylvania. Cultural touchstones of gay New Orleans include Greg Herren's mysteries (*Bourbon Street Blues, Murder in the Rue St. Ann*) and Poppy Z. Brite's novels (*The Value of X, Liquor,* and *Prime*). Special acknowledgment must also be given to Fritz Leiber's *Our Lady of Darkness* and Kingsley Amis's *The Green Man*, two novels which inspired many elements of this novel. Another invaluable touchstone was Charles Jackson's *The Lost Weekend*. And for inspiring the heretical leap of my imagination, gratitude and acknowledgment goes to *The Encyclopedia of Ghosts and Spirits* and *The Encyclopedia of Angels*, both by Rosemary Ellen Guiley.

While the contents of Evangeline Dubuisson's memoir *Out of the Darkness Cometh the Brightest Light* are fictitious, it uses similar historical material to that depicted in many slave narratives of the nineteenth century. I am indebted to the on-line depository of slave narratives compiled by The University of North Carolina at Chapel Hill. Other background sources include period correspondence from the New Orleans archive at RootsWeb. com.

In retelling, suggesting, and creating the myths of the ghosts and other supernatural activity and invoking and describing the rituals and customs of Voodoo and Witchcraft and Magick and other religions, denominations, and cultures, I have tried to be as true as possible to the source material I encountered during my research. I am particularly indebted to *Gay Witchcraft* by Christopher Penczak, *The Complete Art of Witchcraft* by Sybil Leek, *Queer Myth, Symbol and Spirit* by Randy P. Conner, David Hatfield Sparks, and Mariya Sparks, *Queering Creole Spiritual Traditions* by Randy P. Conner and David Hatfield Sparks, *Gods, Heroes and Men of Ancient Greece* by W. H. D. Rouse, *Another Mother Tongue* by Judy Grahn, and *Gay Spirituality* and *Gay Perspective* by Toby Johnson, as well as "Inside a Voodoo Temple" by Brooks Boliek, published by *The Southerner*, "Voodoo in New Orleans," by Barbara-Simone Brandstötter, and *Secrets of Voodoo* by Milo Rigaud. The final Vedic chant used in the requiem of Chapter Six is the Prayer to Lakshmi. Also valuable to this story were *The Grace in Dying* by Kathleen Dowling Singh, *The Good Book* by Peter J. Gomes, and my well-worn copy of *The Bible*. For further details on the Church of God with Signs Following, I suggest an exploration of materials currently available on the Internet.

Some details and background information on wolf legends and myths used in the article "The Wolf at the Door" are from "The Role of Fox, Lynx and Wolf in Mythology" by Astrid Wallner of the Swiss Federal Institute for Forest, Snow and Landscape Research, "Stirring the Cauldron: New Wolf Moon" by Jessica Prentice, "Wolves in American Indian Culture" by Edwin Wollert of Wolf Song of Alaska, and "Wolf Legends and Mythology" published by the Kerwood Wolf Education Centre Inc. All of these materials are available on the Internet.

Once again, my special thanks and appreciation go to Anne H. Wood and Brian Keesling, who have continually read my work and offered me valuable advice on early drafts of this manuscript. For career support and guidance, thanks and gratitude also go to Arch Brown, Edward Iwanicki, Hermann Lademann, Kevin Bentley, Andrew McBeth, Steve Berman, Kevin Patterson, David Feinberg, and the New York Foundation for the Arts.

Special thanks go to Paul Willis, Greg Herren, Greg Wharton, Ian Philips, Mark Sullivan, Wayne Hoffman, Toby Johnson, Craig Gidney, Lawrence Schimel, Richard Labonté, Charles Flowers, Tom Cardamone, NoAIDS Task Force, and the Saint and Sinners Literary Festival for bringing me back to a city I have adored since boyhood. I am also indebted to Dark Scribe magazine and press for their championing of my gay-themed ghost stories, and my gratitude flows to both Vince Liaguno and Chad Helder for their continual support and encouragement.

And none of this would be possible without a supportive family of friends: Martin Gould, Larry Dumont, Jon Marans, John Maresca, Joel Byrd, Deborah Collins, Sean Meriwether, Edward Bohan, Kathleen Corey, Ellen Herb, Jonathan Miller, and Andrew Beierle.

About the Author

Jameson Currier is the author of a novel, *Where the Rainbow Ends*, and four collections of short fiction, *Dancing on the Moon; Desire, Lust, Passion, Sex; Still Dancing*, and *The Haunted Heart and Other Tales*. His short fiction has appeared in many literary magazines and Web sites, including *Velvet Mafia, Blithe House Quarterly, Christopher Street*, and the anthologies *Men on Men, Best American Gay Fiction, Mammoth Book of New Gay Erotica, Best Gay Erotica, Best American Erotica, Rebel Yell*, and *Making Literature Matter*. His gay-themed ghost stories have appeared in *Wilde Stories, Unspeakable Horror, Best Gay Romance, Best Gay Stories, Velvet Mafia, Icarus*, and *All Hallows: The Journal of the Ghost Story Society*.

Black Quill Winner: Editors' Choce-Best Dark Genre Fiction Collection

The Haunted Heart and Other Tales

by Jameson Currier

Twelve stories of gay men and the memories that haunt them.

Jameson Currier modernizes the traditional ghost story with gay lovers, loners, activists, and addicts, blending history and contemporary issues of the gay community with the unexpected of the supernatural.

"Jameson Currier's *The Haunted Heart and Other Tales* expands upon the usual ghost story tropes by imbuing them with deep metaphorical resonance to the queer experience. Infused with flawed, three-dimensional characters, this first-rate collection strikes all the right chords in just the right places. Equal parts unnerving and heartrending, these chilling tales are testament to Currier's literary prowess and the profound humanity at the core of his writing. Gay, straight, twisted like a pretzel… his writing is simply not to be missed by any reader with a taste for good fiction."
Vince Liaguno, *Dark Scribe Magazine*

"I am completely amazed by the range of ghost stories in this collection. These are awesome ghost stories, and the literary connections to gay life are deep and complex."
Chad Helder, *Unspeakable Horror* and *The Pop-Up Book of Death*

"Currier's characters are sumptuous, his plots are freshly twisted and his prose magnificent A perfectly chilling collection of tales from one of the modern masters of the genre. Powerful stuff, indeed."
Jerry Wheeler, *Out in Print* and *Out Front Colorado*

"Jameson Currier is a story teller who weaves his tale around you until you genuinely care about the characters. He has the ability to capture dialogue with an almost journalistic objectivity; this places you in the scene as an eavesdropper, making you part of the story. He is one of the few writers who can be equally literary, erotic, dramatic and damn funny, sometimes all in the same sentence. His collection of ghost stories, *The Haunted Heart*, allows him to showcase these abilities in original stories that are not intended to frighten so much as entertain. There are a multitude of ghosts here, not just the spirits of the dead that you would expect, but the ghosts of abusive relationships, bad decisions, personal flaws, and the ever-present ghost of AIDS that forever hovers in the lives of gay men."
Sean Meriwether, author of *The Silent Hustler*

"Currier's writing is flawless and his knack for conveying emotion, with both the spoken words and thoughts of his characters, is unparalleled. Fans of the author have come to expect that his work isn't exactly light or escapist, which makes it all the more affecting."
Chris Verleger, *Edge*

Available from Lethe Press
ISBN-10: 1590212037 / ISBN-13: 978-1590212035 / Paperback. $15.00

Breinigsville, PA USA
02 March 2010
233400BV00002B/4/P